PATH OF TOTALITY

PRAISE FOR PATH OF TOTALITY

A young woman's desperate search for peace in the midst of global war. A must read! - DiAnn Mills, Award-winning author of over 50 books.

Futuristic tech and hard-hitting action drive this story forward at a breath-taking pace. Don't blink, or you'll miss what's coming next! – James Hannibal, Award-winning author

Captivating and gripping, Heather Kreke's Path of Totality is guaranteed to keep readers turning the pages until they reach the very end. Kreke is a fresh voice to watch for in fiction! - Darlene L. Turner, best-selling and award-winning author

Heather Kreke, author of Path of Totality, *knows the art of creating characters that come to life. Her storytelling enhances this gift and I know she's a writer I'll be watching, anticipating books to come!* - Edie Melson, Director of the Blue Ridge Mountains Christian Writers Conference and Award-winning author.

From the first line to the last sentence, I couldn't put this down. Amazing story with incredible characters so real that you will want to be best friends with them. - Larry J. Leech II, writing coach of award-winning authors

You will not be able to put it down. The fast paced, action-filled suspense will leave you praying for all of the characters to turn to Christ. - Dr. Chrissy Whiting-Madison, Author of *Choosing Happiness* and *Even Happier*.

Heather Kreke is a gifted writer with a talent for delving into uncomfortable human emotions. Presenting a "What if" scenario based on bits of reality, The Path of Totality is both compelling and insightful. Kreke's characters struggle with humanity. There is no perfectly good vs. perfectly bad; there are humans trapped in a dictatorial setting and trying their best to rely on a God who seems to have been abolished. This book fits in with the dystopian genre while holding a light all its own. - Molly Jo Realy, editor, writing coach, and author of the romantic location mystery novel, *NOLA*.

PATH OF TOTALITY

HEATHER KREKE

For all the teachers who helped me along the way, especially Sister Ann Rosalia Devlin IHM, Cindy McNulty, Jean Ann Streiff, DiAnn Mills, and Larry J. Leech II.

CONTENTS

CHAPTER 1
JADZIA

THE DAY my world ended started out normal enough. I sat in calculus class, texting my best friend, Brent, when the teacher broke through my concentration.

"Jadzia, put your PCD away or you're getting detention."

I rolled my eyes, closed my hand, and shut off my Personal Communication Device. "Sorry, Mrs. Ladd."

"I'm sure whatever boy you're texting can wait until class is over."

Classmates snickered. Heat rushed to my cheeks. Brent and I were just friends. Weren't we? I slid low in my chair and pulled my stylus toward me. Maybe if I stayed still, people would stop staring. Using my stylus, I flicked through the pages in my Projection-book, looking for the right place.

Mrs. Ladd turned back to the large Holo-screen at the front of the room, droning on about finding the derivative of a function or something like that.

I startle and dropped my stylus when everyone's PCDs shrieked an ear-piercing alarm. Probably an alert about a severe thunderstorm or a kidnapped kid. Flicking my wrist, I opened my hand to dismiss it. I sucked in a deep breath. The Holo-display between my finger and thumb scrolled with the words *Urgent News: New York, Los Angeles, Houston, and Chicago Under Attack.* Numbness spread throughout my body.

Voices of my classmates filled the room. "What does this mean? What's happening?"

I stared at my PCD, speechless. My heart raced, I had family in Houston. Uncle Nick worked at one of the biggest technology companies in the city. Anyone attacking Houston would target his building first.

"Enough. Everyone, be quiet." Mrs. Ladd's shaky voice filtered through the classroom, but no one listened.

I tore my gaze from my PCD back to the Holo-screen. Mrs. Ladd had replaced the math equations with the National News Channel. The screen split into four different vid feeds, one from each of the damaged cities. Thick smoke masked the flames and rubble of what used to be massive buildings.

I could barely type out a message to my cousin Carina on my shaking PCD. She always replied instantly when I messaged her. But not this time. Seconds turned into minutes and still nothing. Her school wasn't far outside Houston. What if something happened to her or her parents?

Another alarm sounded, drowning out the murmur of my classmates. My attention flew back to the Holo-screen. A woman's voice urged people near large cities to evacuate immediately, as the government expected more attacks.

About half the class jumped up from their seats and made for the door.

Mrs. Ladd moved from her desk and blocked the doorway. "You aren't going anywhere. The news hasn't shown we're in any danger. We're miles away from Pittsburgh. Everything will be okay." She motioned to our desks. "Take your seats. You're safer here than roaming the streets. Your parents know what's going on. They will contact you."

Everyone backed away from the door but remained standing.

The entire world was going crazy. Call me a baby, but I wanted my mom. I tapped her speed dial icon. Her face appeared—flushed and eyes wide. "Jadzia how—"

My voice came out thick. "What's happening? Have you heard from Uncle Nick or anyone?"

"I can't get through. I'm surprised you reached me. Vid service is down almost everywhere." She wiped her cheek. "Do you want me to swing by and pick you up after I get Jonathan?"

"It's okay. I'll probably beat you home, besides I have my bike here."

Her eyes narrowed. "Be careful and don't stop anywhere. Are we clear?"

If Mom wanted to pick me up, things must be worse than I thought. She never panicked. Since Dad had been in the military, both knew the importance of staying calm. Too bad I didn't inherit that trait. "Okay. I love you." I got the words out before my throat closed.

"I love you too, honey. We'll be fine. See you soon."

I squeezed my hand shut a lot harder than I needed to. Poor Jonathan. Mom and I would have to keep it together in front of him. A first grader shouldn't have to go through this kind of terror. Then again, neither should a high schooler. I drummed my fingers on the desk.

If I had to sit here with everyone crying and hugging, I'd lose it. Did Mom already send the school a message saying I could leave? How much longer until the office let Mrs. Ladd know?

My wrist vibrated again. Carina? Nope. Brent wanted to know if I'd give him a ride home. I told him to meet me by my Hover-bike. His house wasn't too far out of my way. I couldn't say no. Especially now.

I threw my school stuff and projection book in my bag and stared at the Holo-screen.

"Jadzia." Mrs. Ladd didn't even look up from her Holo-pad. "You can go."

Finally. I ran to the parking lot. Brent stood next to my bike, stiff and glaring like he expected something to come at him. I glanced over my shoulder. The world looked normal. Trees budded, flowers poked their heads up out of the ground, and a few birds flew over our heads. Not a cloud in the sky. Shouldn't it be pouring or at least dreary or something? Nature didn't know the threat we were under. I launched myself at Brent. He held his arms open, then folded me into his chest.

His breath ruffled my hair. "We're going to be okay."

The sob I'd been holding back broke free, and he tightened his grip.

A sound louder than anything I'd ever heard before ripped through the afternoon. Every muscle in my body tightened, and my light hold on Brent's waist became a vise grip. He dove to the ground, shielding me with his body. I wasn't the only one shaking. The sound faded. We scrambled to our feet.

"What happened?" I pulled a twig from my hair.

He pointed toward the city. A cloud of black smoke rose in the distance. "We have to move."

My legs refused to work. He gave me a gentle shove. "Downtown is under attack. Let's get somewhere safe."

I threw my leg over my bike and Brent settled in behind me. My mind whirled. Somewhere safe. Where on earth were we safe?

I had to get to Mom and Jonathan. I pressed the starter pad. The bike roared to life and I took off so fast we almost dropped onto the pavement before I balanced us out.

"Sorry. Sorry," I yelled over the sound of the engine. I gunned the bike, and we flew toward Brent's house.

"WHERE HAVE YOU BEEN?" Mom stood in the driveway. Her always perfect hair stuck out in every direction. Jonathan peered out from behind her legs, his hand clinging to hers. "I told you to come straight home."

"I dropped Brent off, plus traffic was insane." I got off my bike and plugged it into the charging station. "Everyone's trying to leave the area. We should too."

"When I tell you to come straight home, I mean you need to come straight home. I thought you were dead." Jonathan whimpered, and Mom lifted him. He wrapped himself around her like a baby sloth. She took a deep breath. "I'm sorry. You sca—worried me."

Scared. Mom was going to say scared. I didn't think she ever got scared. I shifted my weight from. My muscles itched to move. I needed to calm down. We're all home. We're all safe. Everything is okay. Except, it wasn't.

"Come on. Into the house." She shifted Jonathan to her other hip, reached for me with her free hand, and guided me to the door. When was the last time she'd held my hand?

"We're going inside?" Mom must not have been thinking straight. "Shouldn't we head for a shelter?"

She led me through the doorway, pulled me into the kitchen, and set Jonathan down. "Most of the shelters are downtown. We're staying here."

"But we can't. What if someone attacks us?"

"This is the safest spot for now. Take your brother downstairs."

"What are you going to do?"

"Go." She gave me a gentle, firm push. "I'll be down in a minute."

I grabbed Jonathan's hand and led him down to the playroom in the basement. With its bright yellow walls and toys scattered on the floor, this was a place to have fun in. Not to hide. My eyes slid to the open laundry room door. Somehow, the smaller, darker space seemed safer.

"Are bad people coming after us?" Jonathan squeezed my hand.

I closed my eyes. He shouldn't have to ask questions like that. I had to pull myself together. I bent down, looked him in the eye, and hoped my voice didn't shake. "We'll be fine. Mom knows what to do." My voice shook anyway. "Come on." We walked to the couch, and I grabbed some pillows and a blanket.

In the laundry room, I created a nest on the floor in the corner, where the dryer butted against the wall and snuggled Jonathan in. "Why don't you watch something?"

He opened his hand and found a cartoon on his PCD. Distraction accomplished. I opened my hand and flipped on the implant in my ear so only I could hear my vid feed. The news rotated images of the original four cities attacked, plus eleven more—including Pittsburgh.

"Jadzia." Mom stood in the doorway, two large guns in

her hands. They looked like they came straight from a battlefield. "Take one of these."

I folded my arms. "Where did those come from?"

Jonathan looked up from his cartoon. "You have guns?"

Mom ignored Jonathan and answered me. "It doesn't matter." She knelt beside me and placed one gun on the floor with the barrel pointed away from the three of us. "You know how to use one of these, right?" She loaded a cartridge into the rifle, laid across her lap.

"Uh, Dad taught me to use a hunting laser, but not one of these things." I looked down. "I'm not a very good shot." Who was I kidding? I can't hit a target the size of a house.

She pressed the laser into my hands, picked up the one from the ground and slammed a cartridge into it. "Just aim at the door. If anyone opens it, shoot. You'll hit them."

I shrank back. "You want me to shoot someone?"

With wide eyes, she remained calm. "We don't know what's happening out there. I want to be ready. In case."

My hands shook. How would I press the trigger, let alone aim the thing? I needed to focus on something else. I turned my attention back to the to the vid feed on my PCD. More smoke, more death. In between were moments of blackness. I'd never experienced a service failure before, not even for a few seconds. Calls dropped and vids froze all the time back when people carried brick-like phones in their pockets, instead of wearing the slim wrist bands like mine. How bad must things be if service was being interrupted? Had someone gotten to the Satellite to Ground Network? Impossible. So was war on American soil.

We sat for hours. Jonathan watched show after show on his PCD. Mom's gaze shifted between the door, her PCD, my brother, and me. I leaned against the washer, trying not to think about—well, everything—but visions of carnage kept replaying in my head.

I couldn't sit anymore. I stood, laser in hand, and paced. Three steps, turn, three steps, turn.

I'm not sure how long I stalked around for.

Mom threw a hand in the air. "Please sit down. You're driving me crazy."

"Sorry." I huddled next to Jonathan this time, laser still in my hands.

"No. I'm sorry. I shouldn't have yelled. I'm just . . ." She took a deep breath and let it out slowly. She laid the laser rifle across her lap, then reached into a bag. Guess I'd focused on the guns too much to notice it before. She pulled out a food packet and some water pods. "Here. Have something to eat. It's well past dinnertime."

I bit into the water pod. Cool liquid burst into my mouth.

"What is this?" Jonathan looked at the package like Mom gave him a snake.

I laughed. "It's food. Don't you remember MRE night?" I took his packet and flipped it over. "See, you've got pizza, a cookie, carrot sticks, and a chocolate milk pod."

He pushed the food away. "No."

"Dad loved these things. We used to have them every once in a while." A small smile played on my face. Visions of Dad passing out MREs. Four-year-old Jonathan giggling. Me teasing him. Mom warming his food with the mini stove that came with the food. Of course, that was before Dad got shipped overseas.

Jonathan stared at the ground and sniffled. It wasn't fair. I had my dad for fifteen amazing years. Jonathan only had five. Stupid war.

"You just had to mention your dad, didn't you?" Mom set her laser next to her and pulled Jonathan into her lap.

Two years had passed since Dad got killed in an attack on his army base. Some of the first causalities of war. Jonathan still shut down whenever anyone mentioned him.

"I'm sorry, kiddo." I patted his hand.

He stared at me, tears running down his cheeks. Mom held him until he calmed down enough to eat. When the half-eaten cookie fell from his hand, she settled him onto the mound of pillows and tucked a blanket around him. She kissed his forehead and scooted over to me.

Mom and I sat together and watched as the NNC alternated between the rescue attempts and newscasters speculating over what had happened. I rested my head on her shoulder.

I jerked awake when an announcer started talking about Operation Resolution, our country's last-ditch contingency plan. My heart raced. I knew what was coming. We'd talked about it at school, but I'd been stupid enough to believe it would never actually happen.

MOM GASPED and grabbed my hand. "No." We locked eyes. Hers were wide and glistened with tears. "Not you too."

Operation Resolution. The military draft, with a twist. Five years ago, during the Second Cold War, the President announced new terms for the Conscription Act and changed the name. Operation Resolution required all males and females over sixteen to register for military service. The government could call us to serve our country at any time.

Being seventeen, I now had seven days to report to the closest military recruitment office and take a physical. If I passed, I'd be forced into whichever branch of the service required my presence the most.

The vid on my PCD shook. It wasn't the feed. My hand shook. I shut off my PCD and implant. I couldn't breathe. If I hadn't been sitting, I'd have fallen. The room was too small. I wrenched my hand out of Mom's. "I have to get out of here."

I jumped up and shot out the door. Mom's voice trailed behind me, but I didn't go back. Halfway through the house,

I stumbled over Jonathan's shoes. A crash sounded. I'd knocked something over, but didn't care. I kept going. When I stepped outside, a chill shot through me. I hadn't bothered to grab a jacket.

I dove for my bike. Fumbling to unlock my helmet from its holder. When the helmet sprung free, it fell from my hands. I caught it before it hit the ground.

Mom grabbed my arm. "What are you doing?"

I shook her off. "Leaving." I jammed the helmet on my head, straddled the bike, and started it.

"You can't go out there." Mom stood in front of me.

I backed up and dodged her. Her face crumpled. A twinge of guilt gripped me, but I needed to leave.

I didn't think about a destination while I flew down the empty streets. Even the parking lots of the grocery store and the movie theater were empty. Everyone else must be home with their loved ones. Except me. Not that it mattered. However far I ran, I couldn't outrun this.

The implant in my ear that connected to my PCD feed also functioned as a tracker. It only turned on if I did something criminal—like murder someone, take part in a terrorist attack, or dodge the draft. I'd never had a reason to care about being tracked before. Now, I didn't relish the possibility. Maybe I'd be able to hack it. Then again, even if I got away with it, should I dodge the draft? Dad would have been crushed. I screamed over the sound of the bike's engine.

Thirty minutes later, my adrenaline ebbed, and I realized I didn't know where I was. Shivering, I pounded the handlebar with my fist. "Great. Just great."

I opened my PCD and swiped past the NNC. I didn't want to see a repeat of the announcement. It played repeatedly in my mind. I punched in Brent's address. He could make me feel safe, no matter what. I transferred the screen to the display in the corner of my helmet's face shield and took off.

Silent darkness blanketed Brent's house. Any other night that would seem normal, but not tonight. Brent and his parents were probably awake, but just to be sure, I sent him a message.

He opened the front door a few seconds later. I hopped off the bike, hung my helmet from the seat, and plugged into one of his extra charging stations.

When I stepped through the door, he tucked me under his arm. "Come on. Mom and Dad passed out about an hour before the announcement. Figured I'd let them sleep."

Everything in the familiar front room was in the same place it had been two days ago—gray couches, dark wood tables, and beige walls hung with pictures of Brent and his parents. But today, the smiles in the pictures seemed sad and knowing.

I pulled away from Brent. "What are we going to do?"

He didn't answer right away. When he did, I didn't want to hear it. "I've wanted to join the military for a while now. It's only been yo..." He dropped his eyes. "I mean, Mom and Dad who held me back."

"Yeah. You're dying to go out there and get killed. Just like my dad. Be a hero and die for your country."

He rolled his eyes. "It's not the same thing. Your dad's entire base got obliterated. It's been two years. They know how the Zealots think now. They can stop those kinds of attacks. An entire base hasn't been taken out since."

"But anything might happen."

"You're exactly right. And we might be just fine."

"We might also get killed."

He glanced toward the stairs. "Shh. I don't want to fight

with you."

I crossed my arms and stared at him.

"Don't give me that look."

"I don't understand how you are so excited about going and getting killed. Or killing someone else." I shuddered.

Brent put a hand on my shoulder. "Look, I don't want to hurt anyone. It's not about that. It's about doing what's right and protecting the lives of those I love. If I have to take out a few Zealots to do it." He shrugged. "Then that's the way it has to be. They're the ones who started this. And we'll finish it."

I scoffed. He didn't understand what the Zealots were like. I'd never showed him the messages. Dad meant them for Mom's eyes only, but he'd underestimated my hacking abilities. He always filled his messages to me with good news and fluff. I wanted to know the truth, so I hacked into mom's PCD. My hacking skills were still new at the time, so it took a month. When I got in, I had access to everything she did.

Zealots thrived on creating fear. When things first started going crazy in Europe, they only targeted churches, temples, mosques, and other religious gathering places. As their cause gathered support, they attacked companies which operated under religious principles or where the CEO professes a specific belief system. They saw people who believed in a higher power as bigots and haters, but they became bigots and haters themselves. So stupid. Who cared which god people worshiped or if they did at all? Apparently, the Zealots did.

I crossed my arms. "And if you die while you're protecting your country?"

He gave me his crooked smile, the one that always made me want to throw my arms around him. "It will be worth it."

CHAPTER 4

JADZIA

MY DAD'S voice sounded in my ears. I stretched and burrowed into the pillow. Wait. Dad? That didn't seem right. I breathed deeply. The smell of eggs and bacon hit my nose. My legs and back ached. I groaned. Was I on a couch? I opened my eyes.

Brent looked down at me. "You gonna sleep all day?"

What. The. Heck? Heat flashed through me. What was I doing with him? We'd never spent the night together.

I threw off a blanket and forced my legs over the side of the couch. "Where did this blanket come from?" I held my hand up. "Better question. What am I doing here?"

Oh right. Operation Resolution, riding around, and ending up here. I ran a hand through my hair. "What time is it?"

"Are you always this alert when you wake up?" He laughed. "It's about noon. I figured I'd let you sleep longer, but Mom thought you should eat something." He set a plate of real breakfast food on the coffee table in front of me.

Mom. Oh, no. "I've got to call my mom. She's going to kill me." I opened my hand.

Before I connected, he put his hand on top of mine and closed it. "I messaged her right after you fell asleep last night. Well, this morning, I guess."

Whew. "Thanks. I should get home, though." I stood and started toward the door.

"Wait a minute." Mrs. Newhams came in the room holding a glass of water. Her red-rimmed eyes were bloodshot, and a grim line replaced her usual smile. She set the cup next to my plate. "When did you eat last?"

My stomach growled. I ate an MRE in the basement with Jonathan over twelve hours ago.

Brent's parents always used actual food. The stuff from the ground or animals, instead of the fabricated mix of protein, carb, and vitamins, most of us ate. The fabricated stuff replicated the texture and flavor of real meat and vegetables—decent enough if you didn't know any better, but I preferred the real thing. Just another reason I ate here often.

My brain warred with my stomach. Brent's casual attitude last night about being drafted still irked me. Even fresh food didn't have enough power to keep me there, especially since the initial shock of the announcement hadn't worn off yet.

It's not like Brent and I resolved anything last night. With nothing left to say, I'd flopped down on his couch and found a dumb movie in his Holo-screen collection. Something to take my mind off everything. At some point, I guess I dropped off.

Now he stood there looking at me with a goofy grin on his face. Ugh. Why couldn't I just stay mad at him? Stupid, I know.

Mrs. Newhams sensed my hesitation and motioned

toward the plate again. "Your mom will never forgive me if I let you leave before you eat."

My stomach and Brent's mom won. I took a bite, and she smiled.

"It's great." I managed through a mouth full of food.

"I'm glad. Well, I guess I'll leave you guys alone. I have to keep trying to check in with my sister." She headed down the hall toward their office.

I devoured the omelet, sausage, and fruit. Brent settled in next to me, his presence a huge emotional interference. To distract myself from his closeness, I turned on their Holo-screen. It defaulted to NNC, as it always did when important information was being delivered.

The scenes changed from last night. Some smoke had cleared, revealing rubble and destruction. Firefighters battled blazes in offices, labs, and production plants. The Zealots even blew up apartment buildings this time. Had they meant to destroy the lives and homes of regular people, or were they just collateral damage? I pinched the bridge of my nose. So much carnage just because people couldn't get along.

The feed switched to Houston. Groups of people trudged through the debris, looking for survivors.

I messaged Carina again. Uncle Nick had to be home by now, even with all the destruction and the mad rush to get out of the blast zones. Within a few seconds, she called. Panic clearly visible on her face and her red hair looked like she'd just rolled out of bed.

"Z, you're okay. Thank goodness. I couldn't get through to anyone."

She and Uncle Nick were the only ones allowed to call me Z. "Are you guys okay?"

She shook her head. Tears spilled down her cheeks.

"Carina. Tell me."

She struggled to control herself. Her voice broke, but through her sobs, I made out what she said. "Dad's building . . . was c-c-completely destroyed. We haven't heard f-from him since yesterday morning."

Brent put a hand on my shoulder and gave it a squeeze.

"Maybe he's still okay." The words sounded hollow, even to me, but Uncle Nick—dad's twin brother—couldn't be dead.

If Uncle Nick died, Dad was really gone. No more calls where I could see my father's face. No double-takes at family gatherings when Uncle Nick walked into the room. No hugs from the man I knew wasn't my father, but looked like him, laughed like him, and sometimes even spoke like him.

Carina took a bunch of deep breaths. "It's been more than a day. He'd have gotten in touch with us by now."

"Maybe he's just hurt." I needed some remnant of my father to still exist in this world.

She shook her head. "Have you seen the footage? There's nothing left. No survivors from his part of the city."

A familiar weight settled on my chest. I leaned into Brent. He tightened his grip on my shoulder and pulled me close. He knew what Uncle Nick meant to me.

Carina turned her head. "Mom's calling me, Z. I'll call you back if I hear anything else. I'm so glad you're okay. Love you."

I choked out. "Love you too."

I closed my hand and stared at the floor, but didn't see it. My mind conjured an image of Uncle Nick sitting in his office, just like I used to imagine Dad at his desk on base, working on some report or something. Then the building exploded.

Carina was right. Just like with Dad, there would be no survivors. I clenched my fists. My stomach rebelled against the food. I gritted my teeth. I imagined ripping apart every Zealot I could find.

Brent's arm never left my shoulders. I lowered my head to my knees and wrapped my arms around myself. My breath came in gasps. My head swam. Darkness rushed up to greet me and I let it take me.

CHAPTER 5

JADZIA

I MADE it home from Brent's house before the new curfew, at 7:00 p.m., went into effect that night. Life had been quiet since the attacks. People stayed in their homes, schools canceled classes, and most stores closed. Drones and bots roamed the streets, delivering food and other essentials. Even in small cities and the suburbs, people were afraid. We waited for the second shoe to drop. When would more cities get hit?

Not to mention, no one really knew who did this. Zealots weren't from a specific country or even an area within a country. They were regular people who went to work every day, lived in regular neighborhoods, and sent their kids to regular schools. And after their regular day, they met and planned to kill thousands of people. It's no wonder they thought people who believed in a god were nuts. Any god who allowed such evil to exist or even caused it to happen wasn't much of a god.

"Whatcha doing?"

I whirled around. Jonathan stood in my bedroom doorway.

I grinned at him. "Hey, Buddy, come in."

He scanned the mess in my room. I had spent the last few days packing and wondering what branch of the military they would throw me into. Clothes and suitcases cluttered my room. Piles of stuff I thought I would need—and piles of stuff I figured I wouldn't—littered the floor.

To be completely honest, I still didn't know whether I was packing for the military or packing to run. The thought of running tempted me. I'd need to find someone whose hacking skills were five thousand times better than my own to scramble the GPS tracker in my implant, but I had no idea where to even begin looking.

"We're mailing you to Grandma's, so I'm packing your stuff."

He put his hands on his hips. "That's your stuff. And I'm not going anywhere. Mom told me you're going away."

My chest ached. "You caught me."

He came closer, hands still on his hips. "I'm not stupid. University isn't until next year. So, where are you really going?"

The kid was getting too smart for his own good. Mom decided it would be too hard on Jonathan to tell him I'd been drafted. The war had taken Dad from him. Now it would take me too.

I closed my eyes and counted to five. Falling apart wasn't an option. "I got in early, because I'm super smart." Great. Now I'd lied to protect him, the same way Dad tried to protect me with his sweet letters. Luckily—as far as I knew anyway—Jonathan couldn't hack his way into a simple chat room, let alone into something as complex as our mom's PCD.

He looked at me, his face filled with doubt. I forced a

teasing tone into my voice. "What? You don't think I'm smart enough to get into University early?"

He pointed at me. "But school's almost over. Not starting."

He was good. I resisted the urge to give him a hug so I wouldn't make him more suspicious. Instead, I threw a balled up pair of socks at him. "I'm taking some summer classes so I can get ahead. This way, I'll be home faster."

He giggled and threw my socks back, which started an all-out sock fight. Socks from the piles on my bed and ones I'd already put in my suitcase flew everywhere. I'd have to repack, but it was worth it. I could practically feel the seconds I had left with him slipping away, and I planned to treasure every single one of them.

After a few minutes of darting around flinging socks at Jonathan, my side ached from the exertion and laughing so hard. I gasped for air. "Stop." I needed to get into shape. Guess the military would do that for me.

"Never." Jonathan laughed and kept pelting me with socks.

I sank to the floor, a sob rising. "I give up."

He jumped on me and tickled me, but I couldn't even fake laughing.

"Tickle fight!" His little fingers ground into my sides.

I grabbed his arms and pulled him into a hug. "Hug machine."

He squirmed, but I held him close. I might never get this chance again.

He stopped trying to escape and looked at my face. "Are you crying?"

I took a deep breath and forced a smile. "Course not. I just . . . got something in my eye." Lame explanation, I knew, but hopefully he didn't.

He did. Of course.

"No, you didn't. You're crying." Tears filled his eyes, too.

My words came out in a jumbled rush. "Oh no, Buddy. Don't cry. I'm just going to miss you. But I'll call, and I'll send you messages, and I'll see you soon. I might make it home after the summer semester ends. We'll go swimming, we'll play and we'll have lots of fun. Okay?"

He rubbed his eyes. "Promise?"

How did I promise something like that? But if I said no, I'd break his heart. I squeezed him, and my voice came out in a whisper. "I promise I'll come home."

He sat with me on the floor for a few more minutes, then wiggled out of my grip. "I'm going to go watch the Holo-screen now. You want to come?"

I considered the disaster in my room. "No. I have to clean the mess someone made."

Walking out of my room, he giggled. "Not me."

Ugh. What a pain. I'd miss him with all my heart.

CHAPTER 6
JADZIA

I HAD one day left to enlist. If I didn't, a police officer would find me and drag me to the enlisting office. Not like I'd be hard to find.

Brent, of course, enlisted two days after the attacks. They didn't give him a choice where to serve, like I hoped they would, but they placed him in the army, which is want he wanted. I wondered if they'd reject me like I wanted.

That afternoon, I stood in line out front of the recruitment office, trying to force the slight shake from my legs. About ten other kids stood out front with me, and who knew how many were inside the building. The news said it had been like this all week. Tons of new recruits arrived to fulfill their responsibilities. How many of them wanted to be there and how many wished they could run away, like I did? Had anyone tried?

Most of us stood like the soldiers we were there to become. Two huge guys, one with blond hair and one with brown hair, horsed around in the line ahead of me. A scrawny-looking boy stood between us. The older looking guys argued about who was tougher and even started punching each other in the arm. I rolled my eyes. Were they showing off to hide their fear or were they just annoying?

"You want in on this, Shorty?" The brown-haired poked the boy in front of me.

The kid ignored him. He didn't even look sixteen, and stood at least three inches shorter than the other two. He shoved his glasses up his freckled nose. Either his parents didn't spring for eye correction surgery, or the glasses were fake, and he hoped poor vision would keep him out of the service.

It wouldn't. They'd fix his eyes, just like they would fix most defects. Lots of people joined the military for the free surgeries alone. Unfortunately, there just weren't many reasons people got rejected. Pregnancy was one of them. Impossible, short of something miraculous.

"Hey, Shorty. We're talking to you." The blond guy jostled the kid, who lowered his head and appeared to study his shoes. He swayed when Brownie shoved him back toward Blondie.

The words left my mouth before I realized it. "Leave him alone."

Now they focused on me. Great. They moved around Shorty until they were in front of me. Good job, Jadzia.

"You got something to say, beautiful?" Blondie looked me up and down. I wasn't a threat to him, and he had to know it, but I couldn't back down now. If I did, I'd be the next target. Taking a deep breath, I drew myself up to my full height, all five feet two inches, and stared Blondie in the eyes. "I. Said. Leave. Him. Alone." I could feel everyone in line looking at me, but I didn't break eye contact.

"Yeah? You gonna make me?" He leaned toward me. My already racing heart kicked into high gear. If he hit me, I wouldn't be able to stop him. Then again, maybe I'd be in bad enough shape to get rejected—for now.

Brownie put a hand on Blondie's arm and pulled him back. "Dude. She's a chick."

Blondie stepped back. "You're right, she ain't got what it takes. Why are you even here?"

Brownie rescued me. In that moment, I realized I didn't want to be rescued. If I backed down now, I'd always back down. I tightened my hand into a tight fist, thumb on the outside, the way Dad taught me. I pulled back and nailed Blondie on the arm. When I pulled away, my hand stung, but I didn't shake it out or anything. Instead, I braced myself for the return punch that was sure to come. It didn't.

Blondie threw his head back and laughed. "Guess I was wrong about you. That's quite a punch ya got there. I'm Garrett." He motioned to Brownie. "That's Sisko."

"Jadzia." I couldn't stop the grin.

Garrett turned to Shorty. "Sorry, man. I got carried away. I'm just excited, you know."

Shorty looked at us like he thought we were going to gang up on him.

"What's your name?" Calling him Shorty just didn't sit right.

A slow smile crossed his face. "I'm Asher."

I offered Asher my elbow, and we all exchanged elbow bumps. "You guys live around here? I've never seen any of you at school."

Garrett shook his head. "Sisko and I went to a private school. Real exclusive, you know." He rolled his eyes.

Sisko laughed. "Yeah. So exclusive you've gotta have your name on a building to get in, don't you, Garrett?"

Garrett's face ran through about five shades of red

before it settled on a deep blush. "Or maybe your dad has to be the dean." He shot a glance at Sisko.

Archer Academy's main hall was Garrett Hall. I gasped.

Asher got his words out before I did. "You're Garrett James Archer the Third?"

"Guilty."

Garrett James Archer the Third, sole heir to the Archer family fortune. This guy's left pinky-toe was worth more than my entire house.

His grandfather, Garrett James Archer Sr., turned Pittsburgh from a blue-collar industrial town to a white-collar medical tech giant. Almost all the technology for corrective surgeries came from The Archer company.

I shook my head. "There's no way." On the net, Garrett's looks were flawless, but this guy had a slightly crooked nose. With his sandy blond hair and blue eyes, the person in front of me wasn't unpleasant looking, but he certainly wasn't the Adonis presented on the net.

He shrugged. "Filters. If I didn't hide how I really look, I wouldn't be able to go anywhere."

Of all the problems to have. "You poor baby. Fame must be so hard."

We all burst out laughing.

"I knew I liked her," Sisko said.

I looked at Sisko, and my suspicions rose, but I couldn't place his name. "What about you? Are you some secret billionaire, too?"

"You've got me. I'm Jacob Sisko Jessup. I like Sisko better than Jacob, though."

I shook my head. Jacob Jessup. The Jessups had partnered with the Archer family to turn Pittsburgh into the country's medical capital. They'd developed cures for some of the world's most deadly diseases.

"Let me guess. Filters?"

He laughed again. "Yep. When our dads were our age, they always got mobbed by girls wanting to marry them, so they used image disguising software for us."

"How awful that must have been for them." I looked at Asher. "And who are you? President Jobs's kid?"

Asher ducked his head. "Actually. . ." Then he cracked up. "No. I'm just regular old Asher. I was homeschooled. That's why you don't recognize me."

A sharp-looking woman in uniform interrupted our playful interaction by tapping Sisko on the shoulder. "Next."

Sisko and Garrett's eyes met.

"Payback time," Garrett said.

Sisko followed the woman inside. I leaned against the wall to keep from dissolving into a heap on the sidewalk. This wasn't a party, or some social function. This was a recruiting center. We were going to war. For a few minutes, I'd let myself forget. "Payback?"

Garrett nodded, his demeanor suddenly serious. "Archer Tech headquarters got destroyed in the bombing. Our parents are all right, but we lost thousands of others. We're here to make life miserable for the people who did that."

CHAPTER 7
JADZIA

BY THE TIME I followed the woman in uniform into the small recruitment building, Sisko and Garrett were nowhere to be seen. Asher sat on one of two blue plastic chairs in the lobby area.

The woman pressed my right thumb onto her tablet and scanned the implant in my ear. She motioned to the chair next to Asher. "Have a seat." She sat behind the desk across from us. Not one hair in her overly tight bun moved the entire time.

Behind her, posters adorned the walls. People in different uniforms held laser guns, jumped from planes, or stood on the bow of naval ships. The posters boasted adventure and every single person wore a giant smile. Fake, obviously. No one could be that happy about being in a war.

I sat next to Asher. Garrett's pronouncement rang in my ears. Payback. Payback for all the lives taken in the bombings, not just a few days ago, but over the past eight months. For Uncle Nick, who was still missing. For Dad. Is that what I wanted? To hurt the people who hurt me? Yes. But could I? Didn't payback mean becoming like the very people I wanted to hurt?

The woman behind the desk rose. "Asher, you may go back now." She motioned to a door on my right. I hadn't noticed it when I walked in. Asher stood and gave me a nervous grin. "Good luck."

"You too." Good luck. It seemed like a natural enough thing to say, but good luck with what? Passing a physical? Getting put in a good unit? Becoming a killer?

I wrapped my arms around myself. The girl who'd been behind me in line outside entered the office. After being checked in, she sat next to me. "Were you really talking to Garrett James Archer the Third and Jacob Jessup?"

I stared at her. "What?"

She frowned. "The guys in line. I overheard you talking."

"Oh, yeah." I shrugged. "That's what they said."

A huge grin split her face. "Can you imagine getting assigned to their unit? That would be amazing." She bounced in her seat.

Blood rushed to my face. All this girl could think about was getting close to Garrett and Sisko? She didn't care about the people buried under the rubble, or the people who did it to them. She didn't care that in a few minutes, we were going to be the ones responsible for stopping those people by whatever means necessary. Which most likely meant killing them. Dad and Uncle Nick flashed across my mind. I wanted to slap her stupid smile off her face.

I fought for control, but my voice came out louder than I intended. "Don't you get what's going on here? People are dying. You—"

"Jadzia, you may go in." I jumped.

The woman in uniform stood behind the desk, pointing to the door Asher had walked through.

I took a deep breath. On shaky legs, I walked through the door. I found myself in another office, now converted into an examination room. An exam table from a doctor's office sat in the center of the room, a privacy screen stood in the corner, and a paper hospital gown lay on a stool near the door.

A middle-aged man with dark, curly hair closed the door behind me. He scanned my implant. "I'm Doctor Nuzzo. I'll administer the physical part of your evaluation." He motioned to the privacy screen. "Please step behind this screen, remove all your clothing, and put on the gown, with the opening in the back."

Sure, because that's not awkward. Most of the time, doctors had the decency to leave the room when they asked you to change. I kept my voice steady. "Okay."

Blood still pounding in my ears, I sat on the table. Dr. Nuzzo moved with the precision of someone who did this a thousand times a day. He took my temperature, checked my ears, eyes, nose, throat, and hooked me up to a blood pressure monitor. "Humm. Blood pressure is high. Are you nervous?"

Nervous. Maybe when I stood in line out front. Now I wanted to take Dr Nuzzo's thermometer and shove it up the girl in the front office's nose.

"A little."

He waved a hand. "That's natural. Enlisting is a big life change, but you'll be fine."

It took everything in me not to scoff in this guy's face. First, he probably couldn't care less whether I was fine or not. I'd leave, and he would examine another fifty patients before the end of his day. Second, nothing was fine, much less me. I'd never be fine again.

As he administered a hearing test and eye exam, I hoped he'd find something that would let me go home and avoid the whole thing. Maybe I could make up some rare, incurable disease which kept me from aiming a gun properly. Of course, Garrett or Sisko's father could probably cure whatever my limited imagination came up with. Finally, Dr. Nuzzo told me to get dressed.

When I finished, he made some more notes on his Holopad. "Congratulations. You're physically fit for duty. Head through here." He opened a door opposite the one I'd entered. "Someone will guide you to the mental evaluation and aptitude tests."

"Yay. More tests." Heat rushed to my cheeks. Oops.

Dr. Nuzzo laughed and ushered me out. "It's not all bad."

I walked into a dim white hallway. I followed arrows painted on the wall to a room with another uniformed woman behind a desk. After another implant scan, she handed me a tablet and led me to a small room with a single desk and a chair. "This is the aptitude part of your evaluation. It will help us determine which branch you'll fit best. You have ninety minutes to complete the task. Just follow the instructions on the tablet and you'll be fine."

I really wished people would stop telling me that.

An hour and fifteen minutes later I finished the test. I thought about failing it on purpose, but I kept seeing Dad's disappointed face when my hand hovered over the wrong answer.

The mental evaluation was next. Simple enough. I just had to talk to a psych doctor. It only took him forty-five minutes to decide I wasn't insane or a danger to myself or anyone in my unit. The doctor spent a large amount of time on how I felt about the war. My answers must have convinced him I wasn't some Zealot spy or something. I'm not sure how he knew I told the truth.

The psych waved me to yet another room, where a gray-hair man saluted me. Bars and medals, representing decades of sacrifice, covered his perfectly-pressed uniform. "Congratulations, soldier. Welcome to the Army. Your country thanks you for your service."

I stood at attention and snapped off the perfect salute, like dad taught me. My voice loud and clear. "Thank you, Sir."

Soldier. I shuddered.

CHAPTER 8

JADZIA

THE NEXT MORNING, my alarm went off at five. Or, rather, zero five hundred. I guess I should think in military time now. I spent a few extra minutes in my bed, knowing it would be the last time in my own rom for a long while.

Last night had been a special kind of awful when I told Jonathan goodbye. I read him a story and tucked him in, but his trembling lower lip and his pleading little voice enticed me. After three more stories, two songs, and a short tickle battle, Mom finally put her foot down. I kissed him on his forehead and told him I'd see him soon. Mom sent me straight to bed.

I'd tossed and turned all night. But now, as I thought about what lay ahead for today, I felt wide awake. Throwing the covers back, I got out of the bed. I pulled on my issued fatigues and threw my hair in a ponytail, grateful I didn't have to shave my head like Brent. I grabbed my military duffle.

All my earlier packing was for nothing. I could only bring whatever fit in this bag. I jammed it with socks, under-wear, my favorite Seneca Valley Senior High School sweatshirt, and two pairs of jeans. The United States Government would provide toiletries, uniforms, and boots, but I wanted a few things to remind me of home.

I kept pictures of Mom, Dad, Jonathan, and Brent stored on my PCD. Not that I really needed Brent's picture —he'd be in basic training with me. Something to look forward to. Yay.

Mom knocked. "Jadzia, are you wake?"

I opened the door. "Yep." The smell of pancakes met my nose. "You made real pancakes?"

Despite standing next to her, I strained to hear. "I know how much you like the real stuff. You most likely won't be getting a taste of it for a while, so I thought I'd make something special. Even added real blueberries."

I dropped my bag and gave her a hug. "Thank you." I sniffled.

"Don't start crying yet. You should eat. Brent will be here in thirty minutes, Private."

Soldier. Private. Ugh. Those words made it too real. I followed Mom down the stairs, dragging my bag behind me.

"Shhh. You'll wake your brother."

I hoped he would wake up. I wanted one more hug from his little arms before I left. "Sorry."

She made me sit at the kitchen table while she waited on me. She hadn't treated me like this since . . . well, I didn't remember when. My stomach growled at the sight of the pancakes dripping with syrup. Even though the glass of orange juice and the syrup were fabricated, everything still looked amazing. I took a huge bite and moaned. "So good."

Mom's lips quivered, and her eyes shone. "I knew you'd like them."

I looked around the room. My mom, the pancakes, the

clean, comfortable kitchen with its pale green walls and tin ceiling. Dad always loved our kitchen.

I pictured Jonathan snuggled in his bed, and how he'd look when he came padding down the stairs. Perfect. How was I supposed to leave? The pancakes blurred. I took a swig of orange juice to clear the lump in my throat. I coughed and sputtered.

Mom ran to my side. "Are you okay?"

My coughing finally stopped. "Just went down the wrong pipe."

The sound of a gentle knock pulled our attention to the door.

"He's early." I'm not sure Mom heard me. Neither of us moved. Another knock, slightly louder this time.

Mom straightened her shoulders, took a deep breath, and headed for the door. "I'll get it."

I stayed cemented to the chair. I wasn't sure I could have moved if I wanted to.

Brent and Mom exchanged pleasantries in the entry-way. Brent's deep voice barely contained his excitement. Mom's voice trembled with fear. They were in the kitchen before I was ready to face him.

"Morning." Brent beamed at me. He faltered when I didn't answer. He crossed over to my chair and put his hand on my shoulder. "You okay?"

I fumbled for words. I commanded my brain to say something, but my mouth didn't obey. My chest heaved, and the walls seemed to move in closer. Just like the night of the announcement of Operation Resolution, except this time I couldn't run.

Brent leaned over so his eyes were level with mine. He took both of my hands in his. "Jadzia, I'll be with you the entire time." His voice grew serious, and his gaze never left mine. "You'll be fine. I'll get you back here. I promise."

That word again. Fine. But the sound of his voice and the feel of my hands in his brought me back. My breathing calmed and my limbs unlocked. "Okay." My voice cracked, but at least I produced speech this time.

He pulled out the chair next to me. "I'll sit right here while you finish your breakfast."

I forced another bite of the now-cold pancakes and managed to swallow, but when I did, my stomach rebelled. Now, I was more than capable of movement. I shoved my chair back so hard I sent it clattering to the floor, but I didn't look back. I ran to the bathroom. Even after I emptied my stomach of what little I'd eaten, I kept dry heaving. A cool cloth touched the back of my neck. Mom's hand rubbed my back.

"My baby girl." She soothed me. "You can do this. You're tougher than you realize. Besides, as a recruit, you probably won't go into any dangerous situations."

I couldn't figure out which of us she was trying to convince. I pulled myself together enough to take some deep breaths and stood to rinse my mouth out. Mom handed me my toothbrush.

"Thanks for taking care of me."

She squeezed my shoulder. "That's what moms are for." Her breath hitched. "Now, come on. You don't want to be late."

I brushed my teeth and wiped my face off.

In the kitchen, someone had picked up the chair and cleared the table. My cheeks burned with embarrassment. Brent saw and heard everything.

"Sorry," I said.

He shrugged. "No big deal. We all get nervous."

Nervous. Sure. Only nerves.

Mom handed us pods of cold water. "Take small sips."

"Okay." I had no intention of throwing up in Brent's Hover-car. At the door I hugged Mom for what seemed like forever, but really must have been a minute or two.

As I broke the hug, she held out a rock, painted blue. "Take this, to remind you of home."

My breath caught. Since I'd been little, I loved painting rocks. Jonathan and I still did it all the time. Mom's garden was full of our creations. No matter how many rocks I painted in a session I always made one blue. Sometimes I put designs on the rocks, sometimes I just did a plain shade of blue. I'm not sure why I did it, I just liked the way they looked in blue.

I pulled Mom into another quick hug. "Thank you." I slipped the rock into my pocket and headed to the car.

Brent opened the door for me, took my bag, and threw it in the back seat next to his.

I got in the car, and he walked around to the other side. "I could have scooted over."

He shrugged. "You know I like to drive."

I laughed. Hover-cars hadn't needed drivers for years, but as a long-standing joke between the two of us, he always sat where the driver would be. That's why I preferred my bike. At least I still got to do something.

"Cranberry Army Recruiting Center." Brent told the car. It confirmed the destination, and we pulled out of the driveway. I looked toward the house and saw Mom standing in the door frame, waving goodbye. The tears she must have hidden from me all week now streamed freely down her face. I waved and watched my home and my mother disappear.

CHAPTER 9
JADZIA

TRAFFIC to the recruiting center was crazy. What should have been a ten-minute drive took more than forty. The stores in the shopping plaza were closed, whether because of the early hour or because they required every available inch of parking lot. When we found a place to pull over, Brent unloaded our stuff and sent the car back to his house. Neither of us were allowed to use it where we were going. At least a dozen Hover-buses idled nearby.

I looked around at the sea of people in the lot. "Now what?"

"Let's go find Staff Sergeant Wallace."

"Who?"

Brent rolled his eyes. "Didn't you read any of the info they downloaded to your PCD?"

"Nothing after the packing list."

He grew serious. "You'd better check it. With so many people here, there's probably more than one squad. I just assumed we'd be in the same one."

My stomach turned again. Oh, no. Please don't throw up. I opened my hand and pulled up the document, scrolling past the welcome pages and the packing list, until I found my orders. I breathed an enormous sigh. "Bravo Company, First Platoon, Fourth Squad, Staff Sergeant Wallace."

He flashed my favorite smile. "Great. Let's go."

I scanned the throngs of people. "How are we supposed to find him?"

The surrounding people pointed and talked at once. I turned to see what caught everyone's attention. A huge Hover-limo came to a stop nearby. I smirked when the door opened and Garrett and Sisko stepped out. Although I doubted anyone realized who they were, people still crowded around them. Getting shipped off to boot camp in a limo wasn't normal.

Garrett and Sisko pushed through the crowds. They seemed unsure. I wanted to get their attention but didn't know how without causing a scene. I'd never get near them if I did that. Then I remembered the public knew Sisko as Jacob. Most people wouldn't know his nickname.

"Sisko." I waved and tried to make my voice heard over the ocean of other voices. After I yelled a second time, our eyes met. A look of relief washed over his face.

Brent leaned down and spoke in my ear. "Sisko? That's Garrett Archer and Jacob Jessup." His eyebrows rose. "How stuck-up can you get? Showing up for boot camp in a limo."

"Shush. They aren't like that."

He started to answer but stopped when Garrett and Sisko pushed enough people out of the way to get to us.

"Jadzia." Sisko wrapped me in a quick hug. "Thank goodness you're here. It's nice to know someone won't mob us."

"Hey, beautiful," Garrett said.

I laughed. Guess I had a nickname too. Then I saw

Brent's face. His mouth set in a thin line and his eyes were dark. I swallowed. What was his problem?

I introduced them and Garrett and Sisko offered their elbows. Brent glared and practically shoved Garrett. My heart fluttered. Was he jealous? I mean, Garrett was good looking and nice, but he was five years older. And Sisko was, well, Sisko. I told my heart to knock it off. Something else about them must bug Brent.

If Garrett noticed Brent's attitude, he didn't show it. "Do you guys know where you're going?"

I motioned around us. "We were just about to find out. What squad are you in?"

Garrett raised his hand to show me the BC, 1P, 4S written on the back in black ink.

Sisko rolled his eyes. "He didn't want to forget."

Brent scoffed.

I covered Brent's scorn, making my voice louder than was needed to be heard over the din. "We're in the same squad."

Brent said something under his breath, but I didn't catch it. A shrill whistle sounded. Every head turned.

Four men, no older than thirty-five, stood on top of a Hover-bus. "Listen up, recruits." A microphone I couldn't see amplified one of the men's voices.

People fell silent.

"I'm Staff Sergeant Wallace." He motioned to the other three men on top of the bus. "This Sergeant Davis, Sergeant Kulyk, and Sergeant DelTurco." He pointed to each man. "You will move to the Hover-bus displaying your squad number. There, we will scan you in. When your entire platoon is aboard, we will take you to Fort Lincoln. That will be your home for the next four weeks, until your training is complete."

I glanced at Brent. "Four weeks seems short."

He shook his head. "You really didn't read anything they gave you, did you?"

I smacked his arm. "I already told you I didn't."

He shrugged. "They know what they're doing."

We moved toward the bus with Bravo Company, First Platoon, Squads 1-4 listed on its Holo-display. When we arrived, another uniform scanned our ears and let us board. I found two empty double seats about halfway back. Brent and I took one, and Sisko and Garrett sat behind us. Within twenty minutes, the bus filled and left the lot.

The adrenaline keeping me awake ebbed when the bus got on the highway. "How far away is Fort Lincoln?"

Brent pulled it up on his PCD. "It's in State College. You know, where the university used to be, before it moved closer to Harrisburg."

"Why would they put it there? That place is a ghost town."

"They set up extra bases all over the place to handle the new recruits. I guess they took advantage of all those empty university buildings and dorms."

"Makes sense." I yawned.

"Here." Brent shifted and patted his shoulder. "Lean on me. Get some rest. Something tells me we're going to need it."

I snuggled against Brent's warm body. Too bad we weren't cuddled like this in his car, going on our first date, instead of on this loud bus filled with other recruits. I closed my eyes and drifted off.

A shrill whistle jarred me out of my amazing dream about Brent and the house, kids, and hamster we'd have one day. I already hated that whistle.

He chuckled. "You okay?"

Maybe if my dream were true. But waking up on this bus, with an aching neck from my cramped position, was the furthest thing from my dream I could think of. I forced a smile anyway. "I'm fine."

Staff Sergeant Wallace stood at the front of the bus. "All right people, we're calling you by squad. When we call your name, you are to exit the vehicle and join your squad."

Wallace read names from his PCD until he got to mine. "Squad four. Archer, Bashier, Jessup, Kauffman, Mills, Maddison, Newhams, Realy, Tomlin, Zimerman" Not that we really needed to be called. We were the last ten people on the bus.

We must have moved too slowly, because about ten seconds later, Staff Sergeant Wallace started yelling. "Let's move it. We don't have all day."

I quickened my pace, exited the bus, and joined the rest of my squad in a grassy field. Beautiful old buildings stood on three sides, and a pile of rubble lay on the fourth. The other buses had pulled into varying locations nearby.

Sergeant Wallace stepped off the bus and faced the small clusters of squads. "I want to see straight lines of five in each group."

Dad told me drill sergeants liked to yell, and he wasn't kidding. Nothing Wallace had said so far was below the tone of someone trying to be heard at a rock concert.

We arranged ourselves in rows, and I stood at attention the way Dad had shown me.

"For those of you with short memories, I'm your commanding officer, Staff Sergeant Wallace. You will address me as Drill Sergeant or Sir. Is that clear?"

"Yes, Drill Sergeant." My voice rang out over the others. Sergeant Wallace caught my eye and nodded but said nothing.

"When I talk to you, I expect an answer. A loud, clear answer. Do you understand?"

"Yes, Drill Sergeant." This time, everyone answered correctly.

Wallace paced in front of us while he spoke. "That's better. We have a lot of work to do to turn you losers into soldiers, and we don't have a lot of time to do it. I expect nothing short of excellence from every one of you. Your training will be grueling and demanding. Some of you will want to quit. I will not allow you to quit." He smiled. "Recruits, welcome to Hell."

CHAPTER 10
JADZIA

THE NEXT TWO weeks passed and hell became an accurate description. As soon as I thought I figured out a skill—or at least got better at one—Drill Sergeant made it harder. Run two miles in sixteen minutes one day. Do it in fifteen the next. Forty-five pushups today. Do fifty tomorrow.

The routine was horrible from day one. Wake up at zero four thirty, run, eat breakfast, then fight battle sims in an area of the base designed to look like war-torn streets. Run again, lunch, marksmanship, more battle sims, dinner. Then one-on-one meetings with Drill Sergeant Wallace where we went over things each person needed to improve. Pretty much everything, in my case.

Finally, at zero eight hundred, we were free for an hour until lights out. Well, not really free, but we could go back to the barracks and sleep or read. Every Monday and Wednesday, they turned off the communication block so we could message home.

The rest of the week, they blocked our PCDs so no one could use them during the day, except to access info related to battle sims. It only took me a week to hack through the block. I limited the messages I sent to Mom in case she remembered the two-per-week rule from when Dad was in boot camp, but I sent messages to Carina and Jonathan almost every night. I made Jonathan swear not to tell.

On the first day of the third week, an officer caught a member of our platoon with contraband pills. Drill Sergeant called him out in front of everyone. After a thorough dressing-down, the private packed his bag, and we never saw him again.

His replacement came into the mess hall during lunch. The day had been rough so far. I'd tripped during this morning's run and fell on my face. I leaned on my elbow and halfheartedly spooned fabricated mashed potatoes into my mouth. Brent tried to cheer me up, but the din of the room made my head pound.

"Jadzia, Sisko, Garrett," a voice called.

"Who's that?" Brent tapped my arm and pointed.

I looked up from my food and saw a boy, with dark hair and freckles, weaving his way between the metal picnic style tables. "It kinda looks like Asher. Don't you think?" I lifted my head in Sisko and Garrett's direction.

They didn't have time to answer before the kid made it to our table.

I stood and gave him a hug. "Asher. What are you doing here?"

"There were a few extra guys in my platoon and yours is short, so here I am." He grinned.

"I almost didn't recognize you without your glasses. Come on, sit down." I scooted closer to Brent and slid my tray over, opening a gap between me and the end of the long table.

Brent muttered something about there being another

one now. Another what? Another one of my friends? Another person who liked me? Brent seemed to have gotten over any jealousy he'd felt toward Garrett and Sisko. Although I wouldn't go as far as calling them friends.

Asher set his tray on the table and plopped next to me. "Yeah, they corrected my eyes before I left the recruitment center. It's amazing. I can see better than I could with the glasses on."

Sisko nodded. "The eye correction technique is the latest and greatest. Dad's been crowing about it for months. The procedure's even approved for infants."

Garrett rolled his eyes. "And my dad won't shut up about the technology that performs it."

They both laughed.

"You guys always make it sound like you don't like what your parents do." Brent shoved his tray away and glared at them. "Aren't you supposed to be leaders of the company one day? They handed you guys everything and all you do is complain. You don't appreciate any of it."

A small wave of hurt rolled through me. Oh. This is what bugged him. He didn't care if they liked me. I should have known better. I shook myself a little. Knock it off. There are bigger things to worry about.

"Like you've never complained," Garrett said.

"We aren't complaining about the work or the things our companies do." Sisko spoke in a quiet and controlled manner, as always. "Neither of us said we aren't grateful. We're complaining about our father's preoccupation with work and the way they present themselves."

I put a hand on Brent's shoulder. "I've never seen them act like they don't appreciate where they are."

He shook my hand off. "You're taking their side?"

"Don't go off on her, man." Sisko motioned toward me.

I reached for Brent again. "Don't be ridiculous. No one's taking sides."

He stood, stepped over the bench, and picked up his tray. "That's me. Ridiculous."

I grabbed his arm. "What are you doing? We still have five minutes." Since it was the only time in the afternoon we got to relax, we usually milked lunch for every second we could.

He ignored me, stormed over to deposit his tray, and left the mess hall.

I watched him leave, then I looked at Garrett, Sisko, and Asher. "What's his deal?"

They just shook their heads.

Sisko reached across the table and gave my hand a light squeeze. "Don't worry about it. He must just be having a bad day."

I smiled at him. Such a sweet guy, always looking out for me. My heart kicked up a notch when he smiled back. Wait. What was I doing? I slowly pulled my hand away and flipped my ponytail over my shoulder. Hopefully, Sisko would think I just wanted to adjust my hair. The glint of pain in his eyes told me I didn't fool him.

A whistle sounded, and for the first time, the sound didn't grate on my nerves.

The entire platoon moved as one. We took our trays to dishwashing line, exited the mess hall, and headed to the weapons building.

I hated marksmanship. While running and PT sucked, at least I seemed to get better at them. Shooting, however, not so much. I couldn't hit the side of a warehouse if it stood three feet in front of my face, even after being here for a little over two weeks. Maybe I'd get lucky, and the Zealots would die laughing at my attempts to shoot, because I certainly wouldn't hit them.

Not to mention the endless taking apart and reassembling of our laser rifles. Drill Sergeant spent the entire time screaming at me because I moved like a turtle. Holding the rifle reminded me of huddling in the laundry room with Jonathan. I missed him and Mom more than I thought possible.

I spent yet another day watching Brent, Sisko, Garrett, and now Asher shoot better than me. At the end, Drill Sergeant told me I had no business being handed a weapon. I fully agreed, but what else could I do?

After marksmanship came battle sims. We marched out to the simulated city. They blew parts of the campus into rubble specifically for this purpose. What a waste of good buildings. Shooters from another platoon set up in strategic areas all around us. We always had some mission we needed to complete without getting shot.

The shooters' guns were loaded with kill laser clips. Not the stun ones that knocked you out for a few hours. The ones that killed you. Doing this made training real. Supposedly, they shot over our heads. If we were dumb enough to get shot, we paid the price. So far, no one was dumb enough.

CHAPTER 11

JADZIA

SIMS WERE EVEN WORSE than marksmanship class. At least the sun was shining. Two days ago, it poured so hard we could barely see.

Brent led today's mission. We were instructed to clear three city blocks and rescue a group of hostages being held by Zealots.

I loved watching Brent take command. Everything about him changed. He stood taller, his gaze focused in a way I'd never seen before, and his voice rang firm and loud. "You all know how this works. Bashier, Kauffman, Maddison, you guys take right. Realy, Zimmerman, Tom. . ." Brent looked at Asher. "What's your last name?"

"Benedict."

Brent nodded. "Realy, Zimmerman, Benedict—left. The rest of you, with me." He looked into my eyes, and a hint of my favorite smile played on his lips. "Jadzia, please try not to shoot any of us this time."

My face flushed. Asher stared at me, wide-eyed. Everyone else cracked up. While the soldiers shooting at us used kill cartridges, we carried stunners. We were actually supposed to hit the shooters.

I rarely fired, but the last time shooters pinned us down, a clear shot of my enemy presented itself. At least, I thought it did. I took the shot, but instead of hitting the girl I'd targeted, I hit Realy in the back.

Someone stopped the sim and medics hauled Realy to the med bay. She swore she felt fine after she woke up and thanked me for the nap, but I still felt awful.

Making fun of me seemed to help Brent get over whatever happened at lunch. "Implants on." All business again. We all turned our implants on and said our names to make sure we could all hear each other.

"Move out," Brent said.

We fanned out in a triangular pattern, grouped as Brent ordered us. My group headed the front, and the other two groups followed about three feet behind. We cleared one block before a chunk of concrete behind me exploded.

"Hit the deck." Brent's calm voice sounded in my ear.

My heart raced, and I threw myself into the dirt. Most of us were on the ground before Brent spoke the last word. I looked through the scope on my rifle, though I had no intention of firing. There. I pointed to the building slightly behind us. "On your four."

Everyone in my group looked in that direction.

"You got eyes on them, Mills?" Brent's gentle voice settled me some. This wasn't real, I reminded myself. They were shooting around me, not at me. I took a deep breath.

"Third floor, seventh window from the left," I said.

"Got 'em." Garrett's voice rang in my ear. He always seemed a little too excited about knocking someone out.

"Take the shot," Brent said.

Garrett fired, and we waited three minutes. No more concrete blasted around us.

Brent gave his next order. "Jessup, see if it's clear."

Sisko didn't move. He was second in command on this mission. The second took over if the leader got killed. Clearing an area might be dangerous and was the job of a grunt, like me, not of the second.

Brent turned and glared at Sisko. "I gave you an order."

"I'll do it." I got to my knees.

Brent put his hand on mine. "I give the orders. You guys obey them."

Sisko shook his head and moved. No shots fired. "Clear."

Brent hesitated a moment, then motioned us forward. We stood and started walking again. A chunk of concrete exploded on my right. Pain flared through my arm. I gritted my teeth to keep from screaming. I curled up in a ball and everyone else dropped on their stomachs again.

Brent jabbed a finger toward Sisko. "You said it was clear."

Sisko put his hand up. "I didn't see anyone."

"I know I got him." Garrett looked through his scope in the shooter's direction. "Wait. There's a second one." He shot twice more. "Got 'em."

I clutched the upper part of my arm. Blood oozed between my fingers. Some kind of weird cross between a scream and a sob escaped my mouth.

Sisko, being closest to me, noticed first. "You okay?"

I couldn't answer. I wasn't sure what would happen if I opened my mouth.

"Jadzia." Sisko sounded farther away this time, but he was close. He pulled me into a sitting position and leaned me against some rocks. He gently slapped my face. "Hey. Stay with me. Come on."

I locked onto his eyes. His words brought my focus back and the pain as well.

"What's going on?" Brent looked at us.

"She's hurt."

Brent crouched next to me in an instant. "What happened?"

I shook my head and a few tears dripped down my cheeks. I closed my eyes.

"Jadzia, I need you to move your hand." Sisko's voice soothed me.

I forced myself to stop panting and took a few deep breaths through my nose. I had to help them help me. My battlefield first aid training kicked in. I moved my bloody hand away from the upper part of my arm. Blood poured down to my wrist. It took everything in me not to slap my hand back over the wound.

Brent tried to shove Sisko out of the way. "I'll do it."

"I've got it." Sisko used a pair of shears to cut my fatigue sleeve above the wound.

"At least give her pain meds."

Pain meds. My eyes flew open. I knew what that entailed. Brent held a wicked-looking needle from the med bag. A whimper escaped my lips. I cringed against the pile of concrete at my back.

Sisko shook his head. "Thins the blood. I can't give it until I stop the bleeding." He examined my arm.

I blew out a deep breath.

Brent clenched his fists and turned to the rest of our unit. "Make sure no one else is out there. Once we get her patched up, we'll move on."

I watched Sisko's lips as he talked and tried not to pass

out. "Focus on my voice. Okay? I have to dig out a chunk of concrete, disinfect, and clean your wound, and it's going to hurt."

Nothing could hurt more than this already did. "Go ahead."

Sisko dabbed a cleaning cloth on my arm. I was wrong. Fire spread up and down my arm. Every muscle tensed. I did my best to focus on Sisko's rambling story about a dog he used to have, but it didn't do much good.

The edges of my vision went black again while he dug inside my arm with a pair of long tweezers.

"Got it. You okay?" He held up a quarter sized ball of blood-covered debris.

Gagging, sweat poured down my face. I kept my jaw clenched so lunch didn't reappear.

He ripped open a packet of anticoagulant powder and poured it into the wound. The bleeding stopped. He broke a water pod and let the cool liquid run over the area, then put a dressing on it. He took the giant needle and plunged it into my arm.

I squeezed my eyes shut, but in a second, all the pain vanished.

I sighed and let my jaw relax. "That's some good stuff."

Sisko cracked a smile. "I know. My dad makes it."

I actually laughed. "Of course he does."

Brent gently touched my uninjured arm. "You okay?"

I sat up straighter. "Yes, Sir."

He handed me a water pod. "Drink this." He turned to Realy. "Stay here with Jadzia while we finish the mission."

"I'm fine. Honestly." I waved my injured arm around for effect.

He wasn't buying it. "I want you safe."

So far, during sims I'd managed to shoot my squadmate

and get injured. I refused to be the first one to stay behind while the rest went on.

"Is it still clear?" I looked at Realy when I said this. I knew she would give me the truth and wouldn't try to protect me.

She nodded.

I stood. "I'm going."

Brent got to his feet and sighed. "Move out."

CHAPTER 12
JADZIA

WE CLEARED the rest of the blocks with no issues. My arm felt totally fine. I might have forgotten about it altogether, if not for the bandage and the drying blood on my uniform. We followed the info being fed into our PCDs by Drill Sergeant Wallace. He sat in a cushy command tent while we got shot at. Lucky him.

We approached a three-story building that looked like it used to be offices or classrooms. No shots rang out. No sound indicated life. Brent ordered two teams to set up a perimeter outside the building. He, Garrett, Sisko, and I would go in.

As we approached the door, Sisko shook his wrist and let out a low growl. "Something's wrong with my PCD."

Nothing seemed wrong with mine. "Show me." The way his projection jumped, glitched, and fizzled, told me everything I wanted to know. "It's just a simple hacking trick. They must not want us using them." I quickly shut my hand. Thanks to the hack I performed to get around the communications lockout, my PCD worked fine. But no one else needed to know that.

Sisko rolled his eyes. "Figures."

"Quiet," Brent said. "Focus."

We all turned back to the building in front of us. I pointed to the simple keypad lock mechanism on the door. "I can hack this."

Brent nodded and gave orders about keeping watch. I focused on the pad, which glowed to life at my touch. After a few keystrokes, I got into the maintenance system. A few more and the lock clicked open. "Got it."

Brent clapped a hand on my uninjured shoulder. "Good job. Now, Mills, you and I will take the right. Archer, Realy left. Jessup, you breach. We'll cover you."

"But —"

"No arguments, Mills. Follow orders."

Sisko and I looked at each other. He shrugged. I didn't know why Brent kept putting his second in command in danger. For sure, Sergeant Wallace would lecture Brent when the sim was over.

Brent leaned against the door frame on the right side. I set up behind him, with Realy and Garrett on the left. Sisko stood between the four of us, ready to kick the door in.

Brent positioned his rifle. "Move. Now."

Sisko kicked the door open, slamming it against the inner wall. We followed and burst into a room that looked like a lobby, except for one thing. Three soldiers from another platoon sat in a circle, in the center of the room, tied to chairs. Unconscious. With a giant plasma bomb in the middle.

We did a sweep of the room, checking behind the desk, chairs, water cooler, and dead potted plants. "Room's clear. Besides that." Sisko motioned to the group in the middle.

Garret's eyes were wide. "Now what?"

"Can't we just cut them free and carry them out?" Sisko said.

Brent switched on his laser knife. He knelt next to the closest chair and moved to cut one cord.

I screamed, "Wait." Every head turned to me.

Brent stopped, a scowl on his face. "What?"

I pointed. "The wires." I pointed frantically at the chairs, willing them to understand my point.

"What about them?"

My heart hammered against my ribs. "Those wires lead to pressure sensors on the chairs." I pointed to the soldiers. "If we move them, the whole place goes up."

"So, what do we do?" Sisko started toward the hostage closest to him. "Wake them up?"

Brent held out a hand. "Too risky. What if they panic? They might set off the explosive."

I knelt and examined the bomb. A display showed rapidly decreasing numbers. "We have nineteen minutes."

Now what? We weren't a bomb squad. Sweat trickled down my temple. I stared at the screen and watched the numbers slip away. There. A hinge under the screen. I pulled out my laser knife and pried it open.

"What are you thinking?" I jumped at the sound of Sisko's voice next to me. When did he get so close?

"A bomb is a computer with a detonator, right? I might be able to hack it."

He looked doubtful. "You're going to hack a bomb?"

"I'm going to try."

"You can do this, Jadzia." Brent's voice came from above my head. "The rest of you, guard the door."

"No pressure." Sisko tried to joke.

I sliced open the console and stared. A bunch of wires, tubes, and a number pad—probably for entering the amount of time until the bomb exploded and an arm/disarm code. I'd have to use my PCD to interface with it, which meant my team would figure out I bypassed the lockout. If Sergeant Wallace found out, I would get in trouble. Then again, if I didn't use my PCD, the bomb would explode, and I would be dead.

I quickly called up the display on my PCD and went to work. I opened the program I used to interface with the devices closest to me. My fingers flew as I worked through the layers of encryption. So much security on the bomb's mainframe. "Sisko, keep an eye on the time for me."

His voice shook. "You got it."

Sisko called off the three-minute mark when I finally accessed what I needed. Just a few more key stokes. "Got it." The timer froze, then blinked off. I sighed and eased back on my heels.

Everyone crowded around me. From their frowns, I guessed they didn't believe me.

"You're sure?" Brent said.

"I'm sure." I wiped the sweat from my forehead.

We all took a breath, and the cheers started. Everyone patted me on the back or gave me a high five.

A grin planted itself on my face and stayed the rest of the day. My shoulders straightened, and I held my head high. I might be a lousy shot, and I got hurt on a mission, but I also defused a bomb. I saved us. I guess hacking is a useful skill in the military, after all.

THE REST of training camp flew by. After the mission, we found out the bomb was fake, and we were never in any real danger. But my hacking became the talk of camp. Drill Sergeant even pulled me aside and commended me on my performance.

No one ever mentioned I broke through the blocks on our PCDs to do it. I guess they were just impressed I could. Instead of running drills until lunchtime, I spent my mornings in an intensive tech class. Which ironically enough taught me how to turn off the location beacon in my implant. Wish I figured that one out before I'd gotten to boot camp.

I missed the time with my unit and Brent. They were my family now. At least I still got the afternoons with them.

Every night for the remaining two weeks, at least five people knocked on my dorm room asking me to hack the communications block. Some wanted news. Some wanted to call home. Some wanted games to take their mind off the war. Everyone had a different reason. In the end, I traded kitchen, laundry, and bathroom cleaning duties away for the rest of my time at boot camp. Being a legend had its perks.

Graduation day arrived without the usual pomp and circumstance. Drill Sergeant congratulated us, then gave the quickest speech in graduation history. "You'll be fine soldiers." High praise coming from him.

Things happened so fast after the ceremony, I didn't even have time to call Mom and tell her I'd graduated. A few camp staff gave us crisp, urban camo uniforms, told us to pack, threw us on a bus, and drove us to New York.

The higher ups stationed our unit near Battery Park. The military had cleared most of lower Manhattan and controlled the area. Our first four days were a blur of activity. We offered aid and support to displaced citizens. We handed out countless water pods, food packets, and shelter boxes. I wondered how many of the people that I helped were in need and how many were Zealots looking to strengthen their supplies.

On day five, our commanding officer assigned our first mission. Our platoon would go in and root out a Zealot stronghold in the remains of the Times Square One building. We'd arrest them if possible and subdue them if they offered no other option.

We left at zero nine hundred. What should have been an hour and a half walk turned into four as we climbed over rubble and checked to be sure areas were clear before moving into them.

The Zealots had paid particular attention to Times Square when they destroyed the city. Piles of smoking rubble surrounded us, and sparks sometimes flew from severed power cables overhead. A mangled hand jutted from a pile of concrete. I gagged and looked away. The sun's glare on a huge piece of broken glass almost blinded me. Maybe it would burn the image out of my mind.

"This place is a lot worse than they make it look on the NNC," Brent said.

Sisko frowned. "The NNC must be showing bits and pieces to keep the public calm. If they showed how bad it really is, people would panic."

Brent ignored him. "Come on."

As in the sims, we moved in three groups, with Brent, Sisko, Garrett, and I in the lead. A hundred yards from our target, Brent held up a fist. Everyone stopped. The face shield on my helmet magnified the building so I could see it clearly, even from this distance. The entire front was gone, shorn off like someone had sliced it with a knife. I could see inside every room. "They're in there?"

"Supposed to be." Garrett shrugged. "Nothing on thermal yet, though."

We moved from rubble pile to rubble pile for cover. An explosion sounded, far away on our left, a distraction to flush out some of the expected security set up around the Zealot hideout.

We crouched and waited. If my heart pounded any louder, the Zealots might hear it. We watched the area through our magnified or infrared face shields. No movement. No sound from the building. Weird.

"I don't like this." My implant amplified Sisko's voice over the second explosion.

"That should get some of them out," Garrett said.

I fiddled with the scope on my rifle.

"Still no movement on our end." Asher chimed in from further west.

Brent waved us forward. "Let's get closer."

We crept forward until our units converged at the target

building. I looked down. The infrared on my helmet showed a few hot spots moving around. "Looks like they moved underground."

"You think they knew we were coming?" Fear laced Garrett's voice.

I glanced up at the surrounding buildings. Hot spots everywhere. My mouth went dry.

"Why didn't they show up on infrared before now?" Brent kept his voice steady, but I heard the apprehension behind his words.

Sisko's voice shook. "They must have some kind of dampening technology."

Garrett flailed his arm. "So why show themselves now?"

I found my voice. "Because we're exactly where they want us."

NONE OF US MOVED. A female voice I didn't recognize sounded in my ear. "We don't want to hurt any of you. If you turn and leave, we'll let you go without a fight."

I swore, moved my infrared display to the corner of my helmet, and looked at Brent. I mouthed without sound. "They hacked us."

"We need to mov—" Garret said.

Brent made a slashing motion across his throat. "If we can hear them, they might be able to hear us."

"We can," the female voice said.

Brent gave the command for everyone to turn off their coms. "Serpent." An easy to remember word, most likely never used in battle. To most people, I'm sure he looked collected, but I saw the tremor in his hand and the glint of fear in his eyes.

Without coms, we were cut off from everyone. No talking to each other. No talking to the other teams in the area. No way to call for help. Not good.

Brent moved next to me and leaned in. I caught a whiff

of dirt and sweat, but also a hint of his aftershave. Unfortunately, I didn't have the luxury of enjoying it.

"Jadzia, can you hack them back?"

"What? Oh, I mean, yes, sir. I can try." This wasn't the same as hacking Mom's PCD or even hacking the bomb. I didn't know how they were hacking us or their location, both things I usually needed when hacking. I opened my PCD, and my fingers flew across the display. A bead of sweat rolled down the side of my face. Minutes passed.

"Hurry, Jadzia," Brent said.

I let out a growl of frustration. Still nothing.

Garrett's voice, so quiet I could barely hear it. "We need to get out of here. They aren't going to wait forever."

Brent shook his head. "If we move, they might open fire."

"She said," Garrett pointed to his com, "we could leave without fighting."

"They're Zealots." Brent shook his head. "We can't trust them."

Garrett opened his mouth, but I interrupted.

"I have something. Just hang on." I typed faster. Electricity zapped up my arm. I cried out and clenched my hand into a fist, shutting off my PCD.

Brent touched my shoulder. "What happened?"

"They spiked me." My eyes watered. I shook my hand to get rid of the pain.

Brent cursed. "Are you okay?"

"I will be. It's not too bad." I hid my wrist so he wouldn't see the burn mark. "But we still don't have secure coms."

He gently took my wrist, turned it over, and looked at Sisko. "Toss me burn salve."

"We don't have time for this." I gave him a useless shove.

He ignored me.

Sisko dug in his pack and threw Brent the salve. He spread some around and under my PCD band. I sighed when the pain vanished.

"Better?"

I nodded. "Thank you."

Brent studied the buildings trapping us on every side. He motioned for us to turn our coms back on. We touched our ears and Brent spoke. "I'd like to speak to the leader of your group."

The same female voice answered. "I'm listening."

Brent took a deep breath. "We're here to prevent any further damage to this city and to rescue any remaining people. If you and your group surrender to us without resistance, we won't harm you."

A soft laugh came over our coms. "Why would I believe that?"

I couldn't help myself. "We aren't the ones who spiked you."

Brent glared at me and put a finger to his lips. He waved us toward him. The five of us crouched behind our pile of rubble and clustered around Brent. He drew a square in the layer of dust on the ground. "I can understand why you don't trust us." While he talked, he pointed to each of us, then drew a line to the square. He wanted us to move in while he pretended to negotiate.

"I don't need to trust you. Our group outnumbers yours. We're willing to let you leave." She paused.

Brent continued to direct us.

The woman's voice changed to an almost pleading tone. "Just go."

"I like our odds," Brent said.

I didn't. Five in our immediate group, four in Realy's group, and four in Asher's. The other two groups had approached, one from the east and one from the west, increasing our number to forty. The building directly in front of us showed at least thirty hot spots alone. Not to mention all the ones in the other buildings.

Since we couldn't communicate our plans without being overheard, we could only hope the other squads could see us and would follow our lead. But, of course, we would follow orders.

Brent finished drawing and looked each one of us in the eye. We all nodded.

My heart beat so fast I thought it might take off. His plan might have worked, but when I moved, shots rang out.

Sisko yelled so loud he almost blew out my implant. "We're taking fire."

Like I couldn't tell.

Everyone took cover again. I sheltered behind a large pile of rubble which allowed me to remain standing. All of us opened fire. Even me. The infrared in the corner of my helmet showed me where the targets were, but instead of aiming for a specific target, I sprayed the front of the building with fire. Maybe I'd actually hit something.

The blasts from both sides sent chunks of debris into the air. I choked on dust.

"We have to move," Brent said.

But I couldn't. Unlike in training, this was real. People were trying to kill us. I needed to stop them. I kept firing. A hand grabbed my shoulder. I swung the butt of my rifle around and clubbed whomever snuck up on me.

"What'd you do that for?" Garrett, his eyes wild, lay at my feet with blood pouring from his nose.

A hunk of concrete blew off the top of the pile of debris in front of us. I threw myself to my knees. Little bits of concrete rained down over us.

Garrett got to his feet, grabbed my arm, and pulled me to him. "We have to go."

We ran from rubble pile to rubble pile. Stopping to shoot when we had adequate cover. Between attempting to avoid getting shot, or being impaled by flying debris, and looking for cover, I didn't have time to look at the ground. I slipped on something and threw my arms out to break my fall. I somehow kept hold of my rifle.

"Garrett." My voice wasn't nearly loud enough to hear over the shots and explosions. "Wait."

He disappeared around a heap of junk.

I started to get up, and an odd shape sticking out from behind a low concrete wall caught my attention. I shook my head to help clear it. The odd shape was a pair of boots positioned as if someone were on their side.

A strange smell, almost like rust, assaulted me. I gasped. Blood on the ground. On me. My stomach revolted. I turned my head and vomited, barely missing the face shield of my helmet.

My ears rang. I recoiled. I pushed myself to my knees, but I couldn't just leave the person. Maybe I'd be able to help.

I crawled around the small wall, and everything stopped.

"BRENT!" I set my gun aside and rolled him onto his back.

Blood gushed from his abdomen. Laser guns didn't cause this kind of wound. I whipped my head from side to side. A string of curse words flowed from my mouth. No med kit within reach.

The stuff in my pack wouldn't touch this kind of injury. But I needed to try. I yanked my first aid supplies out of my bag. Broke a large water pod over his stomach. "No. No. No." Was that buckshot? I screamed. Some of the Zealots were using the old-fashioned weapons we'd learned about in school. Guns that shot balls of lead.

My hands shook. I tore open a small anticoagulant pack. Dumped it on Brent's stomach. Pressed my hands over the wound. Blood gushed everywhere. His blood.

Keep it together. Help him. The tears in my eyes made it hard to see, but it didn't look good.

I yelled his name. His eyes flickered open. His lips moved. I took my helmet off and put my ear above his mouth.

"Jadzia." I could hardly hear him.

"Stay with me."

He gave me a small nod. His eyes closed. I yelled his name again. I couldn't let him go. First Dad. Then Uncle Nick. Now Brent. Pain stabbed me in the chest. My hand flew up to where it hurt. I pawed at my shirt.

I yelled his name again, louder this time. His eyes opened slowly and locked onto mine. His chest heaved with effort. "Go. Save . . . yourse—"

"You said you'd stay. I'm not leaving."

He shook his head. "Please. Go."

I ignored him and kept the pressure on his stomach. Not that it helped.

His hand weakly sought my cheek, and I leaned over him. He tangled his fingers in my hair and pulled me closer. Every breath was a struggle. "I . . . love . . .you." His hand dropped and his chest stilled.

"Brent! No. No." I pumped his chest and breathed into his mouth. I couldn't bring him back. I closed his eyes and crossed his hands at his chest. Sobbing, choking on dust, and trembling all over, I cradled his head and kissed him. His lips were still warm. He couldn't hear me, but I had to say it. "I love you too."

A pile of rubble exploded near me and caught fire. I flinched. Shots fired all around me. I'd been still fifteen minutes too long during a raging fire fight. I should move. But Brent. I couldn't carry him. I couldn't leave him. Another burst of concrete blasted near my head. My survival instincts kicked in. Move. Find Garrett, Sisko, and the others. Get back to camp.

I picked up the gun sitting next to me, and looked at Brent's face one last time, memorizing every feature. Then, I did something I never thought I'd ever do. And it almost killed me. I turned my back. Staying low, I walked away. And left him.

I didn't get far. Maybe a quarter of a block from where I left Brent, the ground in front of me exploded. Terror coursed through my veins, and I jumped behind the nearest shelled out vehicle. I couldn't suck in a full breath.

I stared at the bloody gun in my hands. Brent. How many more people would I lose because of this stupid war? Garrett? Asher? Myself?

Myself. I didn't realize until this moment, I'd already lost her. Who was I? I hadn't wanted to be here in the first place. Now I was running through the streets of New York trying to kill people. Would I tear someone away from their loved-one, like Brent had been torn away from me?

I flinched. Metal pinged off the car I hid behind. I breathed in through my nose and out through my mouth. Once. Twice. I knew what I needed to do.

I squared my shoulders and wiped my tears. No one would die because of me. I refused to cause someone else this pain.

I tore my dog tags off, and threw them near the base of a burning pile of rubble. With luck, everyone would think I'd gotten myself kidnapped or blown to pieces.

A small voice in the back of my mind reminded me of Jonathan, Mom, Garrett, Sisko, Asher, and the rest of my family and friends. But I hadn't seen Garrett, Sisko, or Asher in a while. They might be dead, too.

If the military found my tags, Mom and Jonathan would think I'd died. Mom would survive—she always did. But Jonathan. The thought of his little face pulled me up short. I had promised him I'd be back. I shook my head to clear it. Focus. Where was I? What came next?

Get away.

I crawled to the next intersection, ducked down 47th Street, and ran. Opening my PCD, I pulled up a map. I needed a bridge. If I headed south, I'd eventually rejoin my company. While not all two hundred soldiers in the company knew me, many did. I'd be instantly recognized. If I went north, I'd hit the George Washington Bridge. Maybe I could cross there and get off this stupid island.

The sound of boots pounding pavement interrupted my train of thought. I knew the sound well. I'd heard it over and over during training. I dove through a broken window and rolled behind a counter. Bits of glass cracked and tinkled under my weight. My heart raced. I hadn't even been gone for ten minutes. Surely my commanding offer hadn't sent a search party after me. He shouldn't even know I was missing yet.

The boots grew closer. I held my breath. They passed the store. I waited until they grew fainter and peaked out. I risked a glance out the broken window.

A full platoon rushed down the street toward Times Square. Reinforcements. Of course. I sagged back to the floor.

Pain stabbed at my hands. The tough material of my uniform prevented most of my body from getting cut, but my bare hands weren't so lucky. I winced as I picked shards of glass from open flesh. Luckily, nothing looked too deep, but it was hard to tell what blood belonged to me and what belonged to Brent. I choked back a sob.

No. I couldn't think about him right now. I had to move. I checked the street. All clear.

I turned down 8th Avenue until I came to Central Park. In the park, I stopped at the first pond I found. I plunged my hands into the cool water. The cuts stung and bled, but I didn't stop scrubbing. I shuddered. I might never get all Brent's blood off.

The more I scrubbed, the more hysteria rose in me. I tried to fight it. I needed to move. Get off the island. I needed . . . needed. . . Strange sounds came from my mouth. I gave in and curled up by the side of the pond and sobbed. I cried for Brent. For Uncle Nick. For Dad. I cried for Jonathan, Mom, and Carina. I cried for Sisko, Garrett, and Asher. And I cried for myself. My mind cycled through images of their faces until I ran out of tears.

CHAPTER 16

JADZIA

EVENTUALLY, I pulled myself together enough to take stock of my situation. Night would be here soon. The darker it got, the colder it would get. I needed shelter.

I also needed to do something about my implant. If my tags didn't convince my commanding officers I'd died in the battle, they'd start tracing me. Most likely to find me and render aid. When they saw I wasn't anywhere near the place I should be, and not injured or captured, I'd be in trouble. I didn't know what they would do exactly, but I didn't want to find out.

To hack into my implant, I needed a new PCD. I knew a lot about fixing PCDs, but not enough to save a fried one.

My most immediate issue sat on the northern side of the park—the outer defense perimeter. Somehow, I'd have to get past those soldiers. On the upside, a good number of them ran past me a while ago. On the downside, I didn't know when they would return.

I headed north, trying to figure out a plan as I went. Each blockade should be two blocks deep. The position of the northern blockade stretched from Columbus Avenue all the way down 110th Street to Park Avenue. The east and west blockades picked up at those streets on their respective sides, forming an annoyingly perfect square.

When I approached the defense perimeter, I decided to walk right in and pretend I belonged there. With my uniform covered in blood, they'd likely send me to the medical area. I had to appear desperate enough to go, but strong enough to walk on my own, so they wouldn't send a guard with me. Once inside, it should be easy enough to just keep going. No-man's-land lay north of the barricade. I could lose myself easily enough there.

I walked to 110th Street and saw the barricade. Low concrete walls, barbed wire, a few supply trucks and about thirty soldiers with rifles. When I got within thirty feet of the wall, every soldier zeroed in and aimed at me. Great. I took a deep breath to steady myself and held my rifle over my head with both hands.

In a crisp, southern accent, an officer yelled, "Stay where you are."

I stopped. Too bad I'd ditched my tags. They'd have been useful proof of my identity if my uniform didn't convince them. "I'm one of yours." Well, I used to be. Of course, I wouldn't tell them that.

The guy who'd yelled nodded to the soldiers in line. Five of them broke rank and approached.

As they neared, I saw Brent, Asher, Sisko, Realy, and me. My breath caught in my throat. No. I willed myself to focus, to see the strangers who were actually approaching. I had to pull this off. My rifle grew heavy, but I didn't dare put it down. The only thing that could make this worse would be getting shot.

A few feet away, they stopped. "Identify yourself." A

girl, slightly older than me, squinted at me over her gun sight.

"Private First Class Jadzia Mills. Bravo Company, First Platoon, Fourth Squad." The soldiers relaxed and aimed their weapons at the ground.

"At ease, Private," the girl said.

I shifted and lowered my gun, grateful to get some blood flow back in my arms. The world spun. I slumped to my knees and groaned. So much for walking to the med bay on my own.

Two of the soldiers moved next to me. They gently pulled me to my feet. "We've got you. Can you walk?"

They half-helped, half-carried me through the block-ade. They got me to the med bay, a large white building pod. I tried to take note of every detail. The entry led into a large room with medical equipment and about twenty cots. A few other doors led to what I assumed were restrooms and an office.

The soldiers eased me onto one of the cots. I cringed. Who else would end up in here? Or in a building just like this one. Sisko? Asher? Garrett? I wanted to curl up and cry again, but I couldn't. The medic, a red-haired man around Dad's age, approached. "I'm Staff Sergeant Augustine." He smiled.

I muttered a response, but he didn't correct my lack of protocol, probably used to the injured not caring about rank.

He took my rifle and backpack, set them under the cot, and scanned my implant to confirm my identity. Crap. I'd forgotten about that. Now they had on record what direction I went. Couldn't do anything about it now. Just had to focus on ditching this medic and getting out of here.

"What happened to you? I see a lot of blood on your

uniform, but you don't seem too injured." His voice soft and gentle.

I flinched. "It's . . . not mine."

"I'm sorry." He opened the front of my jacket. "Let's check you over, just in case."

With a pair of scissors, he cut through my T-shirt. Great. How would I get out of here without a shirt?

He used tweezers to remove a few slivers of glass I'd missed and bandaged my hands. His attention went to the wrist with my PCD on it. "What happened here?"

"I got spiked." I closed my eyes to block the memory. It didn't work.

"Looks like you were able to use some burn cream, at least."

I nodded.

He gently removed my PCD and applied a salve. "It's healed enough for you to wear a new PCD. I'll get you one after we're finished."

After my exam, Sergeant Augustine declared me fit, but exhausted. I could have told him that.

He gave me a pair of gray pants, a gray sweatshirt, and new PCD. "It's already activated and coded to your implant."

"Thank you." I took the PCD and snapped it on my wrist, trying to cover my shaking hands. The band vibrated as it aligned itself to my bioenergy.

He left me to sleep. I wanted nothing more than to sink into the gel mattress of the cot and sleep for a week, but I forced myself to stay awake. I almost dozed off a dozen times, mesmerized by the silent medics weaving between cots. I bit my lip to keep myself awake.

A medic brought me a tray of food and some water pods. I forced the food down. Memories of all of us sitting around at breakfast before we left on the mission assaulted me. Sisko had teased me about shooting Realy in training. Brent had assured me there would be something to hack. Maybe I could even defuse another bomb. Except this time I hadn't. This time, the bomb that exploded wasn't physical. If my hacking skills were better, I'd have been able to prevent all of this. I gagged and set the tray on the small table beside my cot.

As the day wore on, injured soldiers filled the remaining cots. No one I knew. I couldn't decide if that was a good thing or a bad thing. Sisko, Garrett, Asher and everyone else could be safely back at base, not in need of medical care. Or they might be dead.

My dad, uncle, and Brent ran through my thoughts over and over. Parties, dinners, holidays. Memory after memory played in my head. Who knew I had more tears?

Darkness fell. Sergeant Augustine approached my cot. "I informed your commanding officers you're here. They asked me to send you back. I told them I want you to rest here for the night. You need it." He patted my shoulder. "Try to get some sleep. I'm going off duty now. I'll see you in the morning."

"Thanks." I forced a half-smile. He returned it and walked away. He pushed through one of the side doors and flipped on a light in what must be a little office.

Sleep. Right. My body tensed.

Shift change. The small amount of medic training I'd had in Basic came back to me. The medics leaving shift would go over charts and discuss patients with arriving staff.

I figured I had about thirty minutes. I swung my legs over the edge of the cot. Time to move.

I GRABBED my bag and rifle from the shelf under the bed. My regular uniform would have been better than these sweats, but they were warmer than my uniform, which would be handy later.

A few of the other injured soldiers looked up at me, but no one said anything. The rest either slept or were too drugged to notice.

The door to the room Sergeant Augustine had disappeared into stood open. I needed to pass that doorway to reach the exit—or the restroom. Hopefully, anyone who saw me would assume the latter. Heading for the med bay restroom with a bag and rifle seemed totally normal. Right? I rolled my eyes. Sure.

I shifted the rifle to hold it upright against the left side of my body, away from the door. Because this looked totally not suspicious. I took a deep breath and hurried past.

"Mills, do you need something?" Sergeant Augustine's voice chased me.

I swore under my breath. "Just going to the bathroom." I hoped he didn't come out of the office.

"Okay. Just checking."

I didn't hesitate. I stepped through the exit and slipped into the night.

The night air cooled my hot skin. I slipped around the side of the med building and crossed a path through the rubble. Sticking close to the different piles, I made my way to the northern edge of the blockade. Since the Zealots were encamped toward the south, this side of the blockade wasn't as heavily guarded.

When I reached the perimeter, a few soldiers—probably supposed to be patrolling the area—played games on their PCDs. In the dark, I avoided them enough and crossed the line into open territory.

I sighed and relaxed. The perimeter alarm went off. I swore and bolted into the dark. Behind me, soldiers shouted.

I hid behind a car that looked like it had seen better days. Through the back windows of the car, I watched the sleepy encampment came alive. Flood lights came on. Soldiers swarmed. But everyone focused in, not out.

Of course. They assumed Zealots had broken into the camp on a raid for supplies or to attack. No one assumed someone sneaking out of camp would trip the alarm. Why would they?

Still, I didn't linger. Someone might realize they were missing a patient and figure I'd tripped the alarm.

Buildings stood like quiet sentries over empty streets, not at all like Manhattan should be. I kept looking over my shoulder. Every noise made me jump. For about an hour, I wandered north. I needed to find a safe place to crash, but first I needed to make my implant untraceable. I collapsed in the alcove of a convenience store.

Hacking would have been much easier with my old

PCD because of the programs I had created on it, but I needed to work with what I had. I broke open one of my water pods and drank while I worked. My eyes were dry. So tired. I shook myself. I had to keep at it.

Finally, I found the code I was looking for. Thank you Sergeant Wallace's advance tech classes. After a few more tweaks, I turned the locator off. I sighed, got to my feet, and stretched.

I needed to find somewhere to sleep. I walked another seven blocks to put distance between me and the spot my implant placed me last.

When I tripped over my own foot, I knew I'd reached my end. I climbed through the nearest broken window. Using the flashlight feature of my PCD, I scanned the smallish boutique clothing store. New clothes would have been great, but looters beat me to it.

This place gave me the creeps. It should be full of clothes and shoes. Instead, racks were overturned, cases broken open, and glass littered the floor. Everything of value was gone.

I jumped. A silhouette leaned against a door. My light shone over it. Just a mannequin. My shoulders sagged. I craved sleep. But first, I had to make sure I was alone.

I walked the perimeter of the store looking for . . . I don't know what exactly. A place to lie down, a chair, a scrap of cloth I could use as a blanket. Anything. Instead, I found a door. I pressed my ear against it to see if I could hear anything. Nothing but my pounding heart. Slowly, with my rifle aimed, I opened the door.

No movement. Just a counter with a coffeepot on it, a fridge, a table, three chairs, and a small couch. This must have been the employee break room. I thanked—well, I didn't know who—but it seemed the right thing to do. The couch would be tight, but I'd much rather sleep there than on the floor.

I pulled the plastic tablecloth from the table, doubled it, sat on the couch, and spread the cloth over my upper half. Better than nothing. I put one arm through the strap of my pack and one arm through the strap of my gun. Both rested on my chest. That way, if I had to move quickly, at least they were attached to me.

I set an alarm on my PCD for six hours. Not as much sleep as I wanted. But hopefully enough. I had a long day ahead of me tomorrow. I lay with my eyes open, staring into the blackness. Despite my exhaustion, my mind wouldn't shut down. I couldn't stop thinking about everything that had happened. A strange numbness washed over me. Exhaustion settled in and darkness took me.

CHAPTER 18

JADZIA

I JOLTED awake and sprang off the couch. Another crash resonated from the front of the store. I slung my pack on my back and raised my rifle. Creeping through the dark room, I tried not to bump the table. I found the door, still slightly open, and hovered behind it. Peering into the darkness, my heart raced. A scuffling noise came from the left. I took a deep breath.

Calm down. Probably someone looking for food. In a clothing store. In the dark. Sure. Maybe if I stayed quiet, they'd go away.

No such luck. The scuffling came closer to the door. I took a deep breath. At least I'd have the element of surprise. When the noise moved as close as I could stand it, I flung the door all the way open with my gun raised in one hand. I opened my other hand, so the flashlight came on, and aimed it toward the noise. A yellow dog let out a surprised yelp. Air escaped my lungs.

I crouched. "Come here, pup." I made clicking noises and held my hand out. The dog stepped toward me. I buried my fingers in fur. "All that fuss for you."

Then I heard it. Footsteps crunching on glass. I froze. Flashlight on, talking to a dog. My position was obvious and everything but defensible.

Move. I whipped up and faced the footsteps. My flashlight illuminated a twenty-something, muscular guy twice my size. I raised my gun and aimed. At least he didn't know I couldn't shoot to save my life. Which is exactly what I might need to do.

"What are you doing here? What do you want?" I tried to sound tough, but my voice cracked.

"I followed the dog. I want food." His voice sounded rough, like he'd swallowed sandpaper. He took a step toward me. The dog cowered behind my legs. Food. He couldn't mean the dog, could he? Surely we weren't at that point yet.

"I don't have any."

"What's in the pack?" He took another few steps. A knife in his left hand flashed in the beam of my light.

Crap. I really didn't want to give up my pack. I carried everything I owned in it. "Don't come any closer." I backed away, nudging the dog as I went. We hit the wall.

He smirked and took another few steps. Any closer and he could grab me. I threw my pack at him. "Now go away."

He caught my bag and set it on the floor. He looked around. "You know, I kinda like it here. The company is real good." His eyes swept up and down my body.

My skin crawled. I could see his eyes clearly now. Red pupils wide, wild. He had to be on something. My voice shook. "I'll shoot."

He laughed, a rasping sound that sent a chill through me. "I don't think you will."

I hedged to the left. Maybe I could get around him and make a run for it. He didn't seem to be in any shape to catch me. The dog moved with me. So did the man. Crap.

The dog poked its head out from behind my legs and growled softly.

The man laughed again. "What're you going do, mutt?" He stomped and lunged toward us.

I jumped.

The dog whimpered and cowered.

He scoffed. "That's what I thought."

"We're going to be okay." I said it as much to the dog as to myself.

I moved my finger to the trigger. "Last chance."

He lunged forward and grabbed at the rifle. I tightened my grip. His knife came up and slashed at my arm. I cried out but didn't let go of the gun. I kicked him as hard as I could, but he didn't seem to notice. He leaned in. Rank breath washed over me. I pulled the trigger.

His body jerked and his eyes widened. He slumped into me. I couldn't take his weight and fell against the wall. I got out from under him and left him in a heap.

My head reeled. I'd forgotten. I still had my kill cartridge in my rifle from the battle. Not a stun cartridge.

I'd just killed someone.

My stomach roiled. I turned away from him. Grabbed my pack and ran. I ran until my legs gave out and I fell to my knees, chest heaving. I couldn't go any further.

I'd killed someone. Sure, he attacked me. But. I. Had. Killed. Someone. What if there was another way? I'd became a fugitive from the army so I wouldn't have to kill anyone, only to end up doing it anyway. I started to laugh. Giant bursts of laughter I couldn't control poured out of me. Tears streamed down my face. Wave after wave of hysteria bubbled up until I couldn't tell if I was laughing or sobbing.

The feel of his hands pulling on the gun. The smell of his breath. The weight of his body slumping against me. His blood on my clothes. For the second time in two days, my clothes were stained with someone else's blood. Brent's blood. This guy's blood. Brent dying in my arms. This guy dying in my arms. One I desperately wanted to save, one whose life I took. I jammed my fingers into my hair and screamed into the breaking dawn.

A whine broke through my haze of emotion. Something licked my arms, my hands, my face. The dog had followed me. I threw my arms around it and cried. I ran my fingers through its warm fur.

Eventually, the tide ebbed. Numbness set in. I couldn't stay here. Focus on the goal.

I needed to get off the island. Get home to Mom and Jonathan. Get somewhere safe. I wiped my eyes and nose on my sleeve. I forced myself to think about my first step. Find an unguarded bridge. Unlikely. Figure out a way past the guards. Figure out a way home after that. Ugh. How on earth could I do this?

I needed a cross street to figure out where I was. "Come on, girl."

She gave a snuff and bounded to my side. A small smile cracked my lips. "At least I have you."

Together, we walked down the war-torn street, away from the rising sun.

CHAPTER 19

JADZIA

MY BEST CHANCE TO get away from this hellhole would be the George Washington Bridge. Being closest, and in the opposite direction of my unit, it made sense. A better swimmer would have tried to cover the distance by water, but I'd likely drown before I got to shore. The dog seemed happy to stick with me. At least I wasn't totally alone.

What would my commanders think? Surely their minds wouldn't jump straight to me running away. Maybe that they'd think Zealots kidnapped me. But why kidnap just me and no one else? I shook my head. It didn't really matter, but it kept my mind off . . . other things.

When we reached the intersection of Broadway and 168th Street, I realized I'd covered more ground than I thought. Good. The bridge stood a few blocks away. I made my way closer, moving from abandoned car to abandoned car until I could see the guards. I waited and watched.

Relief washed through me. The bridge didn't belong to the military, at least on this side. A bunch of heavily armed Zealots guarded the bridge. They'd used a group of cars as a makeshift barrier, and five of them lounged on the hoods of the cars. They also had a few Hover-bikes and trucks nearby.

I snapped a few pictures with my PCD and retreated to a safer location to study them. About three blocks away, I found a dumpster in an alley. I sat on the pavement and groaned.

My stomach rumbled, and I opened my pack. I hadn't eaten since the med bay tried to give me dinner.

Six energy bars and ten water pods, plus the small med kit that had failed to save Brent's life. I quickly stuffed the kit back into the bag. I didn't have time to go there right now.

I looked at the dog. "It's not much food."

I ripped open an energy bar and chewed. While I ate, I fished through the rest of the contents of my bag. Three more kill cartridges for my rifle and three stun cartridges. I switched my rifle cartridge to a stun cartridge. I'd never use a kill cartridge again, but I couldn't bring myself to get rid of them. I replaced everything but a water pod.

I ate almost the entire energy bar, then threw the last bite to the dog. She caught it in midair. I patted her on the head. "Nice catch."

Biting into the water pod, I opened my PCD and looked at the pictures of the bridge and guards. Expressions ranged from frustration to bored out of their minds. Of course. Instead of fighting, they were stuck here on bridge duty. Images of the battle pushed their way past my mental block. No. I forced them aside. Focus. I'd fall apart again later.

Maybe I could just walk up to the Zealots. Pretend I belonged to them. They might let me through. But why would I be leaving? If I could get on a bike, I could escape faster. But how to get a bike?

I rubbed the dog between her ears. "We need a diversion, girl. What do you think? Any ideas?" Less than twenty-four hours since I last talked to someone, I was asking a dog for advice. Maybe I had lost it. At least she didn't answer.

What would be enough of a distraction to draw them away from the bridge? I rubbed my hands together. Maybe if I blew something up. Something big. Something close.

I pulled up a map of New York on my PCD. I found a convenience store three blocks away. Hoping they'd have some flammable items, I set off. The dog followed me. Cool. I could use the company.

I stepped into the store through the broken-out front window. The dog jumped in behind me. Enough daylight filtered in through the gaping hole for me to see some of the shelves still held items, despite it being six weeks since the attack. New York was a big place. I guess the Zealots just hadn't gotten around to clearing out this part of town yet. What if someone came while I was there? I shuddered and picked up my pace.

I found fire-starting packs, rags, and fuel. Arms full, I climbed out the window and headed back to my dumpster.

"We need a target now, girl." I pulled up my PCD and clicked around the map. There. A food fabrication research lab, two blocks from the bridge. We learned about these labs in school. Scientists perfected and created new foods to be fabricated there. Since the building had to be kept impeccably clean, it likely had a stockpile of decontamination chemicals. All explosive or flammable.

The large building sat about five blocks from the bridge. I'm sure there were more strategic targets, but at the moment it would do. My rear-end had gone numb, and I didn't want to move again. My head pounded. I took out the med kit and dry swallowed pain tablets.

I struggled to my feet and walked toward the lab with my load. The dog followed a few steps behind me. I held up my hand. "No girl, you stay here. It's too dangerous."

She looked up at me with her big brown eyes.

"I'll be back. I promise." Seems like I made that promise a lot. "Stay."

It didn't take me long to get to the lab. I ducked down an alley at the rear of the building. The rear door required a retinal scan to get in. I didn't have the time, nor the mental ability, to hack the lock.

I took my rifle out and tried to blast it. Of course I missed. I fired again. Missed. A low growl escaped my lips. I smacked myself in the forehead. Duh. Even I couldn't miss when my gun rested on the target. Placing the tip of my rifle against the lock, I blasted it. The lock crackled and smoked and the door swung open. The building was far enough from the bridge to keep the Zealots from hearing. Hopefully, no one was closer.

I found a supply closet on the ground floor inside a restroom. I added rags from the store to ones I found in the closet and threw them into a cleaning cart. Moving through the building, I gathered more chemicals from other closets. Lucky for me, cleaning supplies aren't coveted items in an apocalyptic wasteland.

By the time I finished, I had enough to soak the closet and most of the surfaces in the restroom. I poured the fuel and chemicals over the rags and cart. My head spun and my eyes watered from the stench of chemicals.

I took off my shirt and undershirt, replaced my shirt and wrapped my undershirt over my mouth and nose. It didn't help much. I fumbled with one of my kill laser rifle cartridges, setting it to overload. My fingers slipped, and I dropped it. My hands flew up to protect my face.

It didn't go off. My hands dropped, and I sighed.

Picking the cartridge up, I finished the programming. I threw the cartridge in the cart and moved as fast as I could. I slipped on the slick floor and went down. Cursing, I used the sink to pull myself up and out the door. The overload would take about seven minutes. I needed to get clear, fast. With all the chemicals, I expected a fairly decent blast range.

I ran hard until I got back to our dumpster. My dog greeted me with a yip. I crouched behind the dumpster and pulled her close. "Told you I'd be back."

The massive explosion sent out a shock wave. The dumpster and my body shook. When it was over, I smiled. That went better than I expected.

CHAPTER 20

JADZIA

SINCE I DIDN'T KNOW which direction the Zealots would take to the lab, I waited about fifteen minutes before moving. The dog and I walked to the spot where I'd first scoped out the bridge, ready to duck behind a tree or around a corner if I sensed someone approaching.

We made it to the bridge ramp undetected. My heart rate kicked up. Now came the tricky part. We moved from car to car.

Only two guards remained. They'd also left most of the vehicles. I snorted. Obviously, these Zealots weren't trained in any kind of military tactics. All the better for me.

Both guards watched the plume smoke in the distance, clearly wishing they were out there instead of guarding a bridge no one was around to cross. No one but me.

I watched for five minutes. Occasionally, the guards seemed to remember their job, and their heads swiveled in my direction, but they mostly talked on their PCDs or stood staring at the smoke.

I didn't have a plan for getting across the giant length of

the bridge, let alone what to do on the other side. Getting rid of the guards had been my priority. Such an idiot. Now what? I rubbed my temples.

Abandoned cars littered the length of the bridge as far as I could see. The military had evacuated people in large groups to take them to designated safety centers. On trucks. Things worked easier that way. It'd be chaos if everyone brought their own vehicle.

I could make my way from car to car, but once I got to the other side, I'd need something fast. A car was too big to maneuver through lines of abandoned cars. I scanned the backup of vehicles on the bridge. My gaze rested on a Hover-bike. That worked.

We moved a few cars closer to the bike.

I heard one of the guards say, "Hey look, a dog."

Crap. I lay flat to watch their feet from under the car. One guard walked toward us.

Maybe this would be where I had to say goodbye to my dog. I took a deep breath and ran my fingers through her fur. "Thank you for keeping me company." I nudged the dog out from behind the car. "Go on."

I watched her feet as she walked down the driver's side of the cars toward the guard. She met him about two and a half cars ahead of me. With the Zealot distracted, I slipped down the opposite side of the cars until I reached the bike.

I crouched next to it and started hacking the starter pad. Hover-bike starter pads sat where gas tanks used to be, in front of the rider. Low enough so the bike still gave me cover, but high enough so I couldn't really see unless I exposed my head.

Bikes were coded to start only with their owner's, or an authorized rider's bio-signature. I needed to tell this bike to recognize my bio-signature as either the owner or an authorized rider.

I glanced at the guards. The one who met my dog took her back to his companion. Both guards knelt, petted her, and fed her bits of something. My heart sank. She'd been good company. But this bike had no way of bringing her with me, and I knew she'd never keep up.

While I worked, I had to keep ducking down to avoid detection. Frustration worked its way past my lips. I should be finished by now.

Finally, I got into the bike's systems and coded it to recognize me. I peeked out. The guards had lost interest in my poor dog. They were back to looking at their PCDs.

I tightened my rifle and backpack straps. Took a deep breath. Jumped on the bike and slammed my hand on the start pad. If the bike had tires, I'd have squealed them.

For a few seconds, the shocked guards just stared at me. I zipped past them before they snapped out if it. I glanced back and saw two things. The guards jumped into a car to give chase, and my dog ran as fast as she could to keep up with me. I blinked back tears and gunned the engine, leaving her behind.

With a good head start on the Zealots, the wind rushed by me. The bike provided much needed speed and freedom —not just from the island, but from my thoughts. It had been too long since I last rode.

About halfway across the bridge, the Zealots dropped back. I let out a whoop. I'd done it. My exhilaration lasted about three seconds. Another blockade faced me, one a lot more impressive than on the pile of cars on the Zealot side. I slowed. Low, concrete walls stood on both sides of a small wooden gate. Guards lined up behind the wall, their rifles aimed.

"Halt," one of them said, his voice amplified by a mega booster.

No way. I opened the bike up as wide as it would go and shot forward. They opened fire.

I crouched over the handlebars, weaving as much as I could. Maybe I'd be harder to hit. Not everyone's aim was as bad as mine, though. The bike took a few shots.

An exit ramp on the right looked like the easiest place to get through. I rammed the bike into the wooden gate. It splintered. The bike shuddered. I slipped backward and almost lost my grip.

The ramp formed a sharp curve, and I had to brake. I didn't turn back to see if anyone followed me, but I heard shouts, and the bike took a few more shots. An engine started up, and I took a side street, then another.

I wove in and out of cars, in and out of neighborhoods, taking random quick turns.

I pulled the bike to the side of the road and looked around. All seemed quiet. Only a few cars and people roamed. No one seemed to notice me, let alone be following me. I pulled up a map on my PCD. No location services. Right. I'd disabled that. My shoulders ached. I rubbed my eyes. I found the closest street sign and did a search on the map for Monroe Avenue. Crap. Best I could tell I was in Jersey now. I had been going farther away from home. I studied the map, then headed out again.

This time I drove less like a fugitive and more like a normal person. Trying to blend in, I should probably switch vehicles and find new clothes, but stealing felt wrong. Manhattan had been overrun with Zealots and crazy dog-eating people. These were normal people trying to deal with a war. I couldn't treat them the same way.

I rode for about five hours before the charge died. I

found a charging station at a local business park, but no power. What day was it? I checked my PCD. Sunday—the day no one worked, even during a war. Of course, the charging stations were closed.

Sighing, I left the bike by the curb and walked toward the woods near the offices. The shadows lengthened and my legs didn't want to work anymore. I made it about thirty feet in and sat against a tree. A chill shot through me. Alone in the woods. What if looters found me . . . or a bear?

I'd be fine. I just needed to calm down.

Yeah, right. Calm down. My best friend lay dead back in New York. I had abandoned my military unit. I had killed someone. A strange numbness settled over me. I wanted to cry. To scream. But I couldn't work up the energy. I was going to need so much therapy when I got home.

I took out an energy bar and a water pod. I drank the water and got about halfway through the energy bar. My eyes closed on their own. I didn't fight them. I slid down and curled up on my side. Sure would be nice to have my dog now.

CHAPTER 21

JADZIA

I WOKE the next day and checked the time on my PCD. One in the afternoon. I could use another five or six hours of sleep. Instead, I sat up and stretched. I finished the energy bar from last night and ate another one. This left me only three bars and seven water pods. Didn't help that I was starving. A full meal and a long shower would do me a ton of good.

The last sign I saw placed me on the outskirts of Williamsport, Pennsylvania. About two hundred more miles until I reached home. A little less than a six-day walk, if I pushed myself thirty miles a day. No way I'd make it home on these provisions.

Since there were no large cities near me, this area of the state hadn't been hit as badly as Pittsburgh and Philadelphia. Essential businesses should be open. I might be able to get someone to take pity on me and give me a handout.

I made my way out of the woods. Maybe I could plug the bike. Lights flashed through the edge of the woods. I crept closer and ducked behind a tree. Two police cars were parked near my bike. Why did someone call the cops on a lone bike? Maybe they thought the rider needed help. I did, but asking for help meant I might be identified, the next stop would be jail for desertion.

I'd have to walk. I muttered a curse. Seemed like I did that a lot more lately.

I pulled up my map and a compass app and headed west. I stuck to woods. No point in being seen and maybe stopped. The woods were deep and quiet. If not for the compass, keeping a straight path would have been impossible. I swear I was being watched, but never saw a thing.

After three hours, I heard a loud buzz above. What the heck? I searched the air. There. A drone. A big one.

Years ago, Dad and I had played with a drone like the one above me. The machine had scanned us, then projected the images as holographic, full color copies of us. I'd giggled. "We're twins!"

Dad had picked me up and thrown me in the air, catching me gently. I'd squealed. He'd showed me an instant replay. The projection of Dad threw the projection of me. I'd seen myself flying up to meet the drone, heard my own squeals. Everything was in perfect focus. The idea had blown my six-year-old mind. "How does it work?"

Dad had chuckled and crouched down. "It's the newest tech from the military. The drone films the video and sends it to the projector. It can film all different angles because there are so many cameras. Watch." He'd pressed some buttons on a controller to move the drone.

"And you get to play with it."

He'd laughed. "Sort of."

The projection had switched to a front view, and I

looked my projection self in the eye. She copied everything I did.

From the ground, this drone looked the same as the one Dad had shown me. But why was it here? Looking for me? I dashed into thick bushes. Sticks jabbed my skin and pulled at my sweats.

Maybe I did something wrong when I hacked my implant. Could I still be tracked? How else would the drone have found me?

I didn't know what kind of range the drone possessed. For all I knew, the operator hid behind the next tree, ready to arrest me. I trembled. Hopefully, they were looking for Zealots and not me.

I opened my hand and double-checked my implant. Location services were still disabled. My shoulders relaxed, and my heart rate slowed.

No one had tracked me through my implant. Routine patrol of the forest, maybe. I doubt the military had sewn any trackers into my sweats. Why would they bother? It wasn't like soldiers were deserting left and right. Were they?

The drone moved off toward the east. The remaining tension eased out of my muscles.

I stayed under the bush for thirty minutes, just in case it returned. I hoped this wouldn't be a regular occurrence. Dodging these things would slow me down.

I stood and moved west again. The terrain grew rocky and steep as the hours passed. My pace slowed. I wouldn't let myself eat or drink. I cringed every time I thought of my limited supply of food and water.

By 8:00 pm, my gait and mind fell into a numbing rhythm. Pick foot up, put it down. Pick foot up, put it down. Every rock and tree looked like the one I just passed. Nothing changed.

I came across a stream and stopped to rest. I splashed water on my face and rinsed my hands. The water looked clean enough. I scooped up handful after handful and slurped it down, not worrying if anyone or anything heard me. My stomach growled. I wished I knew more about edible plants, but with my luck, I'd pick something poisonous. I sighed and moved again.

I wanted to lie down and sleep, but I needed to keep going. I dodged two more drones, hiding in underbrush once and under a rock shelf another time. Stupid things.

At one point, the ground sloped, and I kicked a rock free. It rolled down the hill, picked up speed as it went, and smacked into a larger rock with a loud crack.

I tensed and scanned the area, rifle raised. The trees blurred in and out of focus.

Garrett's voice echoed in my head. "We have to go."

What. The. Heck? I blinked rapidly, trying to dissolve the image of a city not really there. Gun fire sounded. I whipped my head from side to side.

"You're not in New York. You're not in—" I choked on my words. My heart jack hammered against my ribs. The woods disappeared completely.

Chunks of concrete exploded to my right.

Garrett reached for my arm. "Come on."

Could this be real? It felt real. I screamed. Dust and flame filled the air. I trembled. No. Not again. I fired my gun, trying to hit the Zealots shooting at me.

Garrett yelled. "Jadzia move."

I tried to follow, to save myself, but my feet wouldn't work. My legs gave out.

I landed on my hands and knees in a pile of dry leaves. Trees surrounded me. What had happened? Where was I? Panting. Sweat dripping down forehead.

No smoke. No flame. No Zealots shooting at me. No Garrett.

I looked around at the rocks and trees. Not on a battle-field. Woods. I was in the woods. On my way home.

Safe. I was safe. For now, anyway.

CHAPTER 22

JADZIA

THREE DAYS. I had walked for three days. I desperately needed a shower. My legs hated me. My stomach hated me. I hated myself.

At least in the Army, we had beds. And food. My stomach grumbled. My tongue stuck to the roof of my mouth. I couldn't even work up any spit. I had two water pods and one energy bar left. Energy bar. I snorted. Whoever named the bars obviously never had to eat them to stay alive.

I was in the middle of nowhere Pennsylvania. The last sign I saw said State Game Land 100. According to the map, I was far enough north to avoid the State College basic training camp. I hoped, anyway.

Every once in a while, I crossed a dirt road. Other than that, everything stayed the same. Trees. Rocks. Yay.

Around noon, I stepped out of the woods and into the little town of Pine Glen. I walked down a paved street and almost cried at the sight of civilization. The town appeared to be functioning. Main Street boasted a few stores and one restaurant. The smell of roasting meat wafted through the air. I would have drooled, if I could.

I needed to get food. Actual food. Not energy bars. I didn't have any money, though. Using my PCD to access my bank account would give away my location. I might be able to hack it, but my brain was too fried to try.

My eyes flicked to an alley at the left of the restaurant. I shuddered at the thought of eating garbage but headed down the alley to check for trash bins.

The back of the building smelled like a grease trap. Four grimy trash cans stood by the rear door. I gagged. Could I really do this?

I held my breath and opened the lid. Empty. I checked the next one. Empty. Same with the other two. These people still had garbage service? Did they even know about the war going on?

I swore and kicked a can. I cringed at the loud clang it made. Someone might hear me.

Now what? I ran a hand over my face. I was headed back down the alley when the door opened. A guy about my age stepped out and threw a bag into one of the cans.

Our eyes met, and I ran.

"Hey." I heard footsteps behind me. I didn't look back. My legs rebelled against the quick movements, and I crashed to the ground. In basic, they put us through a lot, and I could usually run a long time, but four days with little food or water had taken its toll.

I trembled and panted. Darkness swam at the edges of my vision. I pushed myself to my knees but collapsed again.

Footsteps closed in on me. The guy loomed in my vision. "You need help." He wasn't asking.

I tried to form words. The darkness grew. His deep brown eyes were the last thing I saw.

Voices swam around me as I regained consciousness.

"She should be in a hospital."

My eyes flew open. My throat was scratchy and thick. "No." A hospital might identify me and I'd be thrown in jail.

I struggled to rise, but my head pounded. I lay back on something hard and flat. Squinting, I looked around. I was in an office. On a desk. The trash guy leaned on the door frame. "Water."

He nodded and left the room.

A middle-aged woman with salt-and-pepper hair took his place by my side. "Jason is right. You should be in a hospital, honey."

I guessed Jason was my rescuer. Or captor. I hadn't decided yet. "I'll be fine. Please. No hospital."

She pursed her lips but didn't argue.

Jason returned with a glass of water. "Take it slow."

"Thanks." He helped me sit. Head still pounding, I brought the cool glass to my lips. I longed to chug the glass as fast as I could, but I knew I'd only throw it up. I took a small sip. Then another.

"How long have you been out there? Where are you coming from? Where are you going?"

Jason held up his hand. "Geez, JoAnn, don't interrogate her."

I cracked a smile. "It's okay. I got separated from my family. I'm trying to get home." Better to lie than to get arrested.

JoAnn motioned to me. "Looks to me like you could use some food and about sixteen hours of sleep."

I could. But I didn't have time for that. "Food would be amazing." I took another sip of water.

"We have fresh venison and wild turkey today. I'll fix you a plate." She swept out of the room.

I looked at Jason. "Venison and wild turkey?" Not your normal restaurant fares.

"We ran out of fabricated cartridges about two weeks ago. Luckily there are a ton of hunters around here, and JoAnn knows how to cook real food."

I finished my water and swung my legs off the desk. Already, I felt stronger. Jason pulled the desk chair closer to me. "Sit. After you eat, I'll show you where you can shower."

Heat rushed to my cheeks. "Sorry. I know I stink."

He laughed. "You're okay."

JoAnn appeared, holding a plate heaped with meat and mashed potatoes. My mouth watered. They left me alone to eat. I slowly filled my belly with food and water. By the time I finished, my headache had disappeared and I could solidly stand on my own two feet.

Jason knocked before he entered the office again. He showed me to a shower in the employee break room. "Some of us like to shower before we go home, so we don't smell like grease in our cars." He opened a locker and pulled out a clean chef's uniform. "I'll wash your clothes in the sink while you shower. You can wear my extra uniform until they dry." He eyed the blood still on my shirt but didn't comment.

Tears filled my eyes. "Thank you."

He left me alone, and I stepped into the shower. I stood under the cascading hot water until my muscles relaxed. When I stepped out, I felt like a new person. I threw on his too-big uniform and paced the break room. The chairs around a table invited me to sit, but now that I had my wits about me again, I knew I couldn't stay in one place for too long.

JoAnn's voice came through the door. "Are you decent, honey?"

Such a sweet lady. "Yes."

She entered, holding my wet clothes. "You can use the hand dryer to dry these faster."

"Thank you so much." I reached for my clothes. "For everything."

She eyed me. "If you don't have far to go, I could have Jason drive you. You shouldn't be out there alone."

My heart thudded. As much as I'd love to have a ride home, I didn't dare risk the discovery I was a fugitive. I didn't want to put them in danger. "No, thank you. Besides, I have a long way to go."

"You should stay here a few days and rest then."

I faked a smile. "That sounds nice."

"Then it's settled."

Yes, it was. I'd leave as soon as my clothes dried.

CHAPTER 23

JADZIA

I SNEAKED out the back door of the restaurant as soon as my clothes weren't soaking wet. They'd dry while I walked. I took nothing with me. I refused to steal from people who were so kind.

The energy from the food ebbed a lot faster than I hoped. Exhaustion and hunger set in by the next morning.

For the next three days, I continued along in my now familiar routine of walking as much as possible, barely eating and drinking from every stream I found.

I stuck to the woods and avoided towns as much as possible. I couldn't risk being discovered, whether by another helpful person who wanted to put me in the hospital or by someone in the military who'd arrest me.

Unfortunately, getting close to a town was the only way I knew my location, so I couldn't completely avoid them. At the first signs of civilization, I'd find the nearest street sign and figure out my location on the map and the direction I needed to go. Then I headed back to the woods. The last town I passed was Saxonburg. Finally, in the same county as home. Our football teams even played against each other a few times.

With the mountains behind me, the terrain flattened somewhat. Thoughts of Jonathan and Mom kept me going. Maybe I'd stop in and see Brent's parents, too. I winced every time he crossed my mind. I shook my head. Seeing them would bring back too many memories. Memories I couldn't handle right now.

I hoped Mom would realize why we had to leave. There must be somewhere we could go. If we were together, everything would be okay. When I got home, she'd form a plan. I yearned for a break from planning.

The sun set and I stopped to rest. The little ground I gained by walking through the night wasn't worth running into trees or tripping over roots. I settled down in a pile of leaves for yet another night in the woods. The creaking trees didn't bother me anymore. I'd only seen a few squirrels and rabbits, so the thought of a bear eating me seemed stupid. Anyway, at this point, the bear should be afraid of me. I tried to shoot a rabbit yesterday. Hunger had not improved my aim.

I rubbed my calves through my pants. They didn't hurt. By now, they just felt like they were going to fall off.

I pulled out the last energy bar and one of my last three water pods. A day had passed since I'd last eaten. Or had I eaten this morning? Whatever. I'd be home tomorrow. I imagined Mom's fabricated pancakes with syrup. Surely there'd be enough time for a good breakfast. If the military came looking for me, the first place they'd check would be the house. They'd tell Mom to rat me out if I came home and leave. She wouldn't, though. She'd run with me. At least, I hoped she would. I'd convince her somehow. Our lives depended on it. Well, mine did anyway.

The water pod wet my mouth, but that's about it. The food bar didn't make a dent in my hunger. I wondered if I could eat tree bark.

I closed my eyes and dreamed about a feast of real, not fabricated food. The meat Brent's mom used to make with real vegetables fresh from her garden. Sweet red apples, mounds of ice cream, and yes. Mom's fluffy, delicious pancakes. Stacks and stacks of them—all different flavors, with butter and syrup.

When I woke up, I had leaves in my mouth. Spitting, I wiped my tongue with my shirt. "Gross."

I looked at my PCD. How on earth could it be eight in the morning? The forest still seemed dark. I looked up. Dark clouds clustered above me. Rain. Great. I walked about thirty minutes before the thunder rolled in. I looked around for shelter—maybe a cave I could hide in. No such luck. Crap. I flung my hands at the sky. "Can't I get a break, for once?"

The sky opened and rain pelted me. I sighed. I guess not. My clothes were soaked through in minutes. I finally found a rock ledge that offered a little protection. I huddled under it. Most of the ground was wet. I wanted to close my eyes, but the chill from the rain set in. My teeth chattered. I rubbed my arms and legs to warm up. The action didn't help much.

Lightning flashed. I cowered against the rock. A crash sounded nearby. Just a tree. Just a tree. I squeezed my eyes shut. Images of standing in the school parking lot with Brent, watching the city burn, assaulted me. I put my hands up to my ears and prayed for the images to stop. My breathing quickened. Just a tree. Nothing is under attack. At least not here.

I purposely hadn't watched the news since the mission.

Didn't want to see the destruction. Didn't want to hear the death count. Didn't want to know what kind of danger my friends were in. It might push me over the mental edge I already teetered on. I wiped my eyes. Whether they were wet from the rain or my tears, I didn't know.

I tried to pull up one of my favorite shows on my PCD. TV seemed stupid. I guess war really changed everything. At least while I walked, I had something to focus on. Now my mind was free to wander. I hummed, trying to pick a rhythm out of the rain. Anything for a distraction.

After thirty minutes, the storm moved on. I stood and tried to wring the water out of my shirt. Useless. I stepped from under the ledge. My socks squished around my toes. Ick. I kept humming to keep my mind from the images that still tried to attack. I'd get to Mom and Jonathan and everything would be all right. Sure. Keep telling yourself that.

CHAPTER 24

JADZIA

AS THE DAY WORE ON, I recognized names of the towns I skirted around. Adams Township. Mars. Seven Fields. I imagined Jonathan running to meet me, his mop of brown hair blown back from his face. Could almost feel him in my arms. I needed to go into the heart of Cranberry to get to my housing plan.

No one else walked here. I tried to look like I belonged, but the people in their Hover-cars stared. I ducked my head and hoped no one recognized me.

I laughed out loud. What must I look like? Filthy face, grimy clothes. Hair with bits of leaves in it. I stank again. The shower at the restaurant didn't last long.

I plodded along the roads until I came to my street. A huge grin broke over my face and a warm feeling crept into my chest. "Home." In fewer than five minutes, I'd hug Mom and Jonathan. I broke into a run and stumbled. Okay. Walk. I'd rather it take me a minute or two longer to get there than pass out in the front yard.

When the house came into view, I stopped short. What if the military sent a unit to watch for me? The place looked exactly as it had when I pulled away from the curb with Brent six weeks ago. Six weeks. Funny how nothing—but everything—had changed.

Three houses away from mine, I crossed the street and pretended to head toward my neighbor's place. Keeping my chin tucked to my chest, I walked down their driveway, then ducked behind their house. I peeked around the corner and just watched.

All was still. No sound, except for a random bird. I scanned my front yard, looking for anything out of the ordinary.

Nothing. No one.

I waited another five minutes before I couldn't take it anymore. Home was right there. Mom. Jonathan. If a soldier popped out of the bushes and tried to arrest me, I'd deal with it then. I sucked in my breath and came out of hiding.

I made it across the street and onto the porch without issue but paused at the door. How would Mom react when she saw me? I ran from the very thing her husband, my dad, gave his life for. A chill ran down my spine. Hopefully she'd just be so happy to see me she wouldn't think about how I got there.

I swiped my PCD over the lock and pushed open the door. The scent of lavender and rose filled my lungs. Home. I walked into the living room and fell to my knees.

"Mom. Jonathan." My voice cracked. "I'm home."

Of course, Mom should already know that. Her PCD would have registered movement at the door when my PCD unlocked it. Where were they? My throat tightened and panic rose in my chest. The house was strangely silent. Like it had been after Dad died. I took a deep breath.

"Mom?" I called again. I pulled up the time on my PCD. Almost six thirty in the evening. Even if kids were going to school with the world in this mess, Jonathan would be home by now. And Mom worked from home. Maybe they were shopping? Most of the parking lots I'd passed were empty. But people still needed to eat.

Calm down. Everything is okay. They will be back soon. I repeated it over and over until I almost believed it.

I looked around the room and pinched myself. Yep. Really here. Not an exhaustion-driven delusion. I sank into our couch and ran my hands along the familiar fabric. A smile crossed my face when I noticed the pizza sauce stain Jonathan got on the couch a few years ago. My stomach grumbled. Food. Maybe we had pancakes.

I went to the kitchen, grabbed some food packets, and threw them into the fabricator. Five minutes later, I sat in front of a plate of pancakes, eggs, bacon, sausage, fruit, and a glass of orange juice. I took a bite and moaned. This hit the spot. Now if only Mom and Jonathan would get here. My thoughts fought as I finished my food. One side of me was pretty sure they were dead. The other side held onto the hope they'd walk in the door any minute.

After I finished, I put my dishes into the sterilizer, then back in the cupboard. Mom trained us to be neat. I wouldn't let her come home to a messy house.

I'd been home for more than forty minutes, and they still weren't back. Now what? I caught a whiff of myself when I started pacing the living room. The way I smelt would appall Mom and Jonathan. I ran up the stairs and into the bathroom I shared with my brother. My eyes stung when I saw the few tub toys he like to play with in bins at the base of the tub. None of that. I'll see him soon enough.

I took an obscenely long shower. Staying under the spray until I drained the hot water tank. Thank goodness we still had power and hot water. Being in the water gave me time to think about my next steps.

I couldn't call Mom. The military most likely set up a tap on her PCD and would trace the call, which was why I hadn't called since the last time I'd spoken to her on graduation day.

My chest got tight. I couldn't linger. In fact, I might already have been here too long. The military might check the entry logs to the house. At least I knew for sure they weren't watching the place because I'd already be in a cell.

After I dried off and dressed, I decided to pack. When Mom and Jonathan got home, we'd be ready to go. Where, I didn't know. But go anyway. I went to the living room and picked up my bag. I needed something a lot bigger. My large army backpack was still under my bunk in Manhattan, but one of Dad's should be somewhere in the attic. He had tons of older packs and uniforms up there and Mom never could get rid of his things.

In the hall outside my room, I pulled the attic stairs down and climbed into the warm space. Dad's stuff sat packed in boxes in the corner. I hadn't been through it since I helped Mom put them up here. I choked back my tears and focused on the task at hand.

I opened a box and saw all his clothes. I picked up a shirt and held it to my chest. Wiping my eyes, I replaced it and shoved the box away. I didn't have time for a trip to the past right now.

Each box I opened contained another part of Dad's life. His books, his knickknacks, some medals, and the flag from his funeral. My breath caught as I ran my hand over the flag. I remember when a soldier handed it to Mom after the rifle salute. I sniffled, set it gently inside, and closed the box. The next box contained his large military-issued laser knife, the only thing of Dad's they found when he died. I set the knife aside to take with me. It'd be a good addition to my own. Under some more uniforms, I found his bag. I grabbed it and the knife and climbed down to my room.

I ran my hand over my bedspread. I'd love to sleep in my own bed again. The pale blue walls, the white carpet Dad had given into buying when I begged, despite Mom's protests. I swallowed the lump in my throat. No matter how much I wanted to enjoy being here again, I didn't have time.

I stuffed the pack with clothes for several days and still had plenty of room for food and other essentials.

Next, I moved to Jonathan's room. Might as well pack his things, and Mom's too. I opened his closet to look for a bag he could carry. It seemed strangely empty. All his favorite shirts were missing. I spun around and opened a drawer. Only a few pairs of shorts left. I threw every drawer open.

What was going on? Did they leave? Where were his clothes? I moved to his bed and threw the covers off. His stuffed tiger wasn't there. He never slept without it.

I ran into Mom's room and threw open her closet. Pulled out her drawers. Most of her clothes were gone too. I slumped onto her bed and put my head in my hands. I swore. What the heck should I do now?

CHAPTER 25

JADZIA

WHILE I SAT on Mom's bed, trying to figure out my next move, my eyes grew heavy. My body craved rest. I wanted to stay awake and plan or try to find my family, but I kept nodding off. I stretched out on the bed. So much nicer than sleeping on the ground.

Where had they gone? I racked my brain, but nothing came to me. Sleep tugged and pulled me under.

I woke to my PDC vibrating. I sat up, rubbed my eyes, and opened my hand. Five missed calls and thirty texts from Mom. How long had I been out? Mom never called me. She knew the life of a solider, and always waited for me to call her when I had time. I hadn't talked to her in almost two weeks. Why would she call now?

My PCD vibrated again. My heart quickened. Answering it might lead to my being found. My exact location would be hard to pinpoint without my location services being turned on, but it wouldn't be hard to figure out I was in my hometown, and my house would be the first place anyone would look.

I couldn't just ignore Mom. I wanted to talk to her. To find her. To plan what we were going to do now. I answered it. Mom's pale face filled the projection. "Jadzia? Is that you?" Her voice was frantic.

My voice cracked. "It's me."

Her eyes filled with tears. "Oh Jadzia. They told me you were MIA. Some general called and said you showed up at a base, then disappeared. No one knew what happened to you or if you were even alive. They thought Zealots took you or something. How did you escape? Where have you been? Are you really at home now? Do—"

"Mom, stop. I'm okay." Warmth spread through me. Mom would take care of me. Just like she always did. Her words rolled around my brain. "They thought I was abducted?"

"That's what the general told me."

For the first time in over a week, I allowed myself to fully relax. If the military thought the Zealots had me, no one would be looking for me here. "Where are you? When are you coming home, Mom?"

"You didn't answer my questions. What's going on?"

"I'll explain everything when I see you. Will you be back soon?" The longer we talked, the more likely a trace was.

"Honey, your brother and I are in Houston."

I stopped breathing for a moment. I stared at Mom's face. Neither of us said anything. "What?" I managed.

"We left the night you graduated." She dropped her gaze. "Your aunt called. They found Nick's body."

I gasped. That was it then. No more hope. Uncle Mark had been killed. "Why didn't Jonathan or Carina say anything?"

"When did you talk to them? I thought your communications were blocked?"

Right. She didn't know I hacked my PCD. "Never mind. How did you get there? Are planes flying again?"

"We secured passage on a military transport headed that way because of your father's former position. It took us four days, but we made it." She reached up as if to touch my face. "We thought we'd be back home well before you, but we got word you were MIA. I didn't know what to do."

"It's okay. I promise." I didn't think I'd ever said anything less true.

"Stay put. We'll come home. We'll leave today."

My voice high and loud. "No."

Her eyebrows pinched together. "What do you mean?"

I stood and looked around the room as if the answer might be written on the walls. "You can't come here." My breath quickened. This house was a trap now. It wouldn't take much longer for the military to pinpoint this call, if they hadn't already. I couldn't be here when they got here. They might even arrest Mom if they thought she'd been hiding me. "Just stay there. I'll come to you." Houston must be safer than here. Right?

"But—"

"Mom. I said I'd come to you. Stay there."

Her eyed widened.

I'd never been so firm with her before. I moved to my room and grabbed Dad's bag. How long would it take me to get to Houston? I didn't have the luxury of using military transport. Did I have enough stuff? Clothing, sure. I could wear dirty stuff and wash it in streams if I really needed to. Now I needed food. The time spent walking through the woods, weak, stomach grumbling, came back to me. I did not want a repeat of that.

"What are you doing?" Mom shook her head. "You can't cross the country alone."

"I just spent two weeks walking through the woods. I think I can handle riding my bike to Houston." Slinging the pack onto my back, I headed to the kitchen. "Where are those guns?" I glanced at the projection. Mom's face would have been funny if I weren't thinking of ways to stay alive right now.

Her mouth hung open while she stammered to find words. "You're going to tell me everything that happened. Right now." She used her best mom voice—the one that told me I was in serious trouble.

I didn't have time for a lecture. "Mom, seriously. It's too dangerous for you to come here, and I can't stay here either. I promise to tell you everything when I get to Houston. You can either help me or hang up and let me find what I need."

Her face softened. "You sound just like your father. He always took charge, too." She sighed. "The guns are in a safe, hidden behind the shelf of MREs, in the storage room. There's a knot on the third beam from the door. Push it and you'll see a keypad. The combination is 02032053."

I chuckled. My birthdate, Jonathan's birth year. "Thank you." I rushed downstairs. I didn't even glance in the direction of the laundry room. No time to relive that night.

I didn't want to hang up, but the faster I packed, the faster I'd be on my way to see them. "I have to go."

Mom nodded. "Please be careful."

"I will. I love you and Jonathan."

"We love you too."

I closed my hand and took some deep breaths to steady myself. No crying. Pack and run. I threw some MREs into my bag.

My PCD emitted the sound it played when someone

rang the doorbell. I opened my hand and pulled up the app that allowed me to see out front. A man and a woman, both in military uniform, stood on the porch.

CHAPTER 26

JADZIA

SWEARING, I closed my hand and continued to throw MREs into my pack. I dropped a few but didn't bother to pick them up. Maybe if I didn't answer, they would leave.

I moved to the third beam from the right of the door and ran my fingers along it. Sure enough, I found a knot in the wood that didn't quite seem to belong. I fumbled with it for a few seconds and a keypad lit up on the beam.

My PCD pinged again. Apparently, they weren't leaving. The band on my wrist started talking even though my display wasn't on.

A male voice said, "Private Mills. Can you hear us?" He sounded bored. "We know you're in there. We traced a call to your PCD at this location."

Maybe if I kept quiet, they would think I left.

"Your home monitoring shows you entered at eighteen-hundred-hours and you haven't left the premises."

Well, crap. Why didn't I think of that when I swiped my PCD?

"We're here to help you."

I almost laughed out loud. Help me. They thought

Zealots had taken me, and I—what? Escaped and made my way home? What would they do if I didn't answer the door, break it down?

I opened my hand. I forced a yawn and tried to make my voice groggy. "Sorry, I just woke up. I'll be right there."

I headed up the steps, rubbing my eyes and mussing my hair as I went, trying to make it look like I'd been sleeping. I opened the door and leaned against the frame to hide my shaking legs.

In addition to the two at the door, a military vehicle parked at the curb with a third person in it. Uh, oh. These were Military Police. My voice cracked. "How can I help you?"

"Private Mills?" The thin, blonde woman glared at me. I snapped to attention and gave a sharp salute. "Sorry, Ma'am. Private Mills reporting as ordered."

She returned my salute, and her expression relaxed. "At ease, Private."

I spread my feet and put my hands behind my back, but I didn't move to let them in. They glanced at each other.

The man said, "We're here to take you back to base. We need to debrief you about your encounter with and escape from the Zealots. You will then be returned to your unit. We can also offer you any medical services you may require."

My mind raced. "I should get my gear first." Lame I knew, but literally the only thing I could come up with.

They both nodded. I stepped back, and they moved to come in, but I shut the door in their faces and locked it. I heard the handle rattle, and the woman said, "Private Mills, we can assist you—"

I didn't stay to hear the rest of it. Instead, I turned and fled down the stairs. The bell chime sounded. I ignored it and jabbed the code into the keypad. It flashed red and warned me I had two more tries to enter the correct password or it would have to be reset. I growled.

I took a second to stop my hands from shaking and slowly punched the numbers again. A click sounded in the wall, then a section of wall about three feet long slid out and into the room. "Holy crap," I said, under my breath.

Another door chime.

I moved faster, grabbing the same gun Mom had given me the night everything started. I grabbed about fifteen cartridges, not bothering to check what type they were.

I threw the cartridges into my bag and slung it and the rifle onto my shoulder. Instead of the door chime this time, the male voice sounded from my PCD again.

"Private Mills, you are bordering on insubordination. You will open this door and let us escort you to base or we will be forced to place you under arrest until the situation is resolved."

Muting my PCD so it wouldn't give me away, I ran to the back door. I took one last look around the basement. I never expected to run from MPs. What would Dad think? My stomach twisted, and I ran out the back door.

I was about five feet from the house when I heard the woman yell, "Halt." I knew the tip of her rifle would be aimed directly at me. Hopefully, she was a bad shot like me.

Dirt hit the back of my legs as the ground behind me burst open. Not as bad as I was then. I dug deeper and poured on more speed. Another patch of earth exploded. I couldn't outrun this. I whirled around and fired at the woman. She dropped. My eyes widened. I hit something I aimed at. Laughing, I pumped my fist in the air. Take that, Sergeant Wallace.

The man rounded the corner of the house and I turned

on my heel and bolted into the woods that bordered our backyard. I stopped with my back against a tree and looked toward the house. The man knelt to check on his partner. I glanced at my gun. Thank goodness, just a stun cartridge. She'd be fine in a few hours.

My chest heaved as I tried to regain my breath. I moved again, but the man fired. A chunk of the tree I hid behind blew off. I dropped to one knee, aimed at the man, and pulled the trigger. The shot went wide and hit the house. So much for my aim. We fired at each other a few more times, but I had the advantage of being behind cover. The closer he got, the more I fired. I finally hit him and he went down. I knew there was a third officer somewhere. Probably still in the car, calling for backup. I didn't wait to take him out too.

I turned and ran through the woods, down the hill where I used to play with my brother.

CHAPTER 27
JADZIA

I RAN through neighborhoods and trees until I was sure no one followed me. I'd gotten used to seeing the stars in the night sky over the past weeks. Tonight was no different. I scoffed. I didn't even get one full night's sleep in my bed.

The encounter with the MPs had forced me to leave without my bike. I slowed my steps. Should I go back for it? No, that would be suicide. They were watching the house for sure. Maybe I could steal one. I shuddered. I didn't want to be a thief if I could help it, anymore than I was a killer. Maybe if I headed into downtown Pittsburgh I'd find an abandoned bike. That way, it wouldn't count as stealing.

My legs grew heavy. Each step seemed harder than the last. I desperately needed some sleep. I glanced at my watch. Midnight. If I found a hiding place soon, I could get a decent night's rest. Well, as decent as possible, considering I'd be sleeping on the ground. Again.

I walked another twenty minutes until I came across a drainage pipe. I shined my PCD light into it. Luckily, it hadn't rained here for a while. The pipe looked dry. It also smelled like sewer. Yay.

If anyone happened to be following me, I doubted they'd look in here. Feet first, I climbed into the pipe. Something rattled. I screamed at the top of my lungs. Moving faster than I've ever moved in my life, I pulled my legs from the pipe and jumped to my feet. A three-foot rattlesnake slithered out.

What? I thought rattlesnakes lived in the desert. I stepped back, to get out of striking distance and fumbled with my rifle. Please hit the thing. I pulled the trigger. The leaves next to the snake exploded. I swore. The snake obviously didn't appreciate me trying to kill it and coiled to strike. The rattle still buzzed in my ears.

I backed up and fired a second time, taking a chunk out of the pipe. The creepy thing seemed to decide I could have its napping spot and slithered off into the bushes.

My hands shook, but I was okay. I looked around to make sure the snake was really gone. The area must be abandoned. No one came to see the crazy girl shooting at a rattlesnake. I still needed a place to hide, though, now more than ever. I'm sure anyone with in a twenty-mile radius heard my screams.

I eyed the pipe. Were there more? What if the one I chased away came back? I really did not want to crawl back into that pipe, but it was the least likely place around to hide, which made it the best. Small. Out of the way. Stinky. And full of murderous snakes. Perfect.

I got on my hands and knees and shined the flashlight from my PCD down the pipe. Some leaves, a few pebbles. I found a long stick and jabbed it into the pipe while I shone my light. Nothing slithered. Nothing rattled.

I was either crazy or stupid, but I took my pack off and set it near the mouth of the pipe. Feet first again, I scooted down until I could barely reach the opening with my hands. I grabbed my pack and pulled it in with me, using it to block the entrance. Maybe it would keep out the snakes.

At least it was warm in here. Had it only been an hour ago I'd been at home in Mom's bed? I knew I needed to sleep, but it didn't come easily. Eventually, exhaustion won and my eyes closed.

I woke the next morning with a start and jerked up. I yelped when my head smashed into the top of the drain-pipe. "Oh, yeah." I rubbed my head. Groaning, I pushed my bag out of the pipe and scooted after it.

I took a deep breath of fresh air, clearing the stale smell of the pipe from my nose. Morning sun filtered through the trees. Sun, a good sign. I stretched and opened my PCD.

Mom had called, but I didn't dare return the call or send a message. Until I connected, no one could trace me. I'd see if I could figure out a way to scramble the signal or something, but that needed to wait.

I pulled up a map and compass on my PCD. Sighing, I rubbed the back of my neck with my free hand. I didn't know which direction I'd run in last night. I needed to find a street sign. Not having my location services turned on sucked. Felt like I was on the Oregon Trail or something. At least they traveled with their families.

I slung my pack onto my shoulders, picked a direction, and started walking until I came to a road. Finding the nearest road sign, I figured out my location. Wexford. I'd actually run in the right direction last night. Finally, something had gone my way.

After walking six hours, I reached the North Shore of downtown Pittsburgh. My city had been a natural target for the Zealots. If you wanted to wreak havoc on a population, you destroyed its centers of medicine and science. Without the hospitals, medical research labs, and production plants, the country's healthcare systems would crumble.

I stopped and stared. My once proud city lay in ruins. Piles of rubble everywhere. I couldn't tell where the Jessup or Archer buildings used to stand, and I could barely make out the remains of the football stadium where the ten-time Super Bowl-winning Pittsburgh Steelers used to play.

I saw no usable vehicles in my immediate area. They were all crushed by debris or flipped onto their sides by explosions. What happened to all the people those crushed cars belonged to? I shuddered. Is that why it stank? Was I smelling dead bodies? Better not look too closely.

Get a grip on yourself. I moved toward the Allegheny River. The destruction only increased as I got closer. Pittsburgh was a peninsula. I hoped at least one bridge survived. I hadn't had time to work on my swimming since I left New York.

When I arrived on the shoreline, I gazed across the river and gasped. Pittsburgh looked like it had been bombed in an aerial attack. Zealots didn't have planes. Did they?

I clenched my fist. No way I'd find a working vehicle in that mess. But I still needed to get to the south side of the city, and I really didn't want to walk all the way around. The faster way would be to cross the river.

I trudged up and down the shoreline looking for an intact bridge, but two of the bridges I could see were reduced to support beams half sticking out of the water, and the third ended in a harrowing drop to the river.

My stomach rumbled, and I could really use a drink, but I refused to drink the water. Although the rivers had been cleaned up long ago, anything might be in the water now.

Bridge and building debris for sure, chemicals from research labs, maybe even viral samples, not to mention bodies. Acid rose in my throat. I closed my eyes.

I couldn't think about that. I opened my eyes and kept walking.

CHAPTER 28
JADZIA

I WALKED the shoreline for fifteen minutes before I noticed something bobbing in the water. I hurried over to check it out and found a half-submerged Waverider. Maybe I could turn the small craft upright and float it across the river. The Waverider wouldn't run, but since it floated, I could paddle across.

I grabbed the side of the craft and yanked as hard as I could. Apparently, I used a lot more force than necessary because the craft easily rolled in the water, and I slammed to the ground. I muttered a string of curse words and stood, grateful no one was around to see me rubbing my rear end.

I didn't have too much experience with these things, but Brent took me for a ride on a two-seater once. I'd wrapped my arms around his waist as he sped us down the river, spraying water. We had so much fun that day. I winced and took a deep breath as pain shot through my chest. I missed him so much.

Not now. One day, things would slow down, and I could mourn for everything I'd lost. Now, I needed to keep moving. I had to find something to paddle with.

I found a thin wooden plank on top of a pile of rubble.

I untied the line that kept the Waverider from floating away and gingerly straddled the seat. I held my breath until I confirmed it would keep me afloat.

"It's just a floating bike. Just a floating bike." I did not look forward to falling in. Satisfied the thing would hold me, I dipped the board into the water on my right side and shoved.

The Waverider moved. I let out a whoop and kept paddling. I turned in a circle. This couldn't be right. I wanted to go across the river, not spin around. Maybe if I switched sides? I put the board in the water on my left and paddled a few times. Yep, a circle in the opposite direction. I smacked myself in the forehead. Okay. One stroke on my left, one stroke on my right. I finally moved straight across the river. Why was nothing easy?

After thirty minutes, my arms ached, but I made it across the river. Unfortunately, I still needed to cross a second river. Groning, I laid the board across my knees and rubbed my arms. I let the current carry me toward The Point, the part of the peninsula where the Allegheny and Monongahela Rivers met and formed the Ohio. Memories of hanging out with Brent and our friends at concerts and the art festival in Point State Park washed over me. Now the park stood empty. I sighed. When I got to the tip of the point, I crossed through the Ohio and into the Monongahela.

When I finally made it to shore, I floated down river a bit, looking for a place to tie it off. Maybe someone else would find it useful. A crooked post about ten yards away would work. I stumbled off the craft, tied it to the post, and patted it goodbye.

I stood on the shore and rubbed my forehead. Ouch.

Moving hurt. I swung my arms in circles and massaged them. I'd hurt worse than this during boot camp, and I needed to keep going.

Perilous piles of debris towered over my head. Hardly any effort had been made to clean up this area. I headed into the rubble, climbing over large hunks of building, avoiding piles of glass and pointy bars of metal.

At one point, my foot slipped, and I fell. Pain shot through my left hand. I cried out and examined the wound. Blood seeped around a large shard of glass jammed into the heel of my hand above my wrist. At least it didn't hit an artery.

Breathing hard, I shrugged my backpack off my shoulder. I grabbed part of the pack with my teeth, pulled open the zipper, and dug through the bag until I found the first aid kit. I pulled out anticoagulant powder, gauze, and medical tape. Using my teeth again, I ripped opened the pouch of anticoagulant power.

Now I had to pull the glass out. I closed my eyes, took a deep breath, and yanked. My eyes flew open, and I swore as the glass cleared my hand. Blood poured from the wound. I shook the powder over my hand and the bleeding slowed, then stopped.

I wrapped the wound and leaned back. I took a water pod and a food bar out of my pack. An hour later, I still sat on the concrete slab. Not exactly a comfortable position, but I couldn't bring myself to move. My hand throbbed, and my legs felt heavy. I closed my eyes and enjoyed the late afternoon sunlight and warm breeze on my skin. A perfect day, really. Wispy white clouds dotted the sky. I should be outside, enjoying the end of winter, not traipsing through an apocalyptic city.

My mind wandered from Brent to Garrett and Sisko,

and then to Mom and Jonathan. Jonathan. As usual, the thought of his face and my promise to return to him got me moving again. I could do this. I had to find a car or a bike and get to Houston.

I stood, careful not to put weight on my right hand, and continued through the wasteland that used to be my city.

I DIDN'T GET FAR before I ran into my next obstacle—Mount Washington. While a large patch of the mountain sheared away from the cliff face, the mountain still posed a huge roadblock. I had three options. Around, over, or through. If Pittsburgh's subway tunnel wasn't collapsed, going through the mountain would be easiest.

I picked my way along the base of the mountain, looking for the tunnel. I stopped short. Instead of the empty passageway I expected, the mouth of the tunnel held a tent. Just outside, a guy crouched over a fire, cooking meat. The smell drew me closer. Real food. Where did this guy get fresh meat? Maybe he'd share. He looked at me, eyes as wild as his hair.

"Uh. Hi?" I waved stupidly.

He grinned, set the meat aside, and stood. "Want to join me for dinner?" He motioned to the meat and winked.

Okay. That's creepy. "I—No thanks."

He took a step toward me. I backed up a few paces.

His eyes raked my body. "You sure? You look real good."

Ew. What did the way I looked have to do with dinner? "I just want to get through the tunnel."

He shook his head and stepped closer. "You don't want to go through there. Tunnel's full of crazy people."

As if this guy was the picture of sanity. I took a step back. "Oh. Well, I should probably go then. My boyfriend is waiting for me." I pointed to my left. "He'll come looking for me in a minute."

He leered. "You're alone. I can tell."

Well, crap. Looks like the imaginary boyfriend didn't work any better here than it had that time I tried to use it to get out of a date.

"I really think I should have you for dinner." He lunged for me.

Have me for dinner. The meat. I gagged and ran. His footsteps thundered after me. He grabbed my arm and wrenched me around. I slammed into his chest. I brought my knee up in between his legs as hard as I could.

He let me go and collapsed to the ground, screaming a long list of curse words.

I gripped my rifle and ran as fast as I could until I reached the Monongahela Incline. A Hover-car designed to look like an old style trolly. It carried passengers, on tracks, along the slope of the mountain, from the top of Mount Washington to the South Side and back again. Pittsburgh's two Inclines had been around forever and were historical landmarks. The Hover-cars didn't need the railroad tie tracks anymore, but the city kept the tracks as a part of history. Lucky for me, I could climb the tracks and hide at the top.

The distance between the ties was enough to make gripping the next one difficult, but not enough that I needed to jump from one to the other. My arms almost gave out and my injured hand burned as I pulled myself up each railroad tie. The gauze I'd wrapped around it turned red. I must have reopened the wound. Sweat poured down my face and soaked my shirt. My pack pulled me backwards with every step, threatening to send me careening to the bottom of the hill.

I glanced back. Crap. The crazy guy had climbed onto the tracks below me. I had about a thirty-rail lead on him. Not a huge lead, but it was enough as long as I could hold on to it. I kept climbing.

Crazy guy was gaining on me. I paused and pulled my rifle off my back. I took a few shots, which hit everywhere except the guy. He looked up at me and laughed. Great. Now he knew I couldn't shoot to save my life.

By the time I reached the top, my breath came in gasps. Blood rushed in my ears and my heart beat so fast I thought I'd pass out. I looked down over the edge to see the crazy guy still climbing. How on earth did he have the energy? I remembered the guy from the store in New York. This guy had to be on something that amped him up.

I tried to run, but my legs gave out. I crawled to the edge and looked down. The guy only had ten rungs to go. Another two or three minutes at most. "Come on now. We don't have time for this." I told my legs. They didn't listen very well. I sent a few shots over the edge, but again, nothing hit him.

I lay down with the rifle, braced my arms against the ground, and waited. When the guy popped his head over the top of the ridge, I pulled the trigger and held it, sending blast after blast in the guy's general direction. He never cleared the ridge. He fell four hundred fifty feet to his death.

Two. Now I'd killed two people. Darkness danced on

the edges of my vision. Air. I needed air. My head swam. My vision blurred. I blacked out.

A cool breeze sent goosebumps along my skin. My eyes fluttered open. Why was I on the ground? Oh. Right. Crazy guy wanted to eat me. I shuddered. Needed to move. What if there were more of them lurking about?

I stood and took two steps before my legs gave out. I crashed to my hands and knees. Pain screamed through my injured hand and up my arm. I held the hand in front of my face. The bleeding had stopped again, but I was exhausted. Apparently, the hour or two I'd been passed out wasn't enough. I needed real rest.

There were so many places I could hide, the chances of another person who wanted to eat me finding me were slim. Plus, I'd just lay completely helpless for at least an hour, and no one had bothered me.

The buildings up here looked to be in decent shape. Windows were broken and doors kicked in, but nothing appeared blown up.

On a normal Friday, this place would have been crawling with people. Now, nothing moved. Everyone had evacuated to safe houses or the homes of relatives. Safety. What a joke. No place was safe with guys who wanted to eat people running around—never mind the Zealots.

I made my way to one of the closest town homes. The door hung open, which meant looters had already gotten to the place. I wouldn't find food or anything valuable I could use to buy food, but I hoped for a bed or a couch I could crash on.

The front room was a disaster. Everything overturned and strewn about. I walked down a hall and found several bedrooms in the same state as the main living areas. I picked one that had a bathroom attached and locked the bedroom door.

I went to the bathroom and turned on the faucet. Water flowed from the spicket, and I gulped as much as I could hold. I tried the hot water in the shower, but after five minutes it still ran cold. I took the fastest shower I have ever taken and switched into clean clothes.

I went back to the bedroom and sat on the bare mattress. I couldn't find any sheets or blankets, but I didn't care.

I pulled an MRE from my bag, but the thought of the guy roasting my arm over his fire and happily munching away made me gag. I threw the MRE back into my pack.

Even though the sky wasn't dark, I lay down on the bed and within minutes I fell asleep.

When I woke, sunlight streamed through the window. I stretched. How long had I been out? I looked at my PCD. No. That couldn't be right. I rubbed my eyes and looked again. Ten in the morning. On Sunday. I'd slept for more than a day.

My mouth was dry, and my stomach rumbled. I slowly climbed out of bed. Mom would be worried if I didn't get to Houston soon, and I couldn't risk calling her again. Today, I'd find a vehicle. Today, I'd make real progress. But to do that, I needed food. I grabbed the least meat-like MRE I could find— potato and cheese soup—pushed all images of people eating other people out of my head and ate.

After the sleep and food, strength returned to my body. I couldn't remember the last time I felt this good. The day before our mission in New York, maybe?

I left the townhouse and walked for an hour to reach Dormont. Lights blazed from storefront windows. Hopefully, I could find a vehicle plugged in somewhere.

I walked from the business section of town to more residential streets. Perfect.

Garages and driveways were full of vehicles left behind in the evacuation, but still plugged into working chargers. A car would work, but a bike would be faster and more maneuverable. Unfortunately, I didn't see any bikes. I found a blue minivan, my favorite color, and hopped in. I picked a minivan because I could lie down in the back when I needed to rest.

I drove a few miles before I hit the brakes. A DTF Trident sat in a driveway. I'd wanted one of those forever. This bike held a charge for at least ten hours of riding time, forty-eight hours of off time, and had a top speed of a hundred and sixty. Oh, yes.

I practically skipped to the bike. My fingers ran along the smooth blue paint. I hacked into the bike's systems and authorized myself as a rider. I checked the garage, found a helmet, and jammed it onto my head. The fit was tight, but better than nothing. I climbed on and let out a whop as I tore out of the driveway. With this, I'd have no problem getting to Houston.

CHAPTER 30
JADZIA

FIVE HOURS LATER, I was on the outskirts of Columbus, Ohio. I couldn't believe a three hour-long trip took me five.

I'd risked taking interstate 70. In movies, when a city gets attacked, the travel lanes out of the city are jammed with cars, but the travel lanes into the city are completely empty. Well, that's not how it works in real life.

When the attacks happened, the people driving into the city either tried to turn around—only to crash into oncoming cars—or just stopped their cars and ran. Both sides of the highways were packed with cars.

I had to maneuver around accidents and abandoned cars. Every time I hit a clear patch of road, I could barely get the bike up to full speed before I had to jam on the brakes and go around another backup. As I picked my way around yet another wreck, I kept an almost constant mutter of curse words and complaints running in my head

The closer I got to Columbus, the more destruction I could see. One more city destroyed by the Zealots. I trembled. The military fought this war to stop destruction. They weren't doing a good job. How much longer until there was nothing left to fight over? Or even worse, no one left to fight.

I took Route 71 south of Columbus and rode for another two hours. I stopped near an exit ramp for a place called Jeffersonville, Ohio. The words Safe House All Welcome had been spray painted in bright yellow paint on the sign.

Advertising where you were lying low didn't seem very smart. Any Zealot could come in and blow the place up, but at this point, my stomach gnawed on itself and a wicked headache pounded behind my eyes. I knew I needed to ration my meager supply of food for at least another week. A safe house might be a good idea. I could restock. I also wouldn't mind a comfy bed or people who weren't trying to eat me.

I wonder what kind of security they had. It probably wasn't an official safe house. I doubted there'd be military. Most likely, some people got together and fortified a building. I took the off-ramp and followed spray painted arrows to a giant warehouse store, one of those stores where only members could shop. It probably held lots of food and other supplies, but I didn't know how the occupants warded off looters.

My heart rate picked up. I stashed my bike, my guns, and my pack in the woods near the store, only keeping my laser knife with me. I wanted to look as needy as possible, so I wouldn't look like a threat. Plus, I didn't want them trying to take my bike.

I approached the front of the store. Two guys in their late thirties or early forties, with large laser rifles in their hands, greeted me. "That's close enough," the guy on the left said.

I put my hands up. "Uh. . . I saw the sign." I pointed toward a yellow arrow by the entrance to the parking lot.

The guy on the right chuckled. His blue eyes seemed friendly and reminded me of a middle-aged Garrett. "You don't have to put your hands up."

I relaxed my arms, but my legs were ready to run.

The Garrett-looking guy approached me, and I took a step back. "I won't hurt you." His gentle voice didn't do much to soothe me. He still held a giant gun in his hands, after all. He could kill me any time he wanted to.

He slung the gun over his shoulder. "Name's Larry. That's Dan." He pointed to the guy by the door. Dan caught my eye and inclined his head in greeting.

My voice squeaked. "Jadzia."

Larry grinned. "You look tired. Come sit over here with me and tell me where you're from." He led me to a wrought-iron and wood bench under a tree in the parking lot. The price tag still dangled from the arm. They must have dragged it out from the garden center.

I kept my head down but took in as much as I could without being obvious. I didn't know what, but something about this wasn't right.

Larry sat and patted the seat next to him. I sat as far away from him as I could, ready to spring and run at any second. His leg brushed against mine. I flinched.

"Don't be nervous."

I forced a smile.

"So. What's your story?"

"My story?"

Larry chuckled again. "Yeah, how did you end up here?"

"Oh." I looked at my hands, which were folded in my lap, the knuckles white. "I'm from uh . . . Columbus. We were trying to get to a shelter, and we got separated." I'm not sure why I felt the need to lie, but I did. "I saw the sign and hoped I could get some food and maybe a place to sleep."

He inclined his head toward the store. "We can offer you that."

I glanced at Dan. He leaned against the door and talked to a woman with blonde hair. Both looked in my direction.

Larry motioned Dan and the woman over. "We just have to make sure you don't mean us any harm."

I forced a laugh. "Harm. I'm seventeen. What harm could I do to you?"

Dan and the woman approached us.

Larry motioned to her. "This is Jillian. She's going to check you for weapons."

I jumped up and pulled my knife out of my waistline. "This is all I have."

Dan smirked and pocketed my knife. Hopefully, I'd get that back. Thank goodness I'd left Dad's knife with the bike.

"That's a good start, but we still need to check," Larry said.

I tried to step back, but stumbled into the bench. With Larry sitting on my left, Jillian standing in front of me, Dan standing to my right, and the bench behind me, I had nowhere to go. This was happening. I nodded once.

Jillian patted me down while I wished to disappear. She didn't linger over private areas and seemed very professional about all of it. Maybe she'd been a cop before all of this.

When she finished patting down my ankles, she stood. "She's clean."

Larry looked pleased. "Thanks guys, we'll see you inside."

Dan and Jillian headed back to the store. I moved to follow, but Larry caught my hand. "Not so fast." His voice hardened.

"I'm not a threat. She just confirmed it." I pointed to where Dan and Jillian went through the door.

"You're old enough to be in the military. We don't like military types around here. You can't trust them." He had a strange look in his eyes. "Always trying to get us to leave this place. Go with them to who knows where. Say they'll protect us." He clenched his fists. "We can protect ourselves."

"I'm not military."

"Yeah." He sneered. "Where'd you get those boots?"

Crap. I didn't think about my boots. I sighed. "Okay, you want the truth?"

"That would be a good place to start, young lady."

"I was in the military. I had to join when Operation Resolution went into effect. But I left. I couldn't take it anymore and I left."

Larry studied me. "Sounds like something a spy would say."

I snapped. "I'm not a spy. They killed my best friend." My throat closed. I sucked air in through my mouth and blew it out. "I don't want anything to do with them." I sniffled and tried to think of something else.

His eyes softened. "That, I believe. Come on." He stood and led me toward the storefront.

I'm not sure why I followed when I should've run.

WHEN WE ENTERED THE STORE, I couldn't believe my eyes. A ten-foot barrier made of pallets and fencing formed a passageway just wide enough for us to walk single file. A gate stood at the end of the passageway, blocked by three armed guards.

Larry showed me through the gate into an open area with a bunch of mismatched chairs set up around tables. Groups of people sat, eating and talking.

He pointed to the snack bar and kitchen. "Mess hall. That's where we cook the food. You'll be on kitchen duty tomorrow morning. Everyone pulls their weight." He grabbed an apple and a water pod from a table full of fruit, energy bars, water, and candy.

Candy. My mouth watered. How long had it been since I ate chocolate? After the tour, I'd make a beeline for this table.

"Have a snack whenever you like." He pointed to the table. "Anything else is stealing. And we don't take kindly to thieves."

I gulped and nodded.

He led me past rows and rows of clothes, real food, and fabricated food packets, medical supplies, and tents. Everything was organized and accessible. Two guards patrolled the supplies. Nothing like armed men to keep you honest.

We rounded a corner of pallets, and Larry pointed out another area. "We even have a day care." I peeked over the wall and saw a bunch of kids ranging from infant to about seven years. They read, napped, or played with toys. An exhausted-looking woman sat in a rocking chair holding an infant.

In the back left of the store, he pushed aside some tarps. "This is where the single girls sleep." He motioned toward a group of mattresses, some with sleeping girls on them. "Pick one and get some rest."

"Thanks." I moved to pick a bed.

"Jadzia." He called after me.

I turned.

"Here." He smiled and threw me the water pod and apple.

"Thanks." I couldn't help but smile back.

I picked a mattress and unlaced my boots. I ate the apple and drank the water, then lay down to get some sleep. My body refused to relax. I didn't know who these people were, or if I could trust them. Two mattresses away, a girl snored like a freight train rumbling through the room. I shoved my pillow over my head. It didn't help. I wished I still had my knife. Something, anything, to protect myself with.

I lay there for hours, trying to figure this place out. Larry seemed nice enough. But there was something in his face. In his eyes. In the eyes of the woman, rocking the baby.

Something about this place just didn't sit well with me, and I couldn't put my finger on it.

At four in the morning, I gave up trying to sleep. I pulled my boots on and pushed aside the tarp separating the sleeping quarters from the rest of the building.

Larry hadn't shown me where the bathrooms were. You'd think that would be an important part of the tour. I walked along the back wall, where bathrooms usually were in these types of stores.

I found an unmarked door and figured I'd try it. The door opened into an office, maybe where the manager used to work. I almost backed away and closed the door, but papers on a table in the middle of the room caught my eye.

Huh. Not many people used paper anymore. I walked toward the table, letting the door close behind me. I picked up a random page from the table. Building plans. My heart raced. Why would a group of survivors need building plans?

I looked through the papers. More building plans. Marks I didn't understand. In the corner of one of the papers, I saw the name of the Henry Ford Building, the tallest, most famous building in Dayton. I pulled info about the city up on my PCD. Dayton, a safe city where survivors were being housed, was only about forty miles away and had yet to be attacked by Zealots.

I moved to another stack of papers and found drawings that looked like the inside of the bomb I hacked during basic training. Bomb schematics. I dropped the paper. Backed up a step. Shook my head. These people were planning to bomb Dayton. I was in a Zealot stronghold.

The door flew open and banged against the wall.

I jumped, and my hand flew to my chest.

Larry stood in the doorway, fury on his face, old-fashioned shotgun in his hands, laser rifle slung across his back, my knife in his belt. "Well, well, well. If it isn't our little spy."

I widened my eyes, trying to look surprised. Really, I wanted to kill all three of them. In a voice I hoped sounded innocent, I said, "Sorry I got lost looking for the bathroom."

"So you decided to look at our classified information?"

I stood my ground. These people were the ones responsible for Dad, Uncle Nick, and Brent's death. Not directly, of course, but people who thought like them. It didn't matter. Face to face with Zealots, I found I hated every single one of them. "The door wasn't locked. Lights were on. I didn't think it was a big deal." I shrugged.

Larry entered the room. Dan and Jillian followed. All three carried more than enough weapons to kill me. My palms were sweating, but I wouldn't give them the satisfaction of knowing it.

Larry grabbed my arm. I cried out and struggled against him.

Dan leveled his rifle at my chest. "Shut up and hold still."

I did.

They led me from the room. We walked through the store. Only a few guards were about. I met each of their eyes, silently begging for help. Every single one of them looked away. Either they believed in their cause, or they didn't want to end up like me.

Dan kept the tip of his gun jammed into my back the entire way out into the parking lot. We approached a Hover-truck. the type that shipped large quantities of items across the country.

Larry opened the rear of the truck. "Get in there." He shoved me into the cargo hold. I stumbled, fell forward, and landed on all fours. My right hand throbbed. Jerk.

Larry slammed the door. I jumped up and banged against it. A lock clicked into place. "Don't bother trying to contact your leaders. There's a dampening field around the truck." A loud boom echoed through the empty area. I could picture his large fist slamming into the side of the truck. I cringed against the back wall. The three of them laughed. Their voices faded as they walked back to the store.

The display on my PCD showed me Larry told the truth. No signal. Who would I call anyway? Not the military. They were likely to arrest me along with Larry's group. I'd end up going from one prison to another.

I stood and ran my hands along the walls of the truck, hoping I could find something, anything, to help me. Nothing. Not a stray screw or bolt I could loosen. I growled.

They might plan on keeping me in this truck forever or they might take me some place else. I really didn't want to find out.

I opened my hand. I might not be able to call anyone or access the net, but maybe I could access the truck itself. It took almost two hours, but I finally got into the truck's systems and unlocked the rear door. I pushed the door open an inch at a time, in case someone guarded the truck. When I didn't see anyone, I opened it wide enough to get out, then shut it again, locking it with my PCD so no one would suspect anything when they came to check on me.

I ran through the parking lot toward where I hid my bike. I heard Jillian yell. My heart jumped out of my chest. I didn't wait to figure out what she'd said or who she'd yelled at. I ran down the hill and into the woods. A vehicle started up as I threw my leg over the bike. I didn't have time to worry about the helmet, so I left it strapped to the back. I swiped my PCD. The bike came to life, and I shot out of the woods.

CHAPTER 32
JADZIA

I RODE BACK toward the highway. If I could find a clear patch of pavement, this bike would outrun almost any other vehicle. I heard yelling and looked in the side mirror. Great. Two Hover-cars and a truck gave chase. My heart pounded almost as fast as the bike went.

Twisting the throttle, I poured on more speed. My lead widened a little. I took a turn too sharply and my knee skimmed the road, tearing my pants. I fought for control. My skin stinging from where it scraped, I muscled the bike upright and kept going.

The slide cost me precious seconds and the vehicles behind me closed the gap. Keeping one hand on the throttle, I used my other hand to awkwardly point my rifle over my shoulder. I tried to use the mirror to judge where to shoot. It didn't work well. I gave up the attempt to aim and just pulled the trigger. Besides, I usually hit things better when I didn't aim at them.

Unfortunately, I didn't hear a crash, but I caught sight of the lead car swerving around to avoid my shots. I veered around another car and almost went down again. I pulled the rifle in front of me. Shooting and steering at the same time was too hard.

A four-car pileup blocked the entrance ramp to the highway. I spotted a small path through the cars. I maneuvered through the wreck, then opened the throttle all the way. No car could follow me through that. I relaxed my shoulders and remembered how to breathe. A huge crash sounded. I flinched and crouched low to the handlebars. I checked the mirror and cursed. The truck plowed through the cars on the road like they were toys. All three vehicles kept chasing me.

I cursed again. I really needed to stop doing that so much, but now didn't seem like the time. My lead had grown, but not enough. Now what? I looked around for anything to stop the Zealots from following. An open patch of road allowed me to break a hundred on the speedometer, and I raced ahead. My hair wiped around my head and my eyes watered from the speed but stopping meant death.

Another pileup blocked the road. I'd have to slow way down and pick my way through. I glanced at the charge meter. It flashed red. I had maybe thirty minutes of ride time left. Wonderful. I needed to lose these guys. Now.

A plan formed. Not a very good plan, but a plan nonetheless. I glanced at the speedometer. One forty-five. I was going to regret this. The abandoned cars loomed. I hit the brakes as hard as I dared, almost flying over the handlebars. I squeezed my legs together as tightly as I could to stay on the seat. Pain flared in my left hand, but I refused to loosen my grip on the bars.

Going about forty miles per hour now, I picked my way through the first few cars. I stopped behind a random car and dismounted. Using the hood for cover, I waited a few seconds until the Zealots came into range. I fired. The windshield on one of their vehicles shattered. Hoping to hit a driver, I kept up a solid wave of fire.

One car veered off the road and slammed into a ditch. I'm not sure if I hit anyone or if they just overcompensated to avoid my laser blasts. I didn't stop firing.

The second car and the truck stopped as they approached the lines of cars. Larry opened the truck door and stood behind it. Nice shield, Captain America. He opened fire, and I ducked behind the car.

I couldn't shoot from here. I took a deep breath and came up screaming. All my fire centered on Larry. After a few seconds, he went down.

I aimed at the car next. After a minute, I stopped firing. I waited. Nothing moved. I stood.

Shots rang out from the truck Larry had been in. I cried out. Pain spread through my left shoulder, but I ignored it. There'd be time to feel pain later. I shot another volley into the car's windshield. Again, all was quiet.

This time I waited a solid five minutes. Silence. My muscles relaxed and my breathing slowed. I aimed my gun at the car and stepped from behind my cover.

My conscience wouldn't let me leave without checking to see if they were alive. I slowly walked toward the closest car, the one that veered off the road. I couldn't have killed them with my shots. My gun still carried a stun cartridge in it. But if they died in the crash, it was still my fault.

My eyes flicked among all three vehicles as I moved, but no Zealots stirred. When I got to the car, a Zealot whom I couldn't identify slumped over the steering wheel and Dan lay with his head against the passenger side window frame. I checked the driver first, then moved over to the one in the passenger seat. Both had pulses. Whew.

They'd be out for a few hours. I made my way to the

other car. Jillian's head lolled out the open driver's side window, but she had a pulse, as did the guy in the passenger seat who lay on her shoulder. Two vehicles down and no fatalities.

I walked around the car to check on Larry and the other person in his truck. Blood trickled out from under the door where Larry had sheltered behind. I stopped. There shouldn't be any blood. Unless . . . I edged my way around the door.

I fell to my knees and vomited. Head shot. Maybe two, by the looks of it. Stunner cartridges didn't normally inflict wounds but take a stunner to the face or anywhere in the head, and you weren't recovering from that.

Three. My mind went back to the guy in Manhattan. And the guy on the cliff. I'd killed three people. My body shook. I threw up again. Sure, they'd all been trying to kill me, but I had taken three lives. Not to mention the people I'd hurt. I couldn't move. I knelt there, staring at the ground, looking everywhere except at the man who lay beside me.

My hands balled into fists. I hated this war. Hated everyone and everything involved. I took my rifle off and shoved it away from me. I ran my hands down my face.

A scream bubbled up and burst from my mouth. "Why?" I threw my arms in the air. "What do you want from me? Huh?" I didn't know who I yelled at, but I continued to rage. "First my dad, then Uncle Nick, then Brent. Then you turn me into a killer. And it just keeps happening." I wrapped my arms around my chest and folded in on myself, rocking back and forth. "How much more do I have to give?"

I don't know how long I knelt there. Must have been at least an hour because I jumped when a car door shut. A very groggy Zealot shuffled around the back of Larry's truck. I must have grazed him with a stunner blast. If I'd hit him full on he'd be out for another three hours.

I fumbled for the rifle I'd pushed away earlier and blasted him. He dropped in a heap onto the pavement.

I sighed. No matter how much I wanted to get rid of it, this gun was the difference between my life and death. I stood, wiped my face, and made my way back to my bike.

CHAPTER 33

JADZIA

I RODE AS FAST as I could for the next thirty minutes, pushing the bike to the limits of its charge. The sun rose high, and the heat swelled. I passed a sign for Kings Island amusement park. An amusement park would be empty, but not a likely target for the Zealots, and likely still intact, which meant I could charge my bike. I'd have to dump it soon if I couldn't, and I really didn't want to. The bike would get me to Houston quicker than any other means of transportation, and I really liked riding it.

The parking lot sat empty. Just as I thought, the park hadn't opened for the season yet when the attacks happened. It didn't open after, either, and really, who knew if it ever would again? I pulled my bike to the far end of the lot under some trees and plugged it in. I sat on the curb, ate an MRE, and drank one of the water pods.

As far as I knew, the bike would take two hours to reach a full charge. I set an alarm on my PCD, curled up in the grass, and closed my eyes.

Two hours later, I jolted awake to the sound of my alarm. Eyes still closed, I fumbled with my PCD display to shut off the noise. I pressed a button, and the alarm quieted.

I didn't want to go to school today. I ran my hand along my mattress, looking for my covers. Where were the stupid things? And why did my bed feel so weird? Almost like grass. I opened my eyes, sat up, and tried to figure out why I'd been sleeping on the ground. I groaned and rubbed my eyes. My surroundings came into sharper focus. Oh. Yeah. Stupid war.

I stood and checked the charge on the bike. Ninety-seven percent. Another ten minutes would get me to a hundred, and I could be on my way. I swung my arms and jogged in place to get my blood flowing. I really wanted to lie back down, but I had to get to Houston. If I didn't arrive soon, Mom would worry. It's not like I could call her and tell her I was still alive. I sighed and unplugged the bike.

I pushed myself for six hours, only stopping to dodge the occasional drone. As I rode, I considered different ways to turn in the Zealot group who'd captured me. I'd have to do it anonymously, of course. It's not like I could walk into a police station or military command post. I couldn't even check into a government-run safe city. I had to avoid leaving trackable clues. If I found someone to tell, and asked them to report it for me, would they even believe me?

I shook my head. Images of Larry bombarded me. I slowed and squeezed my eyes shut for a second, willing the mental images to go away. They did, but images of Brent, lying broken beneath my worthless hands, replaced them. I opened my eyes and cranked the speed up, trying to run from something I could never escape.

At dusk, I hit the outskirts of what used to be Nashville, now a gigantic pile of rubble. My vision blurred and my eyelids grew heavy. I swerved even when there weren't cars to go around. I pulled off the highway into an abandoned suburb. Through the headlight of my bike, I could tell this used to be a wealthy neighborhood. Huge houses, all with beautiful porches and lawn decorations that poked through the overgrown grass. What used to be beautiful flower beds were now overgrown with weeds. Most houses had broken windows and doors that hung open, covered in graffiti. Military marks designated the houses had been evacuated and cleared.

I doubted this place had electricity to get the bike back to a full charge, but my head ached, and I couldn't ride anymore today. I'd charge up at some point tomorrow. Now I just wanted a bed.

I found an open garage door, parked my bike, and pulled the door shut. No one was around to steal anything, but I didn't feel comfortable leaving it out. After all, no one had been around to steal the bike in the first place until I came along.

Flashlight on, I stepped from the garage into the kitchen. The house looked as bad as the neighborhood. Everything was overturned. Glass from broken windows littered the floor. Cabinet doors hung open, some of them broken off completely. Even the knives, which could have been useful, were gone.

I walked down a hall and found all the rooms in the same condition. I picked the master bedroom and turned the faucet in the bathroom sink on. Dirty water sputtered from the spout. I let it run until it cleared enough for me to drink it.

After a freezing three-minute shower, I looked around for a blanket, a sheet, or something. Nothing. Oh well. Another night without a blanket wouldn't kill me.

I pulled an MRE from my bag and ate. These things

were getting on my nerves. They used to be a fun tradition with Dad, but now they tasted like cardboard and sadness.

I climbed into the soft bed, snuggled under my jacket as best I could, and within minutes, I fell asleep.

When I woke, the sun streamed through the window. I stretched. How long had I been out? I looked at my PCD. Four p.m. Sixteen hours. My stomach rumbled. I sprang out of bed. Ugh, I needed to remember to set alarms, so I didn't sleep for so long. I ate an MRE and drank more water from the tap in the bathroom. I put my gun and my bag on my back and headed to the garage.

CHAPTER 34

JADZIA

I GOT on Interstate 40 in Nashville and picked my way southwest. As soon as I noticed places with power, I stopped at an empty shopping plaza and plugged into one of the first parking spots I came across. I sat on the curb and took inventory of my supplies.

My shoulders slumped. Crap. Not as much as I thought or needed. Only two MREs left, ten energy bars and twenty-five water pods. At the rate things were going, I wouldn't reach Houston for at least another eight days.

The time on the run had cost me. I'd tightened my belt to the tightest hole and my pants still seemed baggy. My shirt hung on my frame, and I could feel my ribs. When I get to Houston, Mom would put some meat back on my bones. I could almost taste her pancakes.

I repacked my bag and flipped through some news stations on my PCD. I didn't realize how out of touch I'd been. More cities had been attacked. Survivors were being grouped together to help as many people as possible. If you asked me, that just made a more tempting target, but I wasn't the one in charge.

The blame for all the destruction fell on people of faith. They were the targets, so they were the problem. If we just got rid of religion, everyone could live in peace again. Surely, something could be done. Tear down any remaining places of worship and any statues or buildings with religious affiliation. Outlaw religious gatherings, take down net pages, and ban religious books.

I shook my head and closed my hand. I couldn't take much more. It didn't make any sense. Then again, I guess angry mobs never did. The Zealots were the ones running around blowing people up. Why blame the victims? Public opinion seemed too easy to sway. Why couldn't everyone just get along?

The hum of a drone got me moving. I grabbed my bag and my gun and dashed across the parking lot toward the stores. I ducked into one of the broken windows, backed up against a wall, and crouched. The drone flew over the lot and paused at my bike. What the heck was it doing? I guess a lone bike in an abandoned shopping mall seemed strange to whoever operated the drone. Could they tell the bike had been ridden recently? My heart pounded so loud I'm surprised the drone didn't pick up the sound.

The drone moved again and completed its sweep of the lot and store fronts. I sagged against the wall. I couldn't wait to get to Houston. Mom would take care of me. I could stop running for a little while, anyway.

I waited about thirty minutes, trying to think of anything except the last time I hid out in an empty store. The first time I'd killed someone. A lump formed in my throat. I swallowed it. Every time I sat still for too long, the ghosts caught me. I stood and paced. Four sets of feet paced with me. Brent, the guy in the store, the guy on the cliff, and Larry. I wanted to scream at them to leave me alone.

But I knew it wouldn't do any good. I sighed. Time to move on.

I left the storefront and hopped on my bike. I got back on Interstate 40 and continued riding. More drones flew around the area. I stopped often to avoid them, hiding under overpasses, or ditching the bike and running to nearby underbrush. Once or twice, I thought they hovered too long over a bridge or group of trees where I'd taken refuge.

Maybe the one at the store had marked my bike. I pulled over to check but found no trackers. Good. I didn't want to have to leave my ride behind. The drone activity might just be increased because the area had a larger population.

A lone survivor searching for a safe house, a Zealot, or a deserter avoiding capture. At this point, anyone wandering by themselves on the highway either needed help or was running from something.

One of the drones hovered annoyingly long over my bike while I hid under a bush on the side of the road. Maybe they recognized it from before. My heart cracked against my ribs. I wiped my palms on my pants. I heard a ping. The drone had attached a tracker to the bike. Wonderful. The drone hovered for a few more minutes, scanning the area. Looking for me.

When it moved off, I waited another ten minutes. When the machine didn't return, I went to the bike and searched for the tracker. The stupid things were tiny, and I needed to get out of here in case the drone came back. I growled. There. On the frame right in front of the seat. I tried to pry the tracker off, but it zapped me. Like when the Zealots spiked me, but instead of a burn, I just felt pain up my arm. Pain I wasn't keen to repeat.

Ugh. I seriously hated the government. And the Zealots. And this war. Why couldn't I just go back to school and be normal again?

I opened my PCD and started hacking. I stood in the open on the road, a sitting duck for more drones, but none came. Now that they were tracking the suspicious bike, maybe there was no need to keep scanning the area.

I sat beside the bike, took out a water pod and drank. After half an hour of furious hacking, I broke into the tracker's software. After another five minutes, I created a thirty-second loop that made it look like the bike sat still. Good enough. Even if they sent another drone and found the bike missing, they wouldn't know where I'd gone.

I moved on as fast as I could ride. Past small towns, farmland, trees, and a whole lot of nothing. I passed someone in a car taking advantage of an open stretch of road. I wondered about their story. Neither of us stopped. Couldn't risk it.

I rode for three hours and made it about halfway to Memphis. I came upon a nice long stretch of empty highway. No cars as far as I could see, which was a decent way because of the flat, straight road. Strange, but I wasn't about to miss the opportunity to make up lost time.

I opened the throttle up and the speedometer quickly climbed to one fifty-five. The wind blew my hair that stuck out under my helmet. Brent would have loved this. I whooped. Moments of fun were so few in the past couple of months. I found myself smiling.

Miles later, I rounded a bend in the road and had to slow because of a pileup of abandoned cars. Should have known my luck wouldn't hold. This cluster of cars looked different from the other ones I'd come across. Placed on purpose. Cars lined both shoulders, packed in tight. No room even for my bike to pick through. I stopped. My scalp tingled and goose bumps popped up on my skin.

A group of people appeared from behind the cars and the bushes on the side of the road. They all wore heavy duty clothes, camo pants, stun proof vests, and tough boots. Every single one of them had weapons. From laser knives, to rifles, to a baseball bat. Sweat trickled down my neck.

I swung the bike around to find more people standing across the road about five feet away. Dressed the same, holding weapons. A girl about my age, with red hair, leveled a rifle at me and smiled.

CHAPTER 35
JADZIA

HER WORDS HAD a southern twang to them. "Nice bike."

I stared her down.

"I gave you a compliment. The polite thing to do is say thank you." The others around her snickered.

Whipping my head from side to side, I gunned the bike. They closed the ranks. Out of the corner of my eye, I could see a twenty-something guy smacking his palm with a metal bar that looked a lot like part of the hover-drive from a car.

I willed my voice to be steady. "Move. Or I'll run you over."

The girl had the nerve to look offended. "Well, that's not very nice." She tilted her head. "You come into my territory uninvited. You don't thank me for complimenting your bike, and you threaten me."

"You're pointing a gun at me." My hands itched to grab my own rifle from my back. She'd most likely shoot me if I tried.

She shrugged. "All the more reason to be nice to me. Of course, I suppose I should be the one thanking you."

What? This chick was nuts. "Why would you thank me?"

"You brought me this nice present." She motioned toward my bike.

I inched my hand off the throttle and toward the strap of my gun.

She laughed and shot at the ground near the front of the bike. "No, you don't. Off the bike."

I hesitated. The bike was my best chance at getting away from this group. I didn't see any working vehicles around, so I could easily outrun them. I took my helmet off so they could see my face clearly and put on what I hoped was a please don't kill me expression. "Look, why don't we —"

Another shot. "You don't listen very well, do you?"

I dismounted. My legs shook when I stood.

"On your knees."

I looked at her. Definitely insane. She wanted me to, what, bow to her?

She pulled the trigger again. Gravel showered my shoes. "I said, on your knees."

I slumped to my knees. "I don't want to fight you. Let me go and I'll leave."

The butt of her rifle swung around and connected with the side of my mouth. My face exploded with pain. I should have left the helmet on.

She laughed again. "You think you can cross my territory without paying the toll?" The others laughed too. I wanted to cover my ears, but I kept my hands on my thighs.

She bobbed her head at someone behind me. "Nathan, grab the pack and the gun. Tony, check out the bike."

I turned my head. A large guy with a laser knife the size of my forearm walked up to me. He grabbed the rifle and

ripped it over my head. Then he grabbed my pack and practically dislocated my shoulders to pull it off. The other guy
headed to my bike and started messing with his PCD and
the bike. Great. They had a hacker.

The one with my bag opened it. "Not much in here."
He aimed a sharp kick at my legs. I gasped but didn't
cry out.

The girl's sarcastic voice filled my ears. "Well, that's a
shame. I guess we'll just have to settle for the bike."

She looked at Tony. He nodded. "I can hack it. Just give
me a few minutes to make you the new owner."

I looked around for something, anything, to defend
myself with. A few pebbles on the road, but nothing else.
Great.

My hands curled into fists. I spit a mixture of blood and
saliva at the girl's shoes. She recoiled and called me a few
choice names.

"I think you need a lesson on how to be polite to
people," she said. Quicker than I realized she could move
she grabbed my hair and pulled my head back. Another girl
punched me in the face.

I struggled to get my feet under me. Pulling Dad's laser
knife out of my pocket, I switched it on and jabbed the knife
into the leg of the girl holding my hair.

She let go and hit me in the stomach. Three other
people from the group moved in. Fist after fist connected
with my head. My stomach. My arms. Anywhere they
could connect.

The knife got knocked out of my hand. I punched
blindly, trying to get in as many hits as possible. We'd
trained in hand-to-hand combat, but I knew I couldn't win
this. There were just too many of them. However, I'd make
my life cost as much as I could.

I bit an arm as it grabbed my face. Another hard blow to the face rewarded me. My eyes swelled. I fell back to my knees. Blood poured from my nose. I rolled onto my side and kicked out at someone's knee. A sharp crack sounded. He howled in pain. Someone else replaced him and kicked me in the head. Everything went black for a few seconds.

A sharp pain jerked me back to reality. I sat up and saw the handle of Dad's knife sticking out of my left leg.

The redheaded girl got in my face. "Pay back." She cursed.

I hit her square in the jaw. She reeled and fell on her butt. More feet kicked my sides.

The girl stood and straddled me. She grabbed my head and slammed it against the pavement. Once. Twice. I blacked out again.

I'm not sure how much longer they beat me. I saw flashes of reality in between moments of blackness. Flashes of pain between blissful nothingness. The redheaded girl climbed onto my bike. I think I picked my head up. Something that was supposed to be "Get off my bike," came out as "mmfffmmm."

She looked down at me and laughed. "Thanks for the bike." Her foot smashed me in the face. I gratefully surrendered to the coming darkness.

CHAPTER 36

JADZIA

EVERYTHING HURT. I groaned and shifted. Soft sheets caressed my legs. Wait. Sheets. I opened my eyes as wide as I could, which wasn't much. I could barely see. Despite my blurred vision, I made out pale yellow walls with framed pictures of flowers. I sat up against the pillow and gasped. It hurt to move, to breathe. I leaned against the headboard and hoped the dizziness would clear. An IV tube pulled at my arm and my skin stung.

A table with a lamp sat on both sides of the enormous bed. A desk, a chair, and a Holo-screen sat across from the bed. How did I get to a hotel room?

I tried to sit up more, but the room spun. Another groan escaped my lips.

The door clicked. I turned my head and two girls, a little younger than my mom, with dark skin and dark hair, walked into the room. Each girl held a tray with a bowl on it. A few seconds later, the room stopped spinning, and the images merged. Only one girl, one tray, one bowl. My head pounded. I tried to say something, but only managed another groan.

"Don't try to talk. You've been through a lot," she said.

The girl put the tray on the desk and walked to my bed. I cringed.

She stopped and held up both hands. "It's okay. We won't hurt you."

The last person who told me that locked me in a truck. I slid my hand toward the nightstand. Maybe I could knock her out with the lamp. I only got a few inches away from my body before pain shot through my shoulder. I flinched and eased my arm back to my side.

She gave me a sad smile. "Careful. You have a dislocated shoulder and several other injuries. We don't have the means to heal you as quickly as a hospital. You'll just have to let time do its work." She moved to the head of the bed. "Here, let me help." She picked up a glass of water from the nightstand and sat on the side of the bed.

With what seemed like a practiced move, she slid her arm around my shoulders and lifted me into a better sitting position. Only a small shot of pain went through my ribs. She lifted the glass to my lips. I pretended to swallow.

Guess who I wasn't fooling. "You really should drink something. You've been out for days." She tipped the glass a little more. The cool water pressed against my lips. I couldn't help myself. I took a mouthful of the water. She pulled the cup away and chuckled as I tried to suck down more. "Easy does it. Don't want it to come back up."

I nodded. My tongue loosened. My voice was gritty and my throat raw. "Where am I?"

"You're safe." She gave me more water. "I'm Sage. I'm a nurse, and I've been taking care of you. Do you remember what happened?"

Images of the girl with the gun and her gang beating me

flashed through my head. "A bunch of people beat the living tar out of me and stole my Hover-bike. But I don't know how I ended up here."

She sighed. "We figured as much. There's a band of survivors around here that attack anyone passing through. We've tried to stop them but can't seem to track them down." She stood and got the tray, set it on the nightstand and dipped a spoon in the bowl. "Oh, and Ryker found you on a supply run. He carried you a few miles to get you here."

The smell of chicken broth overwhelmed me. My stomach growled. "How long have I been out?"

"Four days. You're pretty banged up. Concussion, dislocated shoulder, at least five broken ribs, broken ankle, probably broken nose, black eyes."

"Four days? Four days!" I tried to push the covers aside and get up. I needed to get to Houston. Mom must be frantic. The room pitched sideways. My stomach turned. Pain shot through me. I collapsed back onto the bed.

Sage put her hands gently on my shoulders. "Whoa, there. Relax. You're in no shape to go anywhere."

I tried to sit up again, but my vision blacked around the edges. I lay back and fought unconsciousness. It didn't work. The blackness pulled me under like an alligator dragging its victim to the depths.

When I woke again, the swelling in my face had gone down enough for me to open my eyes beyond slits, but not quite all the way. Sage and the tray were gone. The only light in the room came from the lamp on the nightstand.

Still alive. At least they didn't poison the water. I pushed myself up and reached for the glass. My body screamed in protest. I moved slowly and took a drink.

Panting, I sank back into the pillows. How was I supposed to get to Houston now? I could barely take a drink. Mom. Jonathan. Carina. Aunt Dawn. They were all waiting for me. I had to get to them. I slid my legs to the side of the bed and tried to sit on the edge. White hot pain flashed through my chest. My vision blacked, and I fought passing out again. I cried out.

The door opened, and my vision cleared about a minute later. A male voice with a southern drawl said, "Easy there. You shouldn't be getting up yet."

I pulled the covers closer around my body. Some strange man didn't need to see my undershirt.

My vision cleared. A guy about my age, with blond hair and sea-green eyes, stood at the foot of the bed. He moved to help me out of my awkward half sitting, half falling-out-of-bed position. I flinched.

He stopped. "My name is Ryker Jenkins."

My brain knew the name Ryker, but it took a minute to remember why. Which seemed stupid because I'd heard it earlier that day. My voice was better than before, but still not quite my own. "You're the one who found me."

"Yeah. Please, let me help you."

I studied him. His face looked sincere, and his voice seemed gentle. Nothing about him looked threatening. I thought of Larry and the bad feeling I had when I walked up to his safe house. Safe house my rear end. But nothing about Ryker seemed unsafe. Besides, in another few minutes, I'd be on the floor, and the thought of that didn't exactly appeal to me. "Okay."

He gently slid his muscular arms around me and rearranged me on the bed.

"Thanks."

"Of course. Can I get you anything? You hungry?"

Before my fuzzy brain a could answer, my stomach rumbled in response.

He laughed. A deep, melodic sound. "I'll take that as a yes. Be right back." He turned and left.

Surprisingly I looked forward to his return.

CHAPTER 37
JADZIA

WHEN RYKER RETURNED, he helped me eat some broth. I wished for something more substantial, but apparently Sage's orders were liquid only. Ryker promised to sneak me some scrambled eggs in the morning if I kept the broth down. Pancakes would have been better, but eggs would do.

After I finished the broth, a little bit of strength returned. Ryker gathered up the bowl and glass of water and turned to leave.

"Wait." I'm not sure why I stopped him. The word just seemed to drop from my mouth.

He turned. "Do you want something else?"

"Uh. . ." Think. I willed my brain to work through the fog. What did I need to know? "Where are we?"

He hesitated.

Well, crap. I'd let myself get comfortable. Stupid. These people could be Zealots or some gang who wanted to make use of me. But then why did they take me in, care for me? My head spun. Ugh. Why couldn't I think straight?

Ryker sighed. "You're safe. I promise. But I can't risk telling you where we are."

"Why not?" I raised my good arm and pinched the bridge of my nose.

"We don't know who you are. You could be a Zealot, or a member of the gang around here. We have people to protect." He locked those beautiful green eyes on me. So different from Brent, but just as gentle. Just as caring. "We'll care for you until you're in better shape. After that . . . we'll see."

I rubbed my forehead.

"I can give you something for your headache, if you'd like."

I shook my head. A mistake. The room spun. Ryker set down the tray and disappeared into what I assumed was an attached bathroom. He came back with two tablets in his hand. I recognized them from my army med kit.

"Those make me loopy." As if I wasn't loopy enough.

"Maybe they'll help you sleep. Sage said sleep and time are the best things for you right now."

I was beyond thinking they were trying to kill me. At least for now, I'd take them at their word. I nodded.

Ryker handed me the pills and the almost empty glass of water.

I swallowed them. Ryker helped me get as comfortable as possible before the meds knocked me out.

The next few days were the same. Sage and Ryker took turns coming in to care for me. I listened to everything Sage told me to help my body heal faster. Mom and Jonathan were waiting for me, and I had to get out of here as soon as possible. I moved from eating broth to solid foods. Sage removed the IV. The swelling in my face went down, and I almost threw a party the first time I took a shower without Sage's help.

Both Sage and Ryker were nice enough, but they

refused to answer my questions about our location, their numbers, or who they really were. Despite that, I couldn't help feeling comfortable with them. No one threw me into a truck or did anything remotely threatening. They were what they appeared to be. Nice people, trying to survive a war, who just wanted to help me.

A week after my beating, a man about my father's age came into my room. Sandy blond hair and blue-gray eyes. His face looked familiar, although I knew I'd never seen him before.

Thank goodness they'd given me my clothes back a few days ago. Ryker and Sage seeing me in an undershirt didn't seem like a big deal anymore, but it would have been really weird with this guy.

He smiled and stood by my bed. "I'm Michael Jenkins. Welcome to our haven."

Ryker's dad. No wonder he looked familiar. "Hi."

He chuckled, the same chuckle I had grown fond of from his son. "Ryker has told me all about you."

Heat crept into my cheeks. Ryker talked about me to his dad? Then I felt stupid. Of course, he had. His dad was in charge of everything here.

Mr. Jenkin's voice focused my thoughts again. "I'd have been in sooner to welcome you, but I wanted to give you time to heal a little first."

"I'm getting there." Who was I kidding? My head still ached, my ribs still screamed every time I moved at any speed other than a snail's pace, and my brain didn't seem to want to work the way it did before.

"You're strong. I know you'll be back on your feet in a few more weeks."

"A few more weeks!" I struggled to sit up, which proved

his point, but I didn't care. "I can't stay here a few more weeks." Mom surely thought the worst by now.

"I know you're anxious to get to Houston."

"I am."

"You're in no shape to go anywhere. Plus as I understand it, you no longer have transportation."

His words hit me like a prizefighter going for the knockout. I knew my bike had been stolen, but my addled brain hadn't put together the fact that without the bike, I was stranded here. I cursed under my breath.

Mr. Jenkins frowned.

"Sorry."

"It's okay, you're obviously upset."

"My mom and brother are waiting for me."

"Yes. Ryker said you got separated during your evacuation."

I nodded slowly. My gut churned. I had told Ryker I was separated from my family when Zealots attacked our convoy. I guess I didn't trust him as much as I thought I did.

The days of walking from New York came back to me. Exhausted. Hungry. Thirsty. Slogging along. Barely getting anywhere. But I had gotten this far. Where that was. I could manage again. And this time I wouldn't be fleeing. Surely these people would give me supplies. "I could walk."

He chuckled again. "How about we see if you're up for a tour of this place before we decided if you can handle a multi-day trek."

CHAPTER 38
JADZIA

MR. JENKINS OFFERED me his arm.

With my good arm, I took it and let him help me up. I twisted wrong and gasped. So much for proving I was strong enough to walk to Houston.

He steadied me. "Are you all right?"

I closed my eyes and counted to five. The pain receded. "I'm good."

He nodded. "Ryker said you were tough."

My cheeks burned, and I ducked my head. He had? "That's me."

Ryker's dad pointed to my feet. "There's some flip-flops at the foot of the bed. I'll get them for you." He let me go, and I managed to remain standing without help while he grabbed the flip-flops.

I slid my feet into the footwear and we walked out the door into a long, white hall with mud brown carpet.

Why did hotels pick such awful colors for their carpets? Every few feet, there was another door frame in the wall. "How big is this place?"

"Oh, we've got plenty of space for a growing

community."

Not really an answer, but okay. "Why not just go to a shelter city?"

A strange look crossed his face. Uneasiness? Fear? "Do you honestly believe shelter cities are safe?"

I thought about the bomb plans in Larry's stronghold. "Good point."

We arrived at an elevator and waited in silence. I ran my fingers through my hair and gave myself a headache trying to figure out something to say. A ding chimed, and the door opened.

Mr. Jenkins motioned. "After you."

A minute later, the elevator opened into the lobby of the hotel. The smell of chlorine filled the air. "There's a pool?"

He bobbed his head. "Oh, yes. We were very blessed to find this place. It has a pool, fitness room, restaurant grade kitchen, and two hundred thirty-two rooms to house people."

"Are all the rooms full?"

"No. But we pick up a few more people each month."

We walked past the pool. A few families and their kids swam and splashed in the water. "How do they find you?"

He frowned. "Some are like you. Victims of desperate survivors. We find others when we're on supply runs. One family just stumbled upon us. We take in and help who we can."

"Then what?"

He shrugged. "People realize we're a safe place and they decide to stay with us."

"No one's ever left?"

"No one's ever had a reason to."

I did.

Mr. Jenkins motioned down the hall. "Let me show you

the dining room."

I turned but stopped moving when my eyes fell on an open door slightly ahead of us. Holo-screens lined the walls. Projection books and communication equipment littered the desk. My heart rate kicked up a notch.

A man rose from a chair, locked eyes with me, and shut the door. My pulse beat in my ears. What was going on in that room? Were they planning to blow up a city? I glanced at Mr. Jenkins, but he continued the tour as if nothing had happened. As we went from place to place, people met my eyes with welcoming looks. A few waved. I could see why people liked it here, but I still couldn't stay.

After he showed me the entire inside of the hotel complex, we returned to my room. My shoulder ached, my ribs throbbed, and my head felt as if a construction crew were demolishing a building inside of it. I forced a happy face when he opened my door for me. "Thanks for showing me around."

"Of course. Now that you know the lay of the place, I hope you'll feel free to venture out when you feel able."

His words rubbed me the wrong way. I hadn't realized I needed permission to leave my room. I smiled again. "Thank you."

"Dinner is at five-thirty. I hope to see you there." He closed the door.

Despite how much my body craved a break, the desire to explore more won out. I waited a full minute before activating the small Holo-screen next to the door frame. Like an old-fashioned peep hole, it allowed me to see if anyone was at the door, except with this I could scroll and see the length of the hall. It also acted like an intercom, so I could talk to whomever stood on the other side.

I scrolled the length of the hall twice to be sure no one

was around and quietly opened my door. I tiptoed to the elevator and pushed the button.

When the door opened, a girl around my age with platinum blonde hair and eyes the color of warm honey stepped off. So much for being stealthy.

She glared at me. "Oh, it's you. Aren't you supposed to be in your room?"

I straightened my shoulders and met her eyes. "Mr. Jenkins said I could walk around."

"Whatever." She bumped my shoulder as she walked past. Pain shot down my arm, but I kept my face calm. Way to make friends, Jadzia. I shook my head, got in the elevator, and watched the blonde girl hurry down the hall as the doors closed. Making friends didn't matter. I wouldn't be here long.

When I reached the ground floor, I strode out the open doors. My dad once told me acting like you belonged was the best way to blend in. Since stealth hadn't worked, I figured I'd try pretending. I headed to the kitchen and grabbed an apple from the fruit bowl. I moaned when I tasted it. Real fruit. Not fabricated stuff. Where in the world did they find real apples?

I crossed the lobby and headed down the hallway where I'd seen the open door. A few kids sat around and played a multiplayer, interactive game on their PCDs. I could make out projections of the characters and recognized it as one Brent and I used to play. This time, my ribs weren't causing the ache in my chest. I sighed and kept walking.

When I approached the end of the hall, all the doors were closed. Ugh. Which one had the screens behind it? I couldn't remember. I chose a door at random, hoping to get lucky. Locked. Of course. I tried a second door. Also locked.

"What are you doing?"

CHAPTER 39
JADZIA

I JUMPED and turned to face the voice. Ryker gazed down at me, his green eyes shining. Heat rushed to my cheeks. "Don't do that to me."

He grabbed my good arm to steady me. "Sorry. I didn't mean to scare you."

I forced a laugh. "No problem."

He leaned against the frame of the door and dropped my arm. A twinge of disappointment surged through me when he let go.

Ryker hid the door handle with his body. It could have been innocent, but I was pretty sure he didn't want me near that door. Now, at least I knew I which one.

"So?"

"So what?" I said.

His face grew serious. "So, what are you doing here?"

My mind raced. What could I possibly be doing at the end of the hallway trying to open random doors?

"Your dad said I could explore."

He crossed his arms. "Not much to explore here. So, again, what are you doing?"

I couldn't tell if he was mad or just cautious. "Looking for you, okay?" Heat flooded through my body, and I wondered if stupidity could cause spontaneous combustion. Why on earth did that come out of my mouth? I fumbled for more words, but nothing came.

He raised his eyebrows. "Dad told you I'd be in the communications room?" He flinched as if he gave too much away.

Communications room. Huh. Good to know. "He didn't say that exactly."

"What did he say?" He took a step toward me.

I took a deep breath, ignoring the pain in my ribs. The more I lied, the more I had to keep straight. My words came out in a rush. "On the tour, I saw an open door. It looked like an important room, but your dad didn't say anything about it, and someone closed the door. I figured since you're kind of a big deal around here, that's where I'd start looking for you."

His tough guy face cracked. A slow smile appeared. He chuckled. Then full out laughed. "I'm kind of a big deal?"

I laughed with him. "Ow." I held my side.

A look of worry crossed his face. He reached for me again but pulled back. "You okay?"

I nodded. "Still tender." Tender. Ha. More like excruciating.

He offered me his arm. "So now that you found me, what did you want?"

I noted the room number before I took his arm. One fifty-three. "Your dad showed me around the inside of the hotel, but I've been stuffed inside forever." I let him lead me toward the lobby. "Can we go outside?"

If Ryker had any suspicions, he didn't voice them.

"Yeah. I know the perfect spot. You might want better shoes, though."

I glanced at my feet. Flip-flops. Right. "Okay. I'll meet you back here in a few minutes."

Back in my room, I pondered the communications room as I grabbed my boots. These people seemed secretive. But they had a communications room. If they sent signals, were they able to keep them from being tracked?

When I bent down to tie my boots, I knew why they gave me flip flops. It hurt too much to bend over. Panting, with tears in my eyes, I headed back downstairs without tying my laces. I'm sure Garrett's father invented some kind of bone-mending machine that could take care of both my ribs and my shoulder in a matter of minutes. I wished they had those machines here.

Thinking of Garrett made me wonder what the rest of my old unit was doing now. The last time I watched the news, Manhattan had been secured and martial law effected. If you broke curfew, you got arrested and interrogated. Who knew what happened after that?

The elevator door slid open, and Ryker strode toward me. He held a jacket and a small pack. He looked at my boots. "Need help?"

Ugh. Being helpless sucked. "Yes, please."

He led me to a bench in the lobby, and I sat. He knelt to tie my left boot.

A howl erupted from the far side of the room. "You could have picked a more romantic spot to propose, Ryker," a guy around our age said.

Ryker met my eyes, his face as red as mine must have been. "Shut up, Cole."

I willed the floor to open and swallow me, but of course it didn't. Ryker finished tying my other boot, and we stood.

He led me to a group of four guys. The oldest had to be around twenty, and the youngest couldn't have been older than six. He pointed to the first three and introduced me to Murphy, Eric, and Billy. My heart clenched at the sight of the youngest boy, Billy. So much like Jonathan, except he had a mop of blond hair and brown eyes. But his mannerisms and even the way he held himself were the same.

I tore my gaze from Billy and focused back on Ryker. "And this idiot is Cole." He pointed to the last guy, a kid around our age with red hair.

"I'm just messing with you." Cole laughed and offered me his elbow. "Sorry about that. Ryker's too easy sometimes."

I gave him an elbow bump. "Hi guys."

"Hi." The group grinned.

"Out for a romantic walk?" Cole said.

Ryker shot him a look. "Yeah, I'm taking her to the same place I usually take your mom."

We all laughed. I hadn't had this much fun with a group of people since basic training. We'd sit around during down time, goofing off. My unit had been my best friends. My family. How could I have abandoned them?

The walls closed in. I shifted from one foot to another.

Ryker glanced down at me. "I promised you some fresh air."

I swallowed the lump in my throat. "You did."

"See you later, guys." Ryker led me to the doors, which opened automatically. We stepped outside. The sun warmed my skin.

"Sorry about those guys. Cole means well, but he can be stupid sometimes."

I fought the lump in my throat. Say something to him. But I couldn't. Not when Brent, Sisko, Garrett, and the rest were breathing down my neck. I wished they'd leave me alone, but they were always there.

We crossed the parking lot and headed to a path in the nearby woods. When we got past the tree line, out of sight of the hotel, Ryker stopped and gazed down at me. Those green eyes peered into my soul. "Are you okay?"

Don't cry. Don't cry. I tried to nod but ended up shaking my head.

"Come here." He pulled me against his chest and enveloped me in his arms. I couldn't remember the last time someone hugged me. Mom before I left for basic? Or was it Asher when he joined our unit? Ryker held me while the dam broke and all my pent-up emotions poured out. His hands stroked my hair.

Even though it wasn't his arms I wanted, I let him hold me until the tide ebbed.

ABOUT FIFTEEN MINUTES passed while I sobbed in his arms. When I gathered myself together, Ryker took my hand, and we walked in silence, deeper into the forest. I couldn't explain what went on in my head, and he probably had no idea what to do with me, either. But he never let go of my hand.

I imagined what it might be like to walk alone in the forest with Brent. I'd most likely be cracking jokes and he would laugh and joke back. Would we be holding hands? We'd probably still be dancing around our feelings, not wanting to admit the truth for fear of scaring the other off. It didn't seem to be the same with Ryker. Holding hands seemed natural, and I didn't mind the silence, but I was confused.

We reached a creek, and Ryker turned downstream. We walked for another ten minutes. The trees thinned, then ended.

I gasped. "This is amazing."

Tall grass waved in the gentle breeze, the scent of multi-colored wildflowers filled the air.

"I found this place by accident after we settled in here."

"Some accident."

He stared into the trees across the meadow from us. "Mom and I used to love hiking. When she passed and we moved here, I kept it up."

His mother had died. That's why I hadn't met her yet. Why, no one even mentioned her. I hadn't thought to ask. I squeezed his hand. "My father passed too."

He took a deep breath. "I'm sorry."

"I'm sorry about your mom."

We stood in silence for a few minutes, watching the bees fly between flowers.

He sighed. "Come on. I packed us a snack." He led me to some large boulders nestled at the edge of the stream. "My favorite spot is at the top of that big one." He motioned to the largest rock, about twice his height. "You can see the whole meadow."

I pointed with my good arm. "You want me to climb that?" My ribs hurt just thinking about it.

"Or we could go around the back where it's easier to climb."

I gave him a small shove and laughed. "Around the back it is."

We climbed the gentle slope of the boulder, my hand still in his. From the flat top, I really could see the entire meadow and into the woods beyond.

We sat, and he opened his pack. He rummaged around and took out some candy and two water pods. "Found it during my last supply run."

Oh, my gosh. Chocolate. I took a bite and closed my eyes, letting the flavor melt on my tongue.

He laughed. "Good, huh?"

"Shush."

We ate the sweets and talked. He pointed to the far tree line. "Sometimes deer wander up from the stream through there."

"I can see why you like this place. It's beautiful."

He caught my eye and held my gaze. "I've never brought anyone here before." His cheeks tinged pink. "I usually come here when I want to be alone. Or to pray."

Pray. My breath caught in my throat. I looked at the rock. Things started clicking into place. The taking in and caring for strangers, the fear of being exposed. His dad even used the word blessed. Why didn't I pick it up then?

"You're a . . ." I took a breath deep enough to make my ribs ache. "You're a believer?"

He shrugged. "Nowadays, believer, is a general term to describe someone who believes in a higher power. Specifically, I'm a Christian."

I tried to recall the World Religions class from school. We learned about everything from Buddhism to a guy named Jesus, but it all blended in my mind.

Wasn't religion old-fashioned? To Brent, it had been stupid. The longer the war dragged on and the more the Zealots and public opinion blamed people of faith for it, being a believer was only one thing. Dangerous.

Ryker's voice came, thick and quiet. "Say something. Please."

"That's why you haven't gone to a safe city. You're afraid."

He sighed. "We were at church one morning, the last week of March." He stared at the meadow with a faraway look on his face. "Nothing out of the ordinary. Then the building exploded."

I gasped.

He wrung his hands. "Dad and I were in the back talking to one of the other pastors. Mom . . ." He choked up.

I put my good hand on his arm.

"Mom was standing in the lobby, greeting people. Dad and I made it out a back entrance. We never saw Mom again."

I rubbed his arm. "Ryker." Nothing I could say would help. Nothing anyone said to me when Dad died helped. I scooted closer to him and put my uninjured arm around his shoulders.

"Believers weren't popular with the public before the war started. Backwards, narrow-minded." He scoffed. "By the first week in April, there were already whispers about believers being the cause of the war. Dad found the hotel then. We contacted other members of our church and here we are."

"So everyone there is a Christian?"

He shook his head. "Sage ran into a few non-believers on a supply run. She invited them to join us. They stayed. Then a Jewish man found us. We have several Muslim families too. They were traveling together when that gang ambushed them in the night. Took all their supplies. Stranded them." He clenched his fists. "Like they did to you. When I think about how I found you—let's just say my thoughts aren't very Christian." His body shook. He took a deep breath. He snugged his arm around my waist, as if to make sure I was still there and okay.

I tucked my head into his chest and listened to his heartbeat.

"My dad's army base got obliterated." I didn't think it was possible, but he pulled me closer to him.

"Tell me."

I took as deep as a breath as I could without hurting my ribs. Ryker had shared his secret, really the majority of his group's secret, with me. The least I could do was tell him some of mine.

JADZIA FOCUSED her gaze on the rock beneath us. "Zealots posed as dignitaries to get a tour of Dad's army base. The news said their credentials were perfect, and the military easily granted access."

The Zealot's hacker must have been amazing. I'd been thinking of changing the identity of everyone in our group, but hadn't had the time to dig into how to do it.

She wrapped her arms around herself. "As the Zealots were shown around, they planted small proton bombs everywhere. After they left, they remotely triggered the bombs." She sniffled, and I had to lean in to hear her. "The military couldn't even find bodies to ship home."

With technology like that, I guess Dad and I were even more blessed to get out of that church alive. "I heard about the base, but not much about what actually happened." I put my hand over hers and rubbed it with my thumb.

"The government kept it out of the news as much as they could." She wiped a tear from her cheek. "Didn't want any copycats."

We sat in silence, comforting each other with our presence. I didn't know anyone else who'd lost a parent before. An awful club to belong to, for sure, but not being alone anymore somehow made it easier.

An alarm beeped on my PCD. "We should head back. It's almost time for dinner." I stood and offered her a hand up.

After a dinner of fresh venison and some of the fabricated veggies I managed to find on my last supply run, Jadzia and I hung out in a conference room we'd dragged some couches and chairs into when we first found the hotel. Most of the other kids who lived with us were there.

I smiled, watching Billy and Jadzia together. She took to him like she'd known the kid her whole life. She got down to his level, asked him about the video games he played, and joined him in playing until his bedtime.

At eleven, she stood and stretched her good arm. "I'm exhausted, guys. I'm going to bed."

I stood and joined her. "I'll walk you to your room."

Cole let out a wolf howl. I rolled my eyes and kept walking. "Sorry about them."

She grinned. "It's okay. It's kinda nice to be around teasing like that again. Like family."

When we got to her room, she opened the door, and I leaned into her. I couldn't help it. She was such an awesome person to be around—and gorgeous.

She shied back. Pain crossed her face. I tried to cover by shifting my weight against the door frame. Idiot. Why did I think she'd want to kiss me? Just because we shared a moment earlier. "I'll . . . see you tomorrow, I guess."

"Yeah." She closed the door.

I walked to my room, mumbling about what an idiot I was the entire way.

Jadzia's face filled my mind as I tried to sleep. Her eyes hid a pain so much deeper than the loss of her dad.

I'd tossed in bed for an hour when an alarm went off on my PCD. Bleary-eyed I checked my PCD. Crap. When I had first set up our communications equipment, I put security systems into place that alerted me if anyone unauthorized used the equipment. Someone was doing so now.

I shot out of bed and hurried to the communication room, still in my gym shorts and tank top.

My heart stopped. I swore, something I rarely did. "What do you think you're doing?"

Jadzia jumped and spun her chair toward me. Expressions of surprise, fear, sadness, and pain crossed her face. "I, uh—"

Shoving her chair aside, I looked at the screen. "Who did you send a message to?"

Her voice rose. "I didn't send a message."

I turned her chair back to what she'd been working on.

Her eye grew wide. "No. No. No." Her fingers went to the keyboard.

I pushed the chair back again. "No way."

"I have to finish." She reached for me. "Ryker, you have to let me finish."

My voice rose louder than hers. "You think I'm just going to let you send a message to just anyone? That's how things get traced. That's how people get found. I don't know you. I don't know who you're contacting."

She looked like I'd slapped her.

I took a deep breath and calmed my voice. "You're lucky I'm good with computers." I typed a few lines of code into it. Our firewalls seemed okay. After a few more keystrokes, I determined the message was secure. "No trace." I turned to her. "Who were you contacting?"

"My mom. Since you had all this equipment, I figured you could send untraceable messages."

I scoffed. "Your mom. Really?" I motioned toward the door.

She trembled. "I'd never put you in jeopardy."

"You used me." I balled my hands into fists. "I opened up to you. Told you who we are. All you wanted was to use the communications equipment."

"Ryker, please. I swear, I only wanted to let my mom know what happened. I didn't get to finish the message, and now she's going to think I got captured by Zealots." Her breath came in frantic gasps. Eyes wide. "I sent it by accident when you walked in and didn't get to finish."

I paced. "Doesn't she already think that? Didn't you get separated because of Zealots? Or was that a lie, too?"

Her mouth moved, but no sound came out. She shrank back into her chair.

"Are you serious? That wasn't even true." I threw my arms in the air, then pointed at her. "Who are you? The truth this time."

She stood and shoved me so she could get by.

I blocked her. If she'd been a guy, I probably would have punched her. "How did you bypass the security programs?"

Her hand formed fists at her sides. "Either let me finish my message or move."

"You're not getting away that easily. You've dodged questions. Flat out lied. Now, you're going to tell me." I pointed to the chair where she'd been sitting.

She tried to push past me again. I grabbed her good arm. She recoiled. Fear flickered in her eyes. I let her go and took a deep breath. I grabbed a chair without letting her pass. Not an easy feat, but I managed. I plopped the chair in front of the closed door and sat.

Her face flushed with fury, she crossed her arms.

I motioned again to the seat in front of the computer. "I can wait here all night."

Jadzia dropped into the chair. "What do you want to know?"

"The truth."

CHAPTER 42

JADZIA

RYKER FACED ME, his disappointment so obvious it might as well have been tattooed on his face. I looked at my hands and twisted my fingers around each other. "If I tell you the truth, will you let me finish sending my mom the message?"

"You're lucky I haven't called my dad and locked you up."

"That's not an answer."

He shook his head. "Let's see if I believe your story first."

My blood boiled. Jerk. "Fine, you want the truth?" The words spilled from my mouth. The draft, boot camp, New York, the ambush.

My hands shook. My breathing came in quick gasps. The room disappeared. I was back in the city. I heard the shouts of my friends, panicked voices trying to escape. Brent's blood covered my hands. I scrubbed them, trying to remove it. His last words rang in my ears. "I love you."

A frantic voice yanked me back. "Hey. Jadzia. Hey. You're okay."

I lay on the floor, scrunched into a ball in front of the

chair. A guy knelt next to me. Where was I? Someone screamed. I took a breath, and the sound stopped. Oh, it was me.

The guy tried to put his arm around me. I flinched away.

He raised both hands. His voice was strong, yet calm. "Breathe." He took a deep breath and let it out. "Come on. Breathe with me." Another deep breath.

Breathing seemed like something I could do. I took a deep, shuddering breath with him. My ribs hurt. Why did my ribs hurt? I clutched my middle.

"Good. Again."

Ryker. His name came back to me as we breathed together a second time. The hotel. I gazed around. The communication room. I remembered.

"Now, tell me three things you can see."

My voice quivered. "What?"

"Three things you can see." He put an arm on my shoulder. I let him keep it there.

I rattled them off. "The chair. The desk. And you."

"Good."

He talked me through three things I could hear, feel, and smell as well. By the end of the exercise, my body had stilled. My breathing returned to normal, and I let Ryker help me back into my seat.

"Where did you learn that?"

He sat in the chair and looked at his hands. The tips of his ears turned red. "After Mom died, I started having anxiety attacks. As a pastor, Dad knew some techniques that helped me." He shrugged. "I thought I'd try it."

I nodded. "It worked. Thank you." I leaned back.

He sighed. "Look Z, I know this is hard for you. I—"

I sat straight up, a hard edge to my voice. "What did you call me?"

Surprise etched itself on his face. He blinked. "I guess I called you Z."

"Only my cousin calls me that." Even as I said the words, I realized his use of my nickname didn't bother me.

"I'm sorry."

My shoulders slumped. "It's okay. I don't mind. You just caught me off-guard."

He kept his gaze on me. "I think I've heard enough for tonight. It's late. We both need sleep." He stood. "Come on. I'll walk you to your room."

I griped the arms of my chair. "I still want to finish sending my message." The image of Mom reading what I sent, getting to the part about being abducted by Zealots, then having the message end abruptly made my throat close. She'd think they still held me captive and they caught me sending something.

And Jonathan. He had to know I was on my way. What would he think? I started shaking again.

Ryker ran his fingers through his hair. "Houston is in the same time zone we are. It's one in the morning there. Your mom is most likely asleep."

"I—"

"We'll talk to my dad in the morning. He'll decide." He moved toward me and held out his hand.

I looked at it. Locked eyes with him and stood. I left his hand dangling. He formed a fist and dropped it to his side.

Ryker followed me back to my room like he wouldn't let me out of his sight. Jerk.

I tossed and turned the rest of the night.

As soon as the first bit of pink tinged the sky, I went to the dining room.

A blond girl stood by the coffee machine. I desperately needed a dose of caffeine after a night of no sleep. She turned when I stepped next to her.

"Well, well, if it isn't the troublemaker." The girl who'd bumped into me outside of the elevator the other day glared.

Great. I forced a smile. "Good morning."

She scoffed. "Not for you, it isn't."

"What do you mean by that?" Girl, it is too early. Coffee first. Cat fight later.

"Don't play stupid. Everyone already knows Ryker caught you sneaking around, sending secret messages."

My cheeks burned.

She leaned in closer to me and dropped her voice. "I just hope I get to be the one to throw you out on your rear."

"Leave her alone, Cassie." Ryker walked over to us.

Cassie gave Ryker a look so sweet it made me want to throw up. "I was just saying good morning to our guest." She held her cup up to Ryker. "Can I get you a coffee?"

She moved closer to him and touched his arm. "After all, you must be so tired, having to make sure a certain someone didn't get into any more trouble last night." She shot another glare my way.

My blood pressure rose. My shoulders tensed. Who did this chick think she was, touching Ryker like that? Wait. I took a step back. I didn't have any kind of claim on him. Nor did I want one. Did I? He helped me, sure. But last night he'd been a jerk. Hadn't he? Or was he just trying to protect his home?

Ryker shook his head and backed away from Cassie. "I'm good."

Cassie's face fell.

I smirked. My shoulders relaxed, and I studied Ryker.

He did look like someone who'd been awake all night. My fault. Well, his too, really. If he'd have just let me finish that message to Mom, we could have both gotten a good night's sleep.

"If you need anything, Ryker, you know you can," her eyes flicked to me, "trust me." She grazed his arm again as she walked down the hall toward the elevator.

I looked at Ryker. "She's one of you guys?"

He chuckled. "I said we were Christians. I didn't say we were perfect."

CHAPTER 43
JADZIA

I TOOK a sip of my coffee. "Is your dad around?"

"He'll be down for breakfast. He takes the early morning to spend time with God."

Waiting was driving me nuts. Didn't anyone realize I was in a hurry here? "I need to send a message to my mom. She's going to be freaking out. I—"

"Let's get breakfast." Ryker started toward the kitchen.

I placed my hand on his chest, forcing him to stop. "Ryker. Please."

He shook his head. "I can't do anything without talking to my dad first."

I motioned in the direction Cassie went. "She knew what happened. I'm sure you already talked to your dad."

He looked down at me. I noticed how close we were and dropped my hand. My stupid heart beat faster. Didn't it know I was mad at him?

"Cassie knows everything that goes on here. Her dad is the head of security. He used to be a cop." His cheeks flushed. "I talked to him last night."

Could he hear my heart racing? I rolled my eyes. "Hasn't he heard of confidentiality?"

Ryker gave me my favorite laugh. Ugh. Why did I have a favorite laugh? "It's a small place. Everyone knows everything about you before you even know it yourself."

He put his hand on my back. Shivers raced up my spine. Gah. Stop it. "Come on. Let's get food."

My stomach didn't want food, but I let him guide me, anyway. Three people worked over pans of scrambled eggs and a food fabricator. The smell of bacon made me reconsider not eating.

"You guys start early." I walked to a fruit bowl and grabbed an apple. Fabricated, but not too bad.

"Lots of people to feed."

I rolled my eyes. "I thought it was a small place."

He made a stupid noise, something between a snort and a scoff, and asked one of the cooks for plates.

"I'm good." I held up my apple.

"Not eating won't make my dad appear any faster."

Frustration practically seeped from my pores. "Fine." I took the plate he offered me and put a pancake and two strips of bacon on it. I forced the food down without really tasting it.

Ryker took his time. As soon as Mr. Jenkins walked into the room, I stood. Ryker put a hand on my arm. "After he's done. You don't want to do this in public."

I wanted to punch him. My fist even tightened, but I sat back down. He was right.

His dad picked at a table diagonal from us and sat, facing away from us.

My gaze bore a hole into the back of his head while he ate.

Ryker touched my knee to stop it from bouncing, and I

blushed. He snatched his hand away so fast I thought I burned him. I looked everywhere but at him.

Finally, both Ryker and Mr. Jenkins finished their food. Ryker stood. "I'll take you to Dad's office. We'll talk there."

He led me to the lobby and behind the front desk. A hallway led to a few offices and an employee break room. We went into the last office on the right. A desk held a few Holo-pads and a box of tissues.

I dropped into one of the chairs facing the desk. Geeze. Like I got sent to the principal's office.

My jailer sat next to me as if I might run off. He didn't have to worry. If talking to his dad would let me send Mom a message, I was all for it. I just wished the man would hurry. My leg started bouncing again. Ryker eyed me, and I stopped.

Mr. Jenkins walked in, frowning.

I gulped.

He crossed the room and sat behind the desk. "Thank you, son. You can go now."

Wait. Ryker was leaving? I glanced over at him. As much as he'd annoyed me last night, I still didn't want to face his dad alone. I tugged at my collar. Had it gotten warmer in here?

Ryker stood, looking sympathetic.

I pleaded with my eyes.

He hesitated. One look at his dad, though, and he headed for the door.

I hated the fact I wanted him around.

"Obviously, I heard about the incident last night." Mr. Jenkins didn't mess around.

I could only nod.

"Ryker explained everything you told him. I won't make you go through it again."

Thank goodness. I slumped in the seat.

"I'd like to hear the rest of your story. What happened after New York?"

My shoulders tightened again, and the beginnings of a headache formed at my temples. I told him about the guy in the store. Walking home. The call to mom getting traced. The guy at the incline. Larry.

The more I talked, the more I wanted the floor to break open and swallow me. I was a horrible person. I killed three people and flat out lied about it to a group who had been nothing but good to me. Breakfast threatened to come back up. Sweat beaded on my forehead. I wiped my face. These people had every right to throw me out on my rear. I just hoped they didn't give the job to Cassie.

Mr. Jenkins handed me a tissue.

I blew my nose, took a few deep breaths, and tried to focus on three things I could see, hear, smell, and touch, like Ryker had taught me last night. It helped.

Ryker's dad gave me all the time I needed. Condemnation never crossed his face. His tone stayed calm and caring. "Would you like some water?"

My stomach churned. I doubted I could keep it down, but a cool water pod might feel good on my hands and face. I nodded.

Mr Jenkins reached under the desk and pulled out a cold pod.

I raised my eyebrows when he handed it to me.

He cracked a smile. "State-of-the-art hotel. Even has a fridge in the manager's desk."

Holding the pod made me realize my mouth was dirt dry. I broke it open and drank. "Thanks."

The break gave me the strength to keep going. There

wasn't much left, anyway. "I rode until the girl with the gang beat me into oblivion. Then I woke up here."

He pressed his hands together. "And last night you were sending a message to your mother?"

"Yeah, but I didn't get to finish it, and now she'll be even more worried than she already is."

"And the reason you didn't ask Ryker if you could send a message?" He opened his hands in front of him.

Why hadn't I just asked him? "I guess I thought he'd say no."

"So, you thought it would be better to break into a locked room, bypass security systems put in place to keep us safe, and risk everyone here?"

CHAPTER 44

JADZIA

I SHOOK MY HEAD. Just like last night, my mouth moved, but nothing came out. When he said it that way, it sounded terrible. Like I'd purposely tried to expose them or something.

My Jenkins leaned back. "Ryker told me you didn't give away our location."

"I assumed the message was secure." I looked down. "I'd never expose you."

He gave me a sad look. "I wish I could believe you. The truth is, the only reason you didn't give us away is because of my son's talent with computers." He ran a hand through his hair, the same thing Ryker did when he thought of something. "Whether accidentally or on purpose, you could have endangered all of us. I can't let that happen again."

"Let me send a message to my mom and it won't." I almost slapped my hand against my mouth. What was wrong with me? These people saved my life, and I was acting like a brat.

He tilted his head. Anger crossed his face for the first time during this conversation. "That's a very bold statement. You took advantage of my hospitality, broke into a secure area, and endangered my people, and you still have the guts to make demands."

Heat rushed to my face. "I'm sorry. I didn't mean it the way it sounded."

Ryker's dad blew out a deep breath. "You're obviously good with computers. You could have been a real asset to us."

"Could have been?"

He stood and paced behind the desk. "You've put me in a difficult situation here. As you know our location, I can't exactly let you go. However, I'd never hold you here against your will. You're also wounded. For your own safety, I shouldn't let you leave until Sage clears you for travel."

My entire body tensed, and the headache came on full force. "You're going to lock me up."

"I'm going to need some time to decide what to do."

"But my mom. Please. I have to—"

"I'm sorry. I want to believe you. But you may be telling me another lie. For all I know, your mother is a Zealot leader. I have no way of knowing your true loyalties. I can't give you access to our communications equipment at this time." He walked to the door and pulled it open. Ryker stood in the hall, leaning against the opposite door. "Ryker will watch after you today, and I will station a guard at your door tonight. I'll give you my decision tomorrow."

I stayed in my seat, trying to think of something that would change his mind.

"Please don't make this more difficult." He sighed. "I could always call Mr. Blanarik and tell him to confine you to your room."

I cocked my head, trying to figure out who Mr. Blanarik was.

Ryker stepped into the room. "Cassie's dad." He offered me his hand. "Come on."

I stood without taking his hand. Muttering a curse word under my breath, I stormed out of the office.

When I got to the front doors, Ryker grabbed my good arm. "Slow down. Where are you going?"

Energy zipped through every cell in my body. I needed to do something. Go somewhere. Be someplace else. I shook my arm free. "Out."

"I'm supposed to stay with you, remember?"

"Then you'd better keep up." I took off running toward the path he'd shown me the other day. Every step sent waves of pain through my chest and shoulder. I got maybe a quarter mile into the woods before I couldn't go any farther. Sergeant Wallace would have had me scrubbing toilets for a week for my performance, but my body couldn't take any more punishment. I turned to find Ryker right behind me.

"Not bad for someone with broken ribs."

I shouted at him. "Shut up. This is all your fault." It wasn't, and I knew it. But the anger and frustration needed to go somewhere. Blaming him was easier than blaming myself.

"My fault?" He raised his eyebrows. "How is this my fault?"

"If you wouldn't have —"

Ryker grabbed me, pulled me close to him, and covered my mouth with his hand. "Shhh. Stop."

What the heck? I made muffled noises and attempted to kick him.

"Stop fighting." He forced us into a crouched position. "Listen."

I stopped struggling to break his hold.

He loosened his grip. "There." He pointed up the path.

Tuning in to my surroundings, I heard the muffled sound of engines getting louder by the second.

Ryker pulled me off the path, into the thick underbrush.

I put my mouth near his ear. The smell of sandalwood hit me, and I smiled. Ugh, stop that. Not the time. "What is it?"

"I'm not sure. I've never heard an engine out here before."

We waited another thirty seconds before a group of Hover-Vs appeared—small all-terrain vehicles. The people riding them must have raided a nearby dealership.

My chest spasmed, and I wrapped my good arm around my ribs. Driving the first Hover-V was the redheaded girl who'd leveled a rifle at me on the highway. She held the same rifle now. One of her minions rode behind her, holding my rifle.

Ryker and I looked at each other. Seven other Hover-Vs rode down the path, each with two or three heavily armed people on them. My body shook so hard my teeth rattled. These people had almost killed me.

Ryker opened his hand.

I leaned closer to him. "What are you doing?"

"Warning my dad."

"You're not worried about the message being traced?"

He smirked. "I told you. I'm good with computers."

When the last Hover-V passed, Ryker stood.

I grabbed his shirt with my good arm and stopped him. "Where do you think you're going?"

He looked down at me. "We have to help them."

"Did you see their firepower? We don't have guns." Not that it would matter in my case. I doubt my aim had improved much over the last month or so.

"They need me." He pointed in the hotel's direction.

"We have a few weapons we mostly use for hunting, but this?" He shook his head. "We're not ready for this. Someone with military experience would be a big help."

I didn't move. I didn't think my legs would support me. He wanted me to—what—lead them into battle? Against the people who beat me silly, and were armed to the teeth. His side had a few guns, and what? Faith? "I can't."

Disappointment and anger flashed across his face. "Fine." He turned his back and ran toward the hotel.

All I could think about was Brent. He died trying to save this country from horrible people. While I cowered behind a pile of rubble. Now, Ryker charged ahead to save his family from horrible people. While I hid in the bushes.

I balled my fists. Ryker needed me. I couldn't sit by and watch someone I loved die. Not again.

I STOOD and ran after Ryker. Not that I loved him, of course. We were friends. And I was mad at him. I shook my head and did my best to ignore the ache in my ribs. I scanned the ground for anything I could use as a weapon. What would work against laser rifles?

A hefty branch lay near the side of the trail. I bent over and picked it up. Tears pricked at my eyes as my ribs sent fresh waves of pain through me. Great. Now I was armed. I rolled my eyes and kept running. When I got to the trail-head, I almost ran past Ryker, hidden low in the bushes.

He grabbed my leg, and I went sprawling. My vision tunneled and I'm almost certain I heard a rib crack—great way to start combat.

Ryker reached out and helped me to my knees. Concern filled his eyes. "I'm so sorry, Z. I didn't mean to trip you." He gently touched my bad arm. "Are you okay?"

I gritted my teeth. "I'm great."

He didn't look convinced, but he let it go. "What are you doing here?"

I sucked in a breath as carefully as I could. "Couldn't let you have all the fun." I cradled my ribs. "Give me your shirt."

The look of shock on Ryker's face made me laugh. Ouch.

"Uh . . . what?"

"Your shirt." I stuck my good hand out. "Now."

He slipped his shirt off, still looking at me like I was insane. Since I was about to attack a heavily armed group that knocked me out for a week with a stick, I probably was. "Turn around."

He turned. I lifted my shirt and bound my chest as tightly as I could. It didn't help.

"Okay." I touched his back.

He faced me and raised his eyebrows. "You have a plan?"

I peered out of the trees and across the parking lot. At the front entrance, I could see all but one of the Hover-Vs lined up. The front doors were closed and most of the red head's followers stood in the parking lot studying the building. "Looks like your dad locked the doors, at least. Your warning gave them time."

"Not enough, though."

I followed the direction of his gaze. His dad stood in an open window on the second floor, looking down at the redheaded girl. They appeared to be talking, but we were too far away to hear what they were saying.

"At least she's a few pecans short of a fruitcake."

He looked at me. "Huh?"

I smiled. "Something my drill sergeant said to me once." I pointed to the Hover-vs. "Look. All but one of them is at the front door." I used my stick to draw in the dirt—like

Brent had before he died in New York. I squeezed my eyes shut for a second and took a deep breath, pushing aside the pain it caused. I refused to lose anyone today. I opened my eyes and drew a square. "Here's the hotel. These are the doors, one on each side." I looked up to see if he followed my crude drawing.

He looked confused. "Okay."

I drew six dots. "That's the main group. The redhead assumes everyone will be focused on the people in the front. These two," I circled the two dots on either end of the group, "can see the side doors. And this guy," I drew a dot in the back, "is covering the back door."

He looked from my drawing to me, then back to the drawing. "And?"

I ran a hand through my hair. "She's overconfident." I pointed to the hotel. "She expects the only threat to come from inside. She thinks she has the advantage, but we do." I held up my branch with a flourish.

He smirked. "Your stick is our advantage?"

I smacked him. "Surprise is the advantage. You and I sneak up from behind and knock this guy out before he even sees us coming." I pointed to the dot I'd drawn at the back of my map.

"That's one of them. What about the rest?" He pointed to the dots in the front of my square.

"One thing at a time." I crept across the path and through the underbrush on the other side. "Come on."

He followed. "I guess they taught you all this stuff in the military."

I shrugged. Troop movement and strategy were hammered into us in the sims. The more I thought about it, the more this situation reminded me of a sim we did in basic —the only sim my team failed.

I gulped. I knew how to get out of this. Now I just needed to convince Ryker and everyone else.

We made it to the back of the hotel without being seen. I picked up a hand-sized rock and held it out to Ryker.

He glanced at the rock, then at me. "What am I supposed to do with this?"

"You're going to distract him so I can sneak up behind him."

He shook his head but took the rock. "Distract him with a rock?"

"Work with me here." I took a deep breath to calm myself. I never thought I'd miss the chain of command so much. In the military, orders were given and people followed them. No one questioned. Ever. "Listen to me. If this is going to work, you have to trust me. You need to do what I say,when I say it. No questions." I locked eyes with him. "Can you do that?"

He hesitated until determination settled on his face. "Yes."

"Good. Then get out there and sneak up on that guy's left-hand side." I squeezed his shoulder. "You can do this."

He nodded and crept out of the tree line. I waited a few seconds before I left the cover of the trees, heading toward the guy on the Hover-V's right-hand side. My military training had taught me how to move quietly, but where had Ryker learned? His footsteps were pretty much as noiseless as mine.

The guy sitting on the Hover-V watched the back door like he expected it to get up and walk away. The idiot never looked behind him. Overconfidence was the downfall of many an enemy.

Ryker made a sound as he approached and the guy whipped around with his weapon, which appeared to be the driveshaft from a hover car, raised. He pulled back to swing. He never got the chance. I used my good arm to bash him in the back of the head with my stick.

The guy slumped forward over the handlebars of the Hover-V.

Ryker let out a soft whistle. "Remind me to not tick you off when you're holding a stick."

I cracked a smile. "Help me with him."

Together, we pulled his body to the ground. I lifted the seat of the Hover-v, grabbed a handful of random wires, and pulled. It stopped running. "Let's get him inside."

Confusion crossed Ryker's face. "You want to—"

"No questions."

"Yes, ma'am." He saluted. Badly.

We dragged the guy inside. "Let's tie him to something so he can't escape."

"Down here." Ryker used his thumbprint to open a door. Shelves filled with bedding and towels lined the walls. A giant washing machine and dryer rumbled in a corner. Tables for folding sat in the middle of the room.

He motioned to the shelves. "These are bolted to the wall. He's not going anywhere tied to these." He dropped the guy's upper body and headed to the door. "I'll get something to tie him up with."

"You don't have to, unless you think your dad would mind us ripping a sheet apart."

He smiled at me. "You're the boss."

Heck, yeah, I was.

Ryker grabbed some sheets and ripped them into strips. I tied the guy's hands behind his back and tied his feet together, then I tied his hands to one of the uprights on the shelves and his feet to the same upright. In the end, he was a ball of knots tied to a shelf.

Sheets might not have been the strongest thing to use, but my knots were secure, and I used two separate strips everywhere. He'd have to get through at least ten knots before he could escape.

On the way out, Ryker locked the door. "Now what?"

CHAPTER 46

JADZIA

"NOW WE FIND YOUR DAD."

We ran up a flight of stairs and down the hall to Mr. Jenkin's room. He leaned out an open window, still talking to the redhead below. A hunting rifle was propped on the wall next to him. He appeared to be casually conversing but could easily grab the gun if needed.

He turned when we walked in. "Ryker. Thank God you're okay. How did you get back?" He motioned around the room. "I thought we were surrounded."

Ryker looked at me, pride glinting in his eyes. "Z got us in. She's wicked with a stick."

Heat rushed to my cheeks. I shifted under Ryker's gaze.

Mr. Jenkins looked at me. "So we can get out?"

I shook my head. "I wouldn't risk it. When the person we knocked out doesn't check in, the redhead will know something is up. Once she realizes he's gone and we disabled the Hover-V, she'll be really ticked off."

As if on cue, a laser blast blew a chunk of wood and cement from the window frame.

"What did you do to Tony, preacher man?" A familiar southern accent came in through the window. I hated that voice.

Mr. Jenkins turned to answer her. I grabbed his arm and pulled him back. "You're going to get shot."

He shook me off. "She's just a kid. I can reason with her."

"No one can reason with that." I pointed out the window.

Mr. Jenkins really didn't want this to come to a fight. "Ryker's message gave us time to prepare and threw her plans off. I can talk her down."

"Then what? They know where you are. You think they're just going to leave you alone?" I spread my arms. "Look at this place. I don't know where they live, but it can't be as nice as this."

He hesitated. "We could come to an agreement. Maybe even take them in. We . . ." His voice trailed as another shot blasted the window. He ran a hand down his face. Then squared his shoulders. "You're right." He paced.

I cleared my throat. My voice firm. "I have a plan."

Ryker's dad raised his eyebrows. "You expect me to follow you just like that? After everything you've done."

Ryker stepped to my side. "We can trust her."

Mr. Jenkins glanced out the window, then back at Ryker and me. He sighed. "What's your plan?"

"In basic there was one sim my unit failed. We were surrounded and pinned down. We got captured because no one called for backup." I took a deep breath. "We need to call for help."

Both Ryker and his dad looked at me like I was the fruitcake missing the pecans.

"You want us to let more people know where we are?"

"We don't have time to debate this." I glanced out the window and saw the redhead pointing toward the woods. She wouldn't be without a plan for long. I faced Ryker. "Please. Trust me."

He tilted his head in my direction. "I do. Have faith, Dad. She's here for a reason."

A warm sensation spread through my body. I had gained Ryker's trust.

Mr. Jenkins looked out the window, then at me. He nodded.

I pulled up my PCD screen. With a few swipes of my fingers, I hacked into a back door of the military software we used in the army.

A crash downstairs sent Ryker and his dad to the window.

"They're trying to break down the front door." Mr. Jenkins ran out of the room.

Ryker looked between me and the door.

I waved him toward the door. "Go."

He ran after his dad. I swiped some more and found a base about twenty miles from here. I hacked into the base's main communication network.

I created an emergency request for assistance, reactivated my PCD's location beacon, and sent our coordinates. I smirked and ordered air support. Okay, maybe I was having a little too much fun doing this, but chances were this would be the last thing I did as a free individual.

When things calmed down and the military operatives realized who had called them here, I'd get arrested and thrown into jail. I shuddered. I couldn't think of another way out. And I couldn't let anything happen to these people. To Ryker.

I signed everything with Sergeant Wallace's security code, a little something I'd picked up on my last night of boot camp. I smiled. Good thing I had.

Now to hold off the gang until help arrived. I started to the door when I saw the laser rifle still leaning against the window. I grabbed it, even though I probably would've been better off with my stick.

When I got to the front door, the lobby was in chaos. Our attackers had broken through the outer set of the front doors. Glass littered the ground. A Hover-V sat in the entryway.

Residents had piled furniture in front of the closed second set. A few believers I didn't know, plus Ryker and his dad, stood braced on the inside of the couches. As if that'd do anything other than get them injured when the Hover-V broke through or if the redhead started shooting.

So far, her M.O. seemed to be fear and intimidation. She beat me unconscious, when she easily could have killed me. She talked to Ryker's dad instead of shooting him. So nuts, but not necessarily deadly.

The Hover-V backed up to make a run for the second set of doors. I stepped behind the couch that blocked the door and leveled the hunting rifle at the guy on the Hover-V.

"What are you doing?" Ryker tried to pull me down.

I shrugged him off. "Clear out. You and everyone else who doesn't have a weapon."

"But—"

I locked eyes with him. "No questions. Remember?"

"Come on." He pulled his dad and the others to a safer spot.

The guy on the Hover-V yelled something out the broken doors. The redhead walked to him, gun in hand, and stopped dead when she saw me on the other side of the glass.

I waved.

CHAPTER 47

JADZIA

THE REDHEAD GLARED at me through the glass and approached the doors. She flashed me what must be her favorite finger.

I stood my ground and glanced at my PCD. Ten minutes had passed since I sent for help. At most, I needed to stall for another ten before my chopper arrived.

She motioned me forward. Her gun pointed at the floor.

I aimed my rifle at her and took a few steps, coming right up against the top of the couch. I raised my voice. "What?"

"I see your manners haven't improved much." She scowled. "Maybe you need another lesson."

"Not going to happen."

She held her arms out to the side. "We just want some supplies. Surely you guys can share."

"Sure you do. Yo—"

Ryker's voice rang out. "Z, watch out."

I hit the ground as a laser blast fired over my head from behind me. Stupid. I'd let her distract me while she had someone hacking their way into a different door.

I popped up into a crouch and spun around. I fired. Once. Twice. I let out a growl. Three times. On the fourth try, I dropped the guy.

People came out from behind pillars and couches. "Did —did you kill him?" Mr. Jenkins looked horrified.

I checked the cartridge on the rifle. A kill cartridge. My hands shook. Of course. A hunting rifle. Meant to kill animals. Why would it have a stun cartridge? I hadn't even considered before I picked it up. No wonder the others didn't use their rifles when the guy started shooting. I was the only killer here.

Mr. Jenkins knelt next to the man and felt for a pulse. He covered his nose and mouth as the smell of death wafted through the air.

A shrill scream sounded. I whipped around, ready to shoot again. The redhead aimed her rifle at me. I threw myself to the floor.

She fired. Glass exploded everywhere. Shards bounced off my skin. People in the lobby ducked behind anything that might protect them. I scrambled to my knees and aimed at her. Before I could shoot, she fell to the ground.

I looked around. Ryker squatted behind a chair, hunting rifle still aimed where the redhead had stood. I started toward him, but people climbed through the broken doors. I fired a few shots above their heads. They hung back and didn't cross the barricade of couches.

A familiar sound resonated through the building. My muscles relaxed. Heads turned toward the parking lot. A military helicopter landed in the lot and about twenty soldiers jumped off.

Our attackers with guns opened fire.

Idiots.

Within five minutes, all our attackers either lay stunned or had their hands in the air.

Ryker remained squatted behind the chair, his gun still pointed at the front doors. I walked over and put my arm around his shoulder. "Hey."

He tuned his head to me. His eyes were blank, and his breath came in quick gasps.

I put my hand atop his and aimed the gun at the floor. He let me move it without resistance. "Ryker. It's okay. Help is here."

Shock blanketed his face. His tone was flat. "She was going to kill you."

"I know. You did what you needed to do."

His whole body trembled. "I couldn't let her kill you." The gun dropped from his hands.

"Come here." I leaned in and held him. "Name three things you see."

He mumbled a response. I walked him through the same questions he'd asked me last night. Had it really been last night?

His breathing returned to normal. "I'm back." He swallowed hard. "I've never shot anyone before."

I let him go, knowing nothing would ever be the same for him.

Soldiers streaming through the front door caught my attention. Believers huddled together in the back corner, with hands up. Mr. Jenkins approached a female soldier. They talked, but I couldn't hear what they were saying. His gaze flitted toward Ryker and me, then back to the woman.

Time to face the music. I started to stand, but Ryker grabbed my good arm. "What are you doing?" He took my hand and led me to the breakfast room.

When we were out of sight of the lobby, we stood, and he grabbed my shoulders. "You need to get out of here. You're wanted. They'll arrest you."

I winced as pain radiated down my bad arm. "I know."

Anger flashed across his face. "I'm not going to let you sacrifice yourself for us."

Just like Brent, Ryker had become my protector. But even he couldn't keep me from this. "It's okay. I knew this was coming."

He loosened his grip. I took a deep breath and rolled my shoulder slightly. The pain turned into a dull ache.

He peered out the door of the breakfast room. I knew what he saw without having to look. Soldiers were gathering everyone in a central area. Others were combing the building, looking for anyone else. They'd bring everyone together and try to figure out who'd issued the call for help. When they found out who I was and what I'd done, they'd arrest me. I deserved it. For so many reasons.

Ryker held out his hand. "Give me your PCD."

"What?" I gripped my PCD around my right wrist with my left hand. "No."

"I'll tell them I found it, and when our backs were against the wall, I hacked the military programs on it."

I took a step back. "You'll get arrested."

"I'll handle it."

"How?"

He rolled his eyes and held out his hand. "We don't have time for this. It's your turn to trust me."

I whipped off my PCD and slapped it into his hand.

He put it on his wrist below the one he normally wore. With a few keystrokes, he made it work for him.

I smirked. "You are good."

He laughed. "Not as good as you. I'd never actually be able to get into the military systems."

He brushed the back of his fingers against my cheek and held my gaze. "Go to the meadow. I'll be there when it's safe."

My knees went weak, but not because of fear.

CHAPTER 48

RYKER

I WATCHED Z head for the back door, praying she didn't encounter any military personnel on her way out. I took a deep breath and walked back to the lobby.

Soldiers carried the bodies of the redhead, and the guy Z shot. People sat or stood in various places throughout the room. A quick glance told me everyone was present.

"Here he is." Dad walked toward me with a military officer trailing behind him. "Where—"

I knew what Dad was going to say and I couldn't let him mention Z. "Looks like we're all here." I stared hard at Dad.

He nodded. "Yep."

I fought the urge to sigh in relief. That wouldn't have looked suspicious or anything.

Dad motioned to the man beside him. "This is Second Lieutenant Archer."

I turned the guy's name over in my mind. "Archer. Garrett Archer? The tech giant's kid?"

He grinned. "Guilty."

Crap. This guy knew Z. They'd served together. I forced a smile. "I'm Ryker." We bumped elbows in greeting.

Lieutenant Archer's face grew serious. "Your dad told me you and your friend could help me figure out what happened. Who's responsible for the orders that brought us here?"

Double crap. Dad had already mentioned Z. Now what? I really didn't want to make him out to be a liar, but I had to protect Z. I ran my hand through my hair.

"Yeah, uh . . . that was me." Sweat broke out on my forehead. I wrung my hand together. Keep it together. I held up my wrist with the two PCDs.

I glanced at Dad and said a silent prayer. Please play along. Red-faced, he looked like his head might explode, but he said nothing. He'd always been big on letting me make my own decisions, no matter how stupid they were.

Lt. Archer pointed to the PCDs on my wrist. "Two?"

"Yeah. I found this one on a supply run. When things got too heated for us to handle, I hacked into the military programs on it to get some help."

"Sure, you did. How did you get the security codes?"

I knew he didn't believe me. My mouth went dry, and my mind raced. "I found a list of them."

He held his hand out. "Let me see it."

I took Z's PCD from my wrist and handed it to him.

He slapped the PCD onto his wrist and typed into it. His eyes widened. "Where did you get this?"

I shrugged. "Told you. I found it on a supply run."

"No. I mean where, exactly."

Something rubbed me wrong about his response. Almost eager. He didn't seem to care that I'd just confessed to hacking into their secure files. This had to be about tracking down Z.

Another solider with brown hair and a lot of stripes on his sleeve walked up holding a laser rifle. "Garrett . . . Uh . .

. Lieutenant, you're never going to believe whose gun this is."

Archer turned toward the officer. His voice was hollow. "It's Jadzia's."

I wiped my forehead again. My mind raced. I needed to come up with a story.

Confusion crossed the brown-haired guy's face. "Yeah, but how did you know?"

Archer held up her PCD.

The new guy turned to me and my dad. His eyes flashed. "Where is she? What did you do to her?"

"Sergeant," Lt. Archer said.

The guy snapped to attention. "Sorry, sir."

Lt. Archer nodded. "At ease." He introduced the guy as Sisko Jessup, the son of the inventor of some of the most groundbreaking meds and surgery techniques. These guys had all the wealth in the world, and they enlisted. Huh.

Jessup relaxed his stance.

Lt. Archer took a step forward. "We know Jadzia is, or at least was, here. So start talking."

"She was here." My voice cracked. "She got beaten up by the crew you just captured. We took her in, got her better, and she took off." Mostly true—they didn't need to know she took off ten minutes ago.

Archer held up the PCD. "Hacking government property, harboring a fugitive, falsifying military orders, dodging the draft." He glared at me. "Those are all serious charges. Are you sure about your story?" He motioned to everyone else in the room. "There are other people we can ask."

My dad shifted his weight from foot to foot.

I glanced toward the others in the room. Cassie stood within earshot, staring at me. Great. She flung her hair over her shoulder and strutted over.

I stepped in front of her and flashed my biggest grin. "Cassie. Why don't you go help Billy?" I pointed to the six-year-old crying in his mother's lap. "He could use a friend."

She waved me off. "He has his parents. Besides, I think this fine-looking gentleman needs my help more." She stepped around me and stood in front of Lt. Archer. She folded her hands and put on an innocent act. "I know where she is."

I ran my hand down my face.

Lt. Archer called a third soldier over. This one looked a lot younger than me. My stomach tightened. Poor kid, being forced into the war so young. Lt. Archer gave some orders I didn't hear them. How could I warn Z? She didn't have her PCD.

He turned to Cassie. "Take us to her," he pointed at me, "You stay here."

I took a step toward him and got in his face. "Not on your life."

He studied me from head to toe. He must have seen something he liked. "Fine."

"I'm coming, too." Dad took a step forward. "Everything that happens here is my responsibility."

Archer nodded. "Fine. Let's go."

Cassie led us through the shattered front doors, glass crunching under our feet. Once we got outside, I jogged a few steps to catch up with her. I grabbed her shoulder and pulled her close. "What's your deal?"

She shook me off. "I'm not about to let you take the fall for her."

"How do you even know where to go?"

Her face got red, and she had the decency to look down. "I followed you to the meadow once. I assume she's there."

I gritted my teeth. Of course, she'd followed.

CHAPTER 49

JADZIA

I SAT on the rock where Ryker and I had picnicked just yesterday. What could he possibly be thinking? Why did he take the blame for me? Twice I started back to the hotel, ready to face my fate. Twice I turned around and waited.

Trust me, he'd said.

Trust him. I sighed and stood, bouncing on the balls of my feet. What was taking them so long? Of course, without my PCD, I didn't know how much time had passed. Hours. Minutes. I didn't know. I walked down the rock and paced. It didn't help.

Voices from the woods caught my attention. I turned. Ryker stepped from the tree line. My heart lodged in my throat. Ignoring the pain in my chest, I ran toward him, but almost tripped over my own feet when Cassie and his dad stepped out behind him. Regaining my balance, I stood still. Two guys in uniform appeared behind them.

Trust him. I swore. He sold me out. I marched toward him, not hesitating now, eyes focused only on his traitorous face.

When I got to the group, Ryker tried to say something, but my hand across his face stopped him.

Cassie laughed.

A look of hurt crossed Ryker's face. "I didn't tell —"

A throat cleared behind him. "Jadzia."

I knew that voice.

My gaze flew to the faces of the soldiers. My heart raced. I took a step back and looked again. "Holy—" A few curse words dropped from my lips.

I sputtered. "You. What—?"

Sisko smiled and waved. "Hi to you too." He stepped around Ryker and swept me into a hug. Picking me up and swinging me.

Fire shot through my chest. I gasped.

Sisko put me on the ground, his face full of worry. "You okay?"

I cradled my side. "A few busted ribs." I shrugged. "Nothing I can't handle. What on earth are you two doing here?"

I reached to hug Garrett.

He hesitated. What the heck?

He sighed and gently pulled me close. "What are you doing here?"

I snorted. "What are you doing here?"

He let me go. "After New York, we all got split up. Realy ended up in Texas, Asher in Colorado." His voice caught. "And, of course, we lost Brent and Bashier."

I shuddered and shoved down the images of Brent bleeding out.

Sisko flailed his arms. "We thought you were dead. Then we heard Zealots captured you. Then someone said Sergeant Barns found you, but you ran away." He touched my arm. "I'm just glad you're okay."

"How did you guys end up on this mission, though?"

Garrett motioned to the Lieutenant stripes on his uniform. "I got notified when your distress call came through. I recognized Wallace's security code and knew something wasn't right." He shook his head. "Wallace is still training new recruits in PA."

I tried to look innocent. "Oops."

He cracked a smile. "I knew you were good. But wow, you lifted Wallace's security code." He whistled.

Sisko laughed. "Told you she's awesome."

Cassie snorted. Sarcasm dripped from every word. "Yeah, she's wonderful."

Garrett ignored her and grew serious. "She's awesome all right, but what are we going to do with her?"

Sisko looked between Garrett and me. "What do you mean?"

I'd never heard Garret's voice so harsh before. "She hacked into a military system with a stolen access code after she deserted our unit and her duty."

My legs trembled. I'd forgotten this wasn't a reunion. I was in trouble. Lots of it.

Ryker stepped in front of me, as if to shield me from Garrett. "You're not touching her."

Garrett pointed at Ryker. "You're on my list too, buddy. You've got to be what, eighteen, nineteen? Draft dodgers rank the same as deserters."

Mr. Jenkins stepped forward. "He didn't dodge the draft. He was exempt from service on religious grounds and moral objections," he motioned to Cassie, "the same as every person between the ages of sixteen and thirty who is part of our group."

My mind spun. Ryker. Cassie. Cole. Murphy. Most of the teenagers at the hotel should have been in the military. My skin grew hot. I'd gone through hell while they got to sit out on a technicality. I'd have done anything to get out of serving. Instead, I ended up killing people. Four so far.

Then again, I should have I had thought of using a religious objection as my way out. Sure, it would have been a lie, and Brent would've been disappointed in me. But maybe he wouldn't have died in my arms. Or at all. Things might have turned out differently without me there. The edges of my vision started to blacken.

Sisko's voice broke through my thoughts and pulled me back. "Dude. It's Jadzia."

Garrett turned and snapped. "You will address me as Lieutenant or Sir and will speak when I ask you a question. Is that understood?"

I cringed. He shouldn't be yelling at Sisko.

Sisko's fists clenched. "Lieutenant." I could tell he spoke through gritted teeth. "She's our friend."

I took a deep breath. "Sisko, it's okay. I—"

Sisko held up his hand. "New York changed all of us. What happened wasn't your fault. If anything, Garrett—"

Garrett's voice rose. "Sergeant Jessup. You are out of line. You will do your duty or you will be relieved."

I'd never seen Garrett this worked up before. My heart ached at the tension between them. Tension I'd caused.

I put myself between them. "You two are best friends. Please, don't fight. Not because of me." I held my hands out in front of Garrett to let him cuff me. "I'll go with you."

Sisko and Ryker both started yelling at Garret.

Cassie just stood there, looking like a kid at Christmas.

Mr. Jenkins crossed his arms. Obviously, he wouldn't interfere. Never mind that I just saved the lives of everyone he knew. Whatever. This was my mess.

Garrett held up his hands. His voice loud enough to be heard over everyone else. "Quiet."

Ryker and Sisko stopped yelling.

Garrett shifted his attention to me. "Jadzia, walk with me."

I took a deep breath.

Ryker threw a punch at Garrett's face. I blocked it with my bad arm. Pain shot up my arm and down my side. I hissed through my teeth and stumbled.

Ryker reached out and steadied me, shock registering on his face. "Oh, no. Z, I'm sorry."

Garrett looked ready to murder Ryker. He reached across me, probably to wrap his hands around Ryker's throat. I shoved them apart. My shoulder throbbed.

I pointed to Ryker. "You. No hitting my friends. And you," I pointed to Garrett, "no killing them." I swallowed hard walked deeper into the meadow. "Let's go, Garrett."

I looked back at Ryker. My heart clenched. I couldn't leave him behind. But I didn't have a choice.

CHAPTER 50
JADZIA

GARRETT and I walked in silence to the tree line opposite of the others. I trailed a step or two behind him.

If only this was a walk catching up with an old friend. Assuming we were still friends. I glanced at Garrett. Judging from his face, we weren't. I swallowed the lump in my throat.

When we got to the tree line, he stopped and turned to me. "I'm really struggling with what to do here." He ran his fingers through his hair. "It would have been easier if you'd never sent that distress call."

I motioned to Ryker's group, still standing on the edge of the meadow. "Then they'd have gotten killed."

He looked down. "You must really care about them. To risk your freedom."

"I do. And I didn't do the right thing in New York. I had to do it now." I sighed. Garrett had yet to meet my eyes.

He ran a hand down his face and said something, his voice so low I leaned in to hear him. "This is all my fault."

"What do you mean?"

His eyes turned glassy. "In New York. One minute you

were with me. The next—when I turned, I couldn't see you, but I figured you were behind me. I ran. I—" He shook his head. "When we got back to camp, I realized you weren't there. I'd left you behind." He cracked a small smile. "Sisko almost killed me when he found out."

I touched his arm. "It's not your fault. No one could have known about the trap. The Zealots planned it well."

"I shouldn't have left you." He blew out a big breath. "And now it's my job to turn you in." He paced.

I bent, pulled a flower from the grass, and picked the petals off. I gazed back toward the group of believers. "It's like I told Ryker. I knew the risk I was taking when I called in the strike."

"You and Ryker involved?"

I fumbled for words. Finally, something came out. "I guess not." I rolled my eyes at myself. Good, strong answer there, Jadzia.

Garrett gave me a chuckle that turned into a sigh.

A strange calm settled over me. "I sent the message knowing I'd get caught. The fact that it's you doesn't change anything. I know you have a job to do."

"Except I don't think I can. You'd end up in jail. I can't send you there." He flailed his arms. His words came out quick and strung together. "Sisko would kill me. I'd never forgive myself. But if I don't, I could wind up in prison. But if I hadn't left you, none of this would have happened."

I held my hands up. "Stop. Stop. You're driving yourself crazy."

He put his head in his hands, then looked me straight in the eyes, his voice more sure now. "I wasn't there for you once. I'm not making that mistake again."

My heart rate kicked up a notch. "You're not going to turn me in?"

"You're family, Beautiful." He used his nickname for me for the first time since New York. "I'm sorry, I forgot for a minute." He opened his arms and enveloped me in a hug.

We held each other for a few seconds, then headed back. The walk across the meadow was different now. I wanted to whoop. I couldn't keep the grin from my face.

When we met up with the others, Ryker stepped forward, his body tense and his hands balled into fists. "You're not taking her."

Sisko stepped up next to him, looking ready for a fight. "Agreed."

Garrett held his hands up. "I'm not."

"You're not?" They all said.

Sisko grinned and stepped back. "I knew it, man."

Cassie's mouth hung open in a stupid look of shock. She swore. "What the heck?"

Mr. Jenkins nodded. "Thank you."

Ryker relaxed a little but kept his eyes on Garrett. "You mean it? You're not taking her."

Garrett put his hand over his heart. "You have my word."

Ryker blew out a deep breath and his hands opened at his sides. He turned and pulled me into a hug. My arms circled his neck. His body pressed against mine. So strong, so solid. He mumbled under his breath. Thanking God I was okay. God. Huh. I thought he should thank Garrett.

Mr. Jenkins cleared his throat. Ryker stopped hugging me, but he kept an arm around my waist, as if he wanted to be sure Garrett wouldn't haul me away.

Cassie dropped another choice word, turned, and stormed out of the meadow.

Sisko laughed. "Who spit in her Cheerios?"

The tension broke completely, and everyone laughed.

Even Mr. Jenkins chuckled. "I'd better go after her." He held his hand out to Garrett. "Thak you for everything you've done here today. You saved a lot of lives."

Garrett shook Mr. Jenkin's hand. "Just doing my job, Sir."

Ryker's dad nodded, then took off after Cassie at a quick pace.

The rest of us strolled back to the hotel. On the way, I filled Ryker in on a few basic training stories about Garrett, Sisko, and me.

I avoided talking about Brent as much as I could. This was a happy moment. I didn't want to ruin it. We laughed about how I shot Realy, and my terrible aim. And of course, Sisko told him about the bomb I hacked.

"You hacked a bomb?" Ryker gazed at me with admiration.

His warm hand still held mine. I liked that. I blushed and rolled my eyes. "It wasn't a big deal."

Sisko snorted. "It only made her the most popular person at boot camp."

When we got back to the hotel, most of the troops had left., taking our attackers who hadn't been killed with them. Sheet-covered bodies lay in the grass by the parking lot.

I shuddered. More deaths on my list. Even if I didn't pull the trigger, I was still responsible.

Ryker must have felt my distress. He pulled me close and whispered in my ear. "We wouldn't have made it without you."

I sighed. I'd saved the believers, but at what cost?

CHAPTER 51

JADZIA

AS THE SUN SET, Garrett, Sisko, Ryker, and I stood near the last military Hover-jeep left at the hotel. For the most part, the believers could breathe again. A few residents went with the soldiers to be placed in safe cities, but most wanted to stay where they were. I understood. This was home to them. Well, for the past few months, anyway.

Home.

I circled my arms around my chest. Where was my home? In Houston with Mom and Jonathan? Here with Ryker? Back in Pennsylvania? Certainly not in the army, I knew that much.

Garrett handed me my PCD and gun.

I raised my eyebrows. "You're not taking these?"

He shook his head. "They only tie this place to you."

"But what are you going to tell your superiors?"

He sighed. "All I know is I don't want your name anywhere near this."

Sisko motioned to my PCD. "As far as anyone at base knows, Wallace sent those orders."

I shook my head. "That won't hold up long, and you

both know it." My chest hurt. I hated the fact they'd take a fall for me. "Are you sure you don't want me to come with you?"

Ryker slipped his arm around my waist and pulled me close to him, as if his actions alone could stop me from being taken.

Garrett shook his head. "Don't worry. I'll work it out."

"You're not very reassuring."

Garrett ran his hand through his hair. "I don't know. Maybe I'll say it was a mistake. It shouldn't have been Wallace's codes. Maybe it was a glitch on orders for a training exercise."

"That's not going to fly." Sisko looked worried.

Garrett fidgeted with a pocket flap on his uniform. "I'll figure it out."

I met Garrett's eyes. "Whatever you do, don't say anything to get yourself in trouble. I'm not worth it."

He stepped forward, arms out. "I've decided you are."

"But—"

"Shush. And come here."

Ryker let go of me, and I stepped into Garrett's embrace.

"I can't thank you enough for—well, for all of this. Coming, here saving us, letting me go." I swallowed the lump in my throat.

Garrett patted my back and released me.

Sisko folded me into his arms. "I'm so glad you're okay."

After letting go, he looked at Ryker, a smile on his face. "You treat her right or I'm going to come back with an entire platoon."

I smacked Sisko on the arm. We all laughed. Garrett and Sisko climbed into the Hover-jeep and drove off.

Ryker and I stood watching, his arms wrapped around my waist, until long after they'd disappeared from sight.

I leaned my back into his chest.

He lowered his head into my hair and neck, just holding me. His body against mine gave me something solid to hold on to.

The sky turned dark, and the first star appeared. Ryker broke the silence. "We should go inside. You haven't eaten anything since breakfast."

I nodded, and he slid his arms away from my waist, capturing my hand in his as we turned. My legs ached and my head pounded. Food and a hot bath. Perfect.

We walked across the parking lot and through the first set of broken doors. The shattered glass had been removed.

A shudder rippled through Ryker, and he turned his head away from the blood that stained the floor where the redhead had fallen. I squeezed his hand.

An older man with gray hair and a yarmulke on his head worked on putting a plank of wood over the broken glass of the interior set of doors. He greeted us when we passed.

In the lobby, people swept and put furniture back into place. I twisted my PCD band around my wrist. They might be able to put the room back in order, but they'd never fully erase the scars of this day.

We crossed the threshold into the dining room, and Cassie's voice rang out above the general din of people talking and eating. "See. I told you they let her back."

The room grew silent. People glared in my direction.

"Look at her. Acting all innocent. Like this wasn't her fault." Cassie pointed at me. "Blood all over her. Gun around her neck. She's a threat to all of us."

I glanced down at my shirt. Sure enough, dried blood

clung to it. The gun Garrett had handed me hung over my good shoulder. Guess I should have changed and dropped the gun somewhere before I waltzed into the dining room looking like Rambo.

I pulled my hand from Ryker's and turned to leave. Maybe I'd just walk out the front door and keep going. He caught my hand and held on tight. He walked to Cassie's table, taking me with him.

When we stood across from her, he dropped my hand and motioned to the room. "I'm not sure what you heard, but I want to set the record straight. Jadzia saved us. All of us." He glared at Cassie.

Cassie stood. "Without her, that gang wouldn't have found us in the first place. We've taken in other injured people, and no one ever raided us before. Funny, how after she showed up, a bunch of bloodthirsty murderers appeared at our door."

Ryker jabbed his finger at Cassie. "Without her, we might not be here."

Everyone stared at me. My cheeks burned. I was sure they were bright red.

I took a deep breath. No. That was the old Jadzia. The Jadzia who'd have sat in the woods, afraid and let her friends fend for themselves. I was the new Jadzia. The one who ordered a military helicopter strike. I grabbed a chair and stood on it.

Ryker, Cassie, and everyone else in the dining room looked up at me. "I had nothing to do with the gang finding you. I'd never turn you over to anyone. You all have shown me nothing but compassion and friendship, and I'd never repay that by hurting you."

Cassie tried to butt in. I held my hand up and talked

over her. "Nothing you or anyone else says can change the truth. I did not, nor will I ever, betray you."

Silence fell. I took another breath and got ready to step down. I should have known Cassie wouldn't back down easily. Fury filled her face. "She's a murder. She's killed people. Some of you saw her do it today."

Ryker fidgeted and looked down. His voice was strained. "I killed someone today, too."

I ran my fingers down Ryker's cheek. Our eyes met. "Killing isn't something I wanted to do." The faces of those I'd killed rolled through my mind. The guy in the store. The guy on the cliff. Larry. The guy earlier today.

Each face was etched in my mind forever. I swallowed hard. "I have only ever killed when I, or someone I loved, was in danger." My voice cracked, and I looked away from Ryker. "I —"

"What's going on here?"

CHAPTER 52
JADZIA

RYKER'S DAD walked into the room. Using Ryker's shoulder for support, I stepped off the chair. I sucked in a breath as my ribs reminded me that they were still there and still broken. Ryker put his arm around me.

Cassie opened her mouth first. No surprise there. Hand on her hip. "What's going on is she doesn't belong here."

Ryker's dad looked at me, Ryker, and Cassie. He turned to the entire room. His voice was gentle, but firm. "What happened here today was not Jadzia's fault."

Cassie let out a snort. Mr. Jenkins locked eyes with her, and she stared at her shoes.

"I firmly believe she was not responsible for anyone finding us. She called in reinforcements, at great risk to herself. She'd never hurt anyone, especially any of us."

He turned to me. "Jadzia, you are welcome to stay here as long as you like."

He directed his next words to Cassie. "If anyone has an issue with that, you can take it up with me." He reached out to shake my hand. "Thank you for saving us."

I took his hand, and we shook.

Cassie whirled toward the exit and stormed out of the room without another word, shooting me a glare as she went. Most everyone else went back to talking and eating.

Mr. Jenkins released my hand. "Meet me in the communications room tomorrow morning and we'll see about getting in touch with your mom."

A huge grin broke over my face, and I actually squealed. Ryker chuckled.

I gave him a playful smack on the arm. "Oh, shush."

Mr. Jenkins sighed. "I'm off to check on repairs and finalize burial plans."

With the war, cemeteries had run out of room. Mr. Jenkins and Garrett had agreed we'd dig a grave near the woods for the fallen. Mr. Jenkins left to plan a ceremony.

Ryker turned to me. "Come on. You still need to eat."

I didn't think I could, but my stomach growled.

Ryker laughed. He took my hand, and we grabbed fabricated sandwiches, sat by ourselves, and ate.

Later that night, I tossed and turned. Excitement over getting to call mom warred with images of the events of the day. And of course, Brent was never far from my mind. Would he like Ryker? I thought so. I hoped so.

Ryker and I had grown close over the past few days. His presence gave me strength today. I found myself being drawn to him. But being close to him also reminded me of what Brent and I never got to have. My chest ached.

Was I betraying Brent by getting close to Ryker? I blew out my frustration. How could I stop the growing feelings I had toward him? I closed my eyes for the eight thousandth time and rolled over. I needed sleep. But no matter how hard I tried, it wouldn't come.

I lay in bed long after sunlight streamed through my window. A knock on my door got me out of bed. I checked the door's vid feed and saw Ryker grinning at the camera. I pressed the button that allowed me to talk to him. "Go away." I yawned.

He laughed. "It's almost nine o'clock. Please tell me you didn't just wake up."

"In order to wake up, I would have had to have fallen asleep."

Concern crossed his face. "You okay?"

I threw the door open. "No, I'm not okay. I haven't slept. I look like crap. My ribs hurt. I was forced to serve in the military. Something you didn't have to do, by the way." I jabbed my finger at him.

Ryker took a step back as if my words had pushed him into the hall.

I kept going, though. "My best friend is dead. I've killed four people. Cassie thinks I'm going to slit all your throats in the night. I have feelings for you I don't understand. My mom and brother probably think I'm dead. Oh, and did I mention I didn't get to sleep last night?" I ran out of breath. My face burned. I leaned against the door frame to hold myself up and buried my face in my hands.

Ryker pulled me into a hug.

My chest heaved. "I'm s-s-sorry."

He stroked my hair. "It's okay. You've been so strong through so much. You can fall apart if you need to. I'm here." He tucked me under his arm, nudged me into the room, and closed the door behind us.

He held me for a long time and let me cry myself out. When I finished, I looked into his eyes. "Thank you."

He brushed the last tears from my face. "Let's go call your mom."

I stepped back from his arms. My stomach tightened. In my exhausted stupor, I forgot his dad said I could call Mom this morning. I should have dragged myself out of bed first thing. I was a horrible daughter. A horrible sister. Poor Jonathan.

I took a deep breath. "Okay. Let's go." I started out of the room.

"Um, Z?" Ryker stopped me.

"What?"

"Maybe get changed?"

I looked down at my pajamas, a grubby, loose tank top and a way-too-short pair of cloth shorts. I turned and grabbed clothes from my drawer and rushed into the bathroom.

I could hear Ryker's laughter through the bathroom door. A smile formed on my face. I must look ridiculous. A glance in the mirror confirmed. On top of my outfit and my tear-stained face, my hair looked like a fuzzy pom-pom.

The more he laughed, the funnier things struck me. I pulled my clothes on and giggled. I opened the door. One look at Ryker, still laughing, and I burst out laughing myself. Suddenly, everything seemed funny. Maybe I was losing my mind, but I didn't care. Laughing was better than crying. I didn't have many chances for fun anymore. Plus, I was going to talk to Mom, and maybe even Jonathan. Today would be an awesome day.

CHAPTER 53

JADZIA

MR. JENKINS MET us in the communications room. Ryker sat at the desk, and I watched his keystrokes as he made sure no one could trace the transmission. Man, he was good.

Now that the gang didn't exist, and the military knew where the believers were, it wasn't as big of a deal. Still, there were other survivors out there who might be looking for a place to loot. And even though Garrett had covered for me, I was still a wanted fugitive. For sure, any communications Mom received were being watched. A contact from the middle of nowhere, Tennessee, would be suspicious.

I leaned over his shoulder. "I'll have to get you to teach me."

His ears tinged red. "It's not too hard. You'll pick it up fast."

Mr. Jenkins cleared his throat. "Hacking used to be considered a felony, you know."

Ryker chuckled. "Funny how things change."

Mr. Jenkins sighed. "I wish you kids didn't have to go through all this. You should be going to college, not riding out a war." A forced smile appeared on his face. "But God is good. Things will turn around."

I fought the urge to roll my eyes. God is good. After everything that happened yesterday, he still believed that?

"Done." Ryker stood and motioned for me to sit.

After I sat, he pointed to a window on the left side of the Holo-projection. "If it turns red, there's a problem. If it stays green, you're good. I'll be outside the door. Yell if you need me."

Ryker and his dad walked out. I interfaced my PCD to the communication console and called Mom.

Her face filled the projection screen, and tears formed in my eyes.

Her voice sounded haunted. "Jadzia. Is it really you?" She stared at the screen.

I smiled widely. "It's me, Mom."

"I thought you were dead." Her eyes glistened.

"Not yet. I—" I took a deep breath. My voice cracked, but I kept going. "I have so much to tell you."

I filled her in on everything, from getting captured to the gang attack to my confusing feelings for Ryker. I lowered my voice. I knew he hovered by the door, waiting to protect me should anything go wrong. He'd keep me safe no matter the cost to himself, much like I'd done when I called in the military.

After a while, she put Jonathan on. I almost broke when his face appeared the screen, smiling ear to ear. "Hi, buddy."

His head bobbed as he bounced on his seat. "Jadzia. Where are you? When can I hug you?"

I swiped my cheek. "I'll get to you soon, I promise." Another promise I might not keep. I cringed.

"Okay." His shoulders slumped. "I'll keep waiting." His face lit up. "Guess what?"

I laughed. "What?"

He told me all about Houston, and how he went to school at our aunt's house and Mom was his new teacher. I laughed again when he said he liked his old teacher better.

After an hour and a half, Ryker knocked, then opened the door. "You're going to wear the solar panels out." He gave a smile that made my heart quicken.

"So, this is Ryker?" Mom raised her eyebrows.

Ryker's face turned bright red. Mine did too.

"Ugh. I got to go, Mom. I'm still coming to Houston. Just need a little more time for my ribs to heal." And I had to find transportation, but I'd worry about that detail later. "I love you."

"Love you too, Honey. We'll see you soon." She paused and looked at Ryker. "Both of you, I hope."

"Goodbye, Mom." I disconnected the call. Mom knew I was alive and okay. One thing off my mind.

Ryker held out his hand. "Sorry to end your call, but I have something I want to show you. And it's kinda time sensitive."

I took his hand and let him help me to my feet. "What are you talking about?"

"You'll see."

"A man of mystery, huh? I like it." Laughing, we walked out the door together.

When we got outside, almost everyone stood in the parking lot. A few were talking, some kids ran around, but no one seemed to be doing anything. "What's going on?"

He grinned like a kid who had planned a surprise party. "You'll see."

Cole ran up to us. "Where are you guys going? It's going to start soon."

Ryker struck a ridiculously formal posture, his tone stuffy. "I've arranged for a private viewing."

Cole winked. "Oh. Have fun." He walked off to join his other friends.

I put my hand on my hip. "A private viewing?"

"Trust me." He led me to the meadow.

I breathed in the fresh air. The scent of grass and wild-flowers filled my nostrils. I'd started to think of the meadow as our place. Funny, since we'd only been here once before. Not counting the time I almost got arrested. "What do you want to show me?"

He led me to the top of the rock again. He pulled two pairs of glasses from his back pockets, and handed me one. "Put these on."

"Uh. . . okay."

He reached up and pressed the side of mine. The glasses instantly darkened.

I looked around. "How are you going to show me some-thing like this? I can barely see."

He laughed. "Lie back and look up. What do you see?"

I did. "The sun." The glasses were so dark I could look directly at it without hurting my eyes. "Whoa. Where did you get these things?"

"Outdoor shop on a supply run. They were pretty much the only things left." He motioned to the sky. "They aren't much use for anything except this event."

"What event?"

He lay back next to me. "Just watch."

I held my breath. What was going to happen? Birds? Rain? Butterflies? I already had those in my stomach. The tiniest hint of a shadow formed on the sun's surface. As I watched, it grew. "An eclipse?"

"Yep. But this one is special."

"Why?"

"We're in the path of totality, the point where the moon blocks the sun entirely."

I rolled onto my side to face him. "Darkness eclipses light. Kinda like the state of the world right now."

He faced me with a serious look. "Don't think like that. It might seem like darkness is taking over, but God is still good. In the end, light wins."

The laugh escaped my mouth before I could stop it. He grimaced and lay back, looking at the sky again.

"Sorry. I just don't understand how you can believe in God—or in anything good—right now."

He shook his head. "That's your fear talking. God is greater than fear."

I sat up and threw my arms out. My voice rose with each word. "Look around you. You've been forced from your home, you're living in a hotel, tons of cities are in ruins, kids are getting drafted to fight in this stupid war, thousands of people have been killed, and you're talking about some God who's supposed to be all-powerful and good?"

He shifted. "I don't have all the answers. I wish I did." He brushed a strand of hair behind my ear. "All I know is God hates what's going on as much as we do."

"Then why doesn't He stop it?"

He shrugged. "We wouldn't have free will."

"You—"

He pulled his sunglasses down. "Let me see your PCD."

Thankfully, the dark glasses hid my disbelief from him. It's not like I wanted to hurt his feelings. His beliefs were just, well, like Brent used to say, silly. I flicked my wrist, opened my PCD, and turned the projection to face him. "Here."

He tapped and swiped for a minute or two. "There." He slipped his shades back up and lay back. "Start in John."

I flipped the image back toward my face and pulled my glasses down. "Really?" The Bible. He'd downloaded the Bible.

He motioned to my PCD. "Really. Read it." He chuckled. "Then you can tell me I'm crazy."

I snorted. The tension broke, and we both laughed.

"I guess I can give it a shot." No harm in humoring him, I guess.

Ryker nodded and pointed to the sky. "We're going to miss everything if we keep talking."

I put the glasses back over my eyes and lay next to him. As we watched, the glasses adjusted the darkness in microscopic increments to protect our eyes.

When the sun hit totality, they were completely clear. Ryker pointed out the corona. For five full minutes, the world was a strange, grayish twilight with barely enough light to see each other.

"Wow."

"Yeah." He looked at me, not the sun. "You know, you said a lot of stuff this morning."

Familiar heat rushed to my face. "I was tired."

He scoffed. "That's what you're going with?"

He leaned up onto his elbow and hovered above me.

"Something about feelings for me?"

My heart rate tripled. He ran the back of his fingers over my cheek. His eyes radiated warmth. He leaned halfway and hesitated. I closed the gap between us, and our lips met.

CHAPTER 54
JADZIA

WHAT AN IDIOT. I paced the floor of my room back at the hotel on shaky legs. Ryker and I didn't speak much after I kissed him. We just watched the rest of the eclipse in each other's arms, then walked back. He went to the dining room, expecting me to join him for lunch, but food was the furthest thing from my mind.

I ran my fingers through my hair. Pent-up energy coursed through me. I took a deep breath and counted. It didn't help.

The image of Brent's face, bloodied and pale, warred with Ryker's in my mind. The feeling of both of their lips meeting mine, under such different circumstances. If Brent had lived, where would be right now? I swiped at my cheek. My fingers came away wet.

Could I move on with Ryker? Did I want to? Ryker would want answers I couldn't give because I didn't know them myself.

I forced myself to stop pacing. I had more important things to worry about. Mom and Jonathan were my number one priority. Houston. I needed to get to Houston.

Leaving here solved my Ryker problem. A bonus and only a bonus. Sure. Keep telling yourself that.

I threw open the door to my room and walked to one of the storage closets at the end of the hall. After hacking the lock, I rummaged around until I found a pack, food rations, and water pods. I pushed aside the twinge of guilt at stealing from the people who had taken me in, but desperate times and all that.

With food taken care of, I hacked my way into the supply closet where they kept the weapons. Looking over my shoulder to make sure no one was in the hall, I slipped in and found my rifle. Holding it felt like welcoming an old friend. I grabbed as many spare stun cartridges as I could hold, stepped out of the closet, and closed the door behind me.

Running back to my room, I ignored the ache in my ribs and threw some clothes in the pack. I needed to be gone before Ryker came looking for me. I'd just have to grit my teeth and bear any pain on the trip, including the rapidly growing one around my heart.

I left my room without leaving a note and took the three flights of stairs to ground level. Slipping out a side door, I took one last look at the place that had saved my life and turned to the woods. The afternoon sunlight streamed through the trees. So pretty. I sighed. Did I really want to leave here? Jonathan's face popped into my mind. Yep. I wanted to leave.

When I got out of sight of the hotel, I pulled the compass and a map up on my PCD and figured out my exact location. My shoulders slumped. Walking would take at least three weeks. Maybe more. Plus, I still needed to cross the Mississippi River.

Sighing, I leaned against a tree. I could kick myself for

not stealing a Hover-V from the hotel. Sure, a Hover-V's speed was no match for my bike, but who knew where that ended up.

Maybe I should go back. I shook my head. Going back meant risking getting caught. I got out of there once, but I might not be able to do it again. Ugh. I'd have to find something on the way.

I made my way toward Memphis, staying as close to the highway as I dared. Drone activity seemed to be heavier in the area. I smirked. I'm sure my calling in a fake military strike and finding two large groups of survivors had something to do with the increase.

My shirt stuck to my skin. I stopped often but refused to break into my water supplies yet. My chest burned. I gritted my teeth. Had to keep going. At this rate, I'd never make it to the next town, let alone Houston.

The sound of an engine approached. I looked around and practically dove behind a cluster of bushes. Fire ripped through my chest, and I willed myself not to scream. When I could breathe again, I peeked through the branches. A Hover-V approached and stopped a few feet from where I'd been standing. Ryker got off the vehicle and looked around.

I muttered a curse. Seriously? He'd come after me.

He stood directly in front of the bush I hid behind. His voice carried through the woods. "Z. Where are you?"

I crouched lower and hoped he'd move on. Of course, he didn't. He examined the ground, then looked closer at the bush. "I know you're here, somewhere, Z."

Might as well give in. I stood. "How'd you find me?"

"I'm the one who hunts the most for a reason. Now, what the heck are you doing?"

I squared my shoulders. "Going to Houston."

He ran a hand down his face. "I thought we were going together after your ribs healed more."

"I don't have time for that."

"This isn't because of what happened in the meadow, is it?"

I held up a hand. "Let's not even go there."

"What happened in the meadow?" Cassie stepped out from behind a tree.

My voice high and loud. "You brought her?"

Ryker took a step back. "N—I did not." He turned to Cassie. "What are you doing here?"

"I saw her sneak out with our stuff and I followed."

My hands curled into fists. I gritted my teeth. "You've been following me all day?"

She looked at the ground and moved some leaves around with her foot. "Yeah."

I swore. "Did you plan to follow me all the way to Houston?"

"I . . ." She picked up her head and glared at me. "I just wanted to make sure you were leaving for good."

I looked at my PCD. "It took you four hours to figure that out?"

"Enough." Ryker's voice rose louder than ours.

We both stopped and looked at him. He sighed. "Z, if you're really set on leaving today, we'll take Cassie back and—"

My legs shook, but I held my ground. "I'm not going back."

"Z, you can't walk to Houston alone."

"I was doing fine until—"

"Until you got beaten within an inch of your life?"

My turn to look at the ground. Why did he have to complicate things by following me? Going back meant losing time, not to mention facing Ryker's dad and who knew who else. But it also might mean better transportation and a much better supply situation and—if Ryker came with me—I ran my fingers through my hair and tugged. A growl slipped from my throat. So many possibilities crowded my brain.

"She obviously wants to be left alone. Just take me back, Ryker." Cassie ran her fingers up his forearm.

I reached to pull her off but stopped. I didn't have a claim on him. Nor did I want one. Getting close to Ryker meant betraying Brent, didn't it? And I couldn't think of either of them now.

He stepped toward me. "I'm not leaving you."

All our heads swiveled at the sound of an approaching drone. My eyes widened. "Hide."

FEAR ETCHED itself on Z's face. She rushed toward Cassie and me, pushing us behind a thick tree trunk. "What about the Hover-V?"

She swore. "No time. It's painted camo. We'll have to hope they miss it somehow."

"This is stupid." Cassie stepped out from behind the tree and waved her arms. "They can help us."

Z grabbed her and yanked her back. "Yeah, and they'll arrest me."

Cassie smirked and tried to shake Z's grip on her shirt. "Even better."

Z didn't let her go.

I grabbed Z's hand and jerked her away from Cassie. "Stop it." I looked at Cassie. "Stay put."

She let go of Cassie and they both glared at me. Great.

Peering around the trunk of the tree where we hid, I scanned for the drone.

Z pressed her back against mine and leaned out the other side. "There."

I turned and saw the drone flying through the trees

about fifty yards north of us. I leaned into Z's ear. The scent of her hair sent a pleasant shiver through me. Focus. "We might still have time to get the hoover-v under that bush."

She nodded.

We moved together. Cassie tried to step out with us. "Please don't move." I looked into her eyes. "She's not the only one who'll be in trouble if we get caught. I shot some-one, remember?"

She crossed her arms. "Fine."

We reached the Hover-V and started to drag it along the ground. Stupid thing was heavy when it wasn't on and hovering. We got a few feet when the drone turned our way.

"Duck." Z grabbed me and pulled me down behind the Hover-V.

"Do you think it saw us?"

The buzz of the drone grew closer. Fear filled her eyes.

"I have an idea, but I don't want you to get upset."

"Anything."

I leaned in and kissed her. If the drone couldn't see our faces, it couldn't identify us. Hopefully who ever operated the drone would assume we were two kids who slipped away from the nearest safe city for some privacy.

Cassie gasped from behind the tree, and I willed her to stay put.

Z's body went rigid. So different from earlier today when she welcomed my touch. What turned her away from me? She didn't smack me or pull away, so she must have realized my reasons, at least.

The buzz hovered over our heads. Maybe the operator was trying to get a good view of our faces, or maybe they were just enjoying the show. I know I was enjoying myself.

The feel of Z's lips on mine sent warmth through my body, not just physically. She belonged to me, and I belonged to her. I never wanted this moment to end. But, of course, end it did, with the ping of a tracker hitting a metal part of the Hover-V and the sound of the drone buzzing away.

Z broke the kiss the second the whine of the drone faded.

Disappointment coursed through me. "Did you hear the tracker hit?"

She held her arms out. "I did. Now what?"

"I could try to disable it." I scanned the frame of the Hover-V, looking for the small disc-shaped tracker.

"You can't mess with those. It'll shock you." She shrugged. "I can hack the thing, but it will take some time."

I jumped at the sound of Cassie's voice. "Can I come out from behind this stupid tree now?"

"Yeah, coast is clear. Sorta."

She flounced over to join us. "What's the problem?"

I pointed. "Tracker."

"So?"

I sighed.

Z yelled at her. "So, I'm a wanted criminal, not only for deserting the army, but for hacking a military system and calling in an air strike. You think they want me running loose?"

Cassie rolled her eyes. "You two aren't thinking straight."

I grabbed Z, since it looked like her next move would be to rip Cassie's head off. "What do you mean?"

"We take the Hover-V back to the hotel. The military already knows we're there, so no big deal." She motioned to Z. "It's not like they can run facial recognition. You were sucking her face so hard I doubt they got a look at her."

I mulled over what she'd said. "But why would we be so far out?"

Cassie shrugged. "Supply run. Looking for other people. Trying to get help. There are lots of reasons." She stepped closer to me, and I tightened my grip on Z. While Z didn't struggle against me, I wasn't ready to let her go just yet.

Cassie got on the Hover-V. "Get on. It's going to be a squeeze with three of us, so you'll have to sit close to me." She threw me a coy look.

I smirked and turned to Z. "She's right. It makes sense."

Z planted her feet. "I told you, I'm not going back."

I pinched the bridge of my nose and paced between her and the Hover-V. These girls were going to drive me insane.

"If we don't take the tracker someplace the military already knows is housing survivors, they'll show up to find out who we are." Cassie sounded like she was talking to a first grader. "Since your friends," she made air quotes on the word friends, "already identified our group, they'll leave us alone."

Z couldn't argue with the logic. She spread her arms. "Fine. You two take the Hover-V back."

I guess she could. Both girls had made it walking this far without me. Cassie could make it back, no problem on the Hover-V. Z had hundreds of miles to go, and who knew what she'd run into. I ran my hand down my face. Neither one of them would like this.

I walked back to Cassie. "Look, Cass." She loved it when I called her by her nickname. "Can you do me a favor?"

Her face brightened. "Anything for you."

I hoped so. "You're right about the Hover-V needing to

get back home." Her smile brightened. I took a deep breath. "So I want you to take it there for me."

Her face fell and her shoulders slumped. She opened her mouth to protest, but I cut her off. "Please."

"Ryker, I want you to go with her." Z rubbed my back. She was trying to pull the same thing with me as I tried to pull with Cassie. I ignored her and stayed focused on Cassie.

Cassie bobbed her chin at Z. "See. Even she wants you to come with me." She patted the back of the Hover-V seat.

An involuntary sound I can only describe as a growl resonated in my throat.

Both girls spoke at the same time. "What?"

"Look, I'm done arguing. Cass, I really need you to do this for me."

She huffed. A sly look crossed her face. "I'll do it on one condition."

"What?"

"You have to kiss me."

My eyebrows raised so fast they practically flew off my forehead. I stepped back and tripped over a stick. "You want me to kiss you?"

"You kissed her to hide. If you want me to do this, that's my price."

My head swiveled from Cassie to Z and back again.

Z shrugged and turned her back as if she didn't care.

I flinched. If someone had presented her with that offer, I'd have punched them. Why didn't she care?

Gah. I took a deep breath and slowly let it out. I stepped up to the side of the Hover-V. Cassie's eye widened as I leaned in. I gave her a quick peck on the lips.

Before I backed away entirely, she wrapped her arms around my neck. "Oh, no. I want a real kiss."

She tugged me down and her lips met mine again. I tried to pull away after a few seconds, but she held me close.

After much too long, she released me with a disappointed sigh. "At least now I know for sure."

"Know what?"

"I know you'll never feel for me what you feel for her." She started the Hover -V "A deal is a deal. I'll get this home." She maneuvered the vehicle until she pointed toward the hotel. "Goodbye Ryker. I hope I see you again someday."

"I'll be back, Cass."

She gave me a half-smile and drove away.

I turned to Z to figure out what to do now, but she'd disappeared.

RYKER'S VOICE followed me through the woods, but I trudged on. I knew trying to lose him wouldn't work, but try I did. I zigzagged around trees and looked for small places to hide myself in. At most, I had a five-minute head start. I attempted to convince myself the underbrush was enough.

It wasn't. Ryker caught up with me. "What are you doing?"

"Hiding. What does it look like?"

"Are you mad because of the kiss thing?"

I crossed my arms. "You mean when you kissed me or when you kissed Cassie?"

"Both."

I stopped walking and turned to him. "Look. I left alone because I wanted to be alone. You should have gone with Cassie." I jabbed my finger into his chest. "You shouldn't have followed me in the first place."

"If I hadn't followed, you'd be out here alone with Cassie."

I shuddered at the thought. "Before you found me, I

didn't even know she was here. She'd have gotten bored eventually and gone home."

"You sure about that?"

"Cassie doesn't strike me as the 'spend the night sleeping on the ground' type."

He chuckled. "She's not."

I turned and kept walking.

"We need some kind of plan, Z."

"I have a plan. Get to Houston. Find my mom and my brother."

He held up a backpack. "And how are we going to do that? I have some food and water pods, but not enough to get us to Houston. Especially if we're walking the whole way."

I gritted my teeth. "Then go back."

"I'm not leaving you."

I picked up my pace, but he stayed in step with me. He kept trying to convince me we needed a plan, a mode of transportation, more supplies, and anything else he could think of to get me to stop.

Eventually, his stream of words became like the sound of the wind, something there, but I wasn't really conscience of. Finally, after at least forty-five minutes, he stopped talking. Thank goodness.

We walked in silence for a few hours.

He rummaged in his pack and handed me a water pod. "Here."

"No, thanks."

"You need water."

I did need water. I just didn't want him to tell me I needed water. "Fine." I took the pod and drank. The liquid cooled my anger some and cleared the ache that had formed around my temples.

"Thanks." I looked around, noticing more than my PCD screen or the ground in front of me for the first time. The light filtered low through the trees.

"We're going to have to find a place to sleep." I pulled my PCD up and looked at the map for the two hundredth time today. "Looks like there's supposed to be an overpass a few miles ahead." I pointed. "If it's still standing, we could sleep under there."

He pulled up his own map and nodded. "That'd work."

We walked toward the highway. The trees grew thinner and the ground less filled with brush as we approached the side of the road.

"We could sleep in one of these cars." Ryker pointed to the abandoned vehicles sitting in the middle of the road. "Drones might check under an underpass, but they can't check every car. It'd take way too long."

I shook my head. "I tried on my way down here. None of them have power anymore, so you can't pick the locks." I headed toward the overpass. A loud crash sounded behind me. I jumped, spun, crouched, and brought my gun up into firing position in one fluid movement.

Ryker stood next to a car, his hands in the air. A shirt wrapped around his right hand, which held a giant rock. "Whoa. Calm down. Just me." He pointed to the broken-out window. "There's more than one way to get into a car, you know."

I lowered the gun and stood on shaky legs. "Sorry."

He walked over to me and raised his arm like he was going to touch me, but then he let it drop. "You okay?"

No. "I'm fine." I walked to the car, a large family vehicle with lots of storage room for groceries or sports equipment. I reached through the empty window and opened the door. "You coming, or what?"

He shook his head. "Not that one."

I flailed my arms. "Why did you bust the window out, then?"

He stepped up to another car and broke that window. "If a drone comes by and sees one broken window, they'll check it out." He moved to another car and broke both windows on the driver's side. "If they see a bunch of busted out windows, they'll assume someone looted them and moved on. Whomever is operating it won't check every car." He busted out a fourth car window.

He actually made sense and breaking a window might feel pretty good right now.

I reared my rifle back and, picturing Ryker's face, I rammed the butt of my rifle into the window closest to me. The glass shattered. I smashed the rear window in the same car. I whirled around and shattered another window. A giggle escaped me. Another window met its demise.

"Having fun?" Ryker watched me, a look of amusement on his face.

I smirked. "Maybe."

He motioned to the surrounding cars. "You done yet?"

"No." I broke out three more for good measure.

He picked a small hatchback, opened the door, and climbed in.

I frowned and walked over, peering into the cargo space. We'd be completely squished together in there. "Why not the van?"

"Too obvious."

Ugh. I'd risk obvious if it meant I'd have room. But I climbed into the car next to him and squished myself against the side of the vehicle. Our shoulders and legs still touched.

He went through his pack and frowned. "I could have sworn I threw a blanket in here."

I rolled my eyes. "It's the middle of June. We'll be fine." I pulled my pack out and grabbed two food rations and two water pods. I handed one of each to Ryker, and we ate in silence.

When he finished, he looked at me. "We're just not going to talk this whole trip?"

"Not if I can help it." Childish, I know, but I wasn't ready to forgive him for . . . well, I didn't know what. But I'd figure it out, eventually.

I stowed my pack in the front seat, lay down on the rough carpeted floor of the car, and turned my back to him.

He shifted and thrust a jacket into my field of view. "For your head."

I grabbed it and shoved it under my head.

He sighed.

Even though light still shone in the sky, exhaustion swept over me. I closed my eyes and welcomed oblivion.

CHAPTER 57

JADZIA

I WOKE UP SCREAMING. I managed to stop myself, but my breathing still came rapidly. The vision of Brent bleeding out in my arms faded. I couldn't help but rub my hands on my pants, trying to get rid of the blood that wasn't there.

Someone touched my arm. "Z. You're okay. You're safe."

I whipped my head to the left. Hands clenched into fists, I let one fly, and struck the person in the face.

He groaned. "Geez, Z. It's me."

I blinked a few more times and my eyes adjusted to the darkness. Ryker sat next to me, holding the right side of his face.

My hands flailed. I reached for him. "Oh, my gosh, Ryker. I'm so sorry. I didn't m—mea—" A weird hiccup-gasp type thing took my ability to speak.

He tugged me toward him. "I know, I know. It's okay."

I trembled, leaned into his chest, and let him stroke my hair.

I let him hold me for a few minutes while I caught my

breath, but then I pushed back. I couldn't decide if I actually wanted Ryker's arms, or if his arms were just a pale representation of the arms I needed.

"I'm really sorry about your face." I was glad for the darkness because he couldn't see how red my face must be.

"You have quite a right hook." He rubbed his cheek. "Lucky you didn't catch my eye. It would be black for sure."

I looked away.

He kept his voice low. "Hey, I'm kidding. I'll be fine."

I pushed myself to my knees and turned to the front seat. I grabbed his pack and, by the light of my PCD, started rummaging. "Did you bring any medical supplies, ice packs, anything?"

"I grabbed a few things, but no ice packs."

"I found pain pills. Do you want some of those?" I held the package of pills out to him.

"Really, Z. I'm fine." He patted the floor next to him. "Lie back down. We can still get a few hours of sleep before it gets light." He lay down and rolled onto his side, his back to me.

I assumed he did this because it's what I had done earlier. I longed to have his arms holding me again. Comforting me. But did I really? Ugh. I wished I could figure out what I wanted. I was better off alone.

I tossed and turned as much as I could in the cramped space of the car, afraid to fall asleep again because I knew Brent would be lurking in my dreams. I pulled up the Bible Ryker had downloaded onto my PCD.

Interesting to read, but I wasn't sure I believed it. I read until my vision blurred and the sky tinged pink on the horizon. I let my eyes close and fell into a peaceful, dreamless sleep.

When I woke, light filtered through the windows. Ryker

had left. Had I finally chased him away? I sat up and realized he had taken my gun with him. That jerk left me defenseless.

I swore and grabbed my pack. At least he left me that. I opened my hand to send him a lengthy text conveying exactly what I thought of him, when I noticed a message from him. Reading it, I slumped back onto the floor. He'd gone to find transportation and hunt for food. I sighed. Well, if the Boy Scout thought he could find us some food, we'd need a fire to cook it when he got back.

I had a nice pile of wood and had started to form a pile of kindling when I heard an engine. I dropped to my stomach, thankful I hadn't lit the fire yet. No smoke to give me away.

The engine cut off and Ryker called my name.

Whew. Just Ryker. "Coming." I stepped out of the woods, stopped, and grinned. "You found a bike." This bike was older than my last one and not as fast—plus it was an awful shade of purple, but still.

"We wouldn't be able to pick through the wrecks and abandoned cars on anything else."

A shudder ran through me. The last time I got stopped by a traffic jam, I ended up unconscious for four days. I looked at him. "Oh, my gosh, your face."

His cheek was swollen and purple.

My hands flew to my mouth. "I'm so sorry."

"I'm sure it looks worse than it is." He tried to smile, but it turned into a wince.

"Uh huh." I decided to drop it. "Did you find any food?"

He shook his head.

"No problem. Here." I dug through my pack and threw him an energy bar. "This should hold us till dinner."

We ate our bars, organized the gear, and hopped on the bike. He drove, and I sat behind him, with my arms wrapped around his waist. I longed to pull myself closer and lean my head against his back. Wait. No, I didn't. Ugh. Snap out of it, Jadzia.

The wind whipped through my hair. Between the noise of the bike and the sound of the wind, we couldn't talk to each to each other. Fine by me. I didn't want another lecture about the need for a plan.

I kept watch for drones. Stupid things. Whenever I spotted one, I tapped Ryker's shoulder, perhaps a little too aggressively. Leaving the bike in the middle of the road just another abandoned vehicle on the highway, we'd run for whatever the closest cover might be. Once, we dove under some cars, and another time it we hid out in a large drainage pipe. Thankfully, no rattlesnakes this time.

About twenty miles east of Memphis, Ryker took an exit ramp off the highway.

I tapped his shoulder and yelled over the wind. "What are you doing?"

He pulled over and pointed toward the city. "Memphis is a safe city. We can't go through it without passing through a military checkpoint." He opened his PCD and showed me an aerial view of Memphis. Sure enough, even from this vantage point, I could see the now-familiar military block-ade. "I don't have the time or expertise to change our DNA patterns or create fake identities for us."

I nodded. "So we go around."

Ryker started to get back on the bike, but a sound I'd heard before ripped through the air. It took a second to identify. We stared at each other. Without saying a word, we both turned toward Memphis. A large black cloud rose into the sky.

CHAPTER 58

JADZIA

RYKER SWORE. "This is why the whole safe city idea is stupid." He threw his arms up in the air. "Even with all the security, no one knows who's a Zealot and who's not."

I stood rooted to the spot. I couldn't tear my eyes from the cloud. The last time I saw smoke erupting from a major city, Brent stood next to me. Everything—and nothing—had changed. Brent lay dead, probably in an unmarked grave somewhere, and the world still fell under attack.

My legs gave out, and I sank to my knees.

Ryker knelt next to me. I looked at him and saw his mouth moving, but the sound seemed to have cut out.

I think I asked him what he said. I'm not sure I actually spoke. He shook me. I focused on his face. Tried to name three things I could see. Three things I could hear. Something. Anything to not remember. I could feel myself slipping. I curled into a ball on the pavement. Flashes of memories pulled me away.

I was back in New York. Explosions sounding around me. I crouched behind a wall of rubble. Firing my laser rifle at everything and anything. Running through debris, slipping on something warm and red. Brent dying. Crouching in a store. Shooting someone. The guy on the top of the incline. Larry. The person who attacked the hotel. Everyone I'd hurt. I'd killed. I screamed at them to leave me alone. But they just stood there condemning me.

Someone slapped me on the cheek. Someone called my name. Someone shook me. Hard. My eyes flew open. My breathing came in small, quick gasps. Where was I? I shuffled back.

He didn't move with me. "It's me, Z. You're safe. I promise. We're on the side of the highway just outside of Memphis. We are not in danger. You are okay."

His familiar voice calmed me. I blinked rapidly. Ryker crouched a few feet away from me. He was close but didn't touch me.

I sucked in air and tried to hold it for a few seconds. My lungs couldn't handle that yet, and air forced itself from me in bursts.

"Good, Z. Breathe." He took a deep breath and slowly let it out.

I tried to follow. After four breaths, I fell into rhythm with him. I straightened my legs.

Ryker scooted over and slowly put his arm around me.

I leaned into him.

He rubbed small circles between my shoulder blades. "I think we should just camp here for the night."

"We've barely made any progress today." My hands fluttered to my throat.

"I know, but it's already been a long day. Besides, we're going to hit the Mississippi River soon. We have to figure out how to cross if we can't find a bridge that's still standing."

I nodded. I didn't want to form a plan for an impossible

task right now. Even finding a place to hunker down seemed too much. I sighed. I should stand. Maybe I could handle that. It'd be a start, anyway. I pushed up from the ground and wobbled to my feet. So far, so good.

Ryker held my elbow to steady me.

I took a step. Then another. Okay, I could do this.

"Where are you going?"

I turned to Ryker, a sad smile on my face. "Just making sure I can walk."

He pulled me into a hug. "We're going to get through this. We're going to find your family and get somewhere safe."

I wondered if he really believed that or if he just said it to make me feel better. Maybe believing in God made you an eternal optimist. There was really no other reason to believe we were still going to be alive tomorrow, let alone make it to Houston.

I pulled away from him. "You said something about setting up camp? We're sleeping in a car again?"

He shook his head. "People will be pouring out of Memphis. We have to find somewhere to hide."

"We could use that. Get lost in the crowd."

"No. The military will be looking for survivors, wanting to relocate people." He paced. "Shove them all back together again. Make them targets." He kicked a rock. "Stupid. At least until they get these Zealots under control."

Maybe he wasn't such an optimist after all. I tilted my head and peered at him. "Come on. Let's find cover."

We pushed the bike into the woods and wandered south through the trees.

After about thirty minutes, Ryker pointed out a dense cluster of underbrush and bushes. "I'll bet we can huddle in there."

I looked at the tangle of branches and cocked my head. "Maybe behind it."

"Trust me." He circled the mess of tangled branches. He knelt, then popped back up. "Yep. Over here."

I joined him. Sure enough, there was an opening in the brush. I got on my knees and crawled inside an igloo-like opening. "What is this place?"

"Deer probably use it."

I moved to crawl back out. "I'm not fighting deer for a place to sleep."

He chuckled and studied the ground. "We'll be fine. Look at the fresh growth." He pointed at a few green shoots. "It hasn't been used in about a month."

We settled in, took out water pods, and ate energy bars. Again. Too bad we didn't have any pancakes. Timed passed slowly. We made a few attempts at conversation, but it didn't really go anywhere. There wasn't a ton of space in the hideout, so I stepped out to stretch my legs.

I wandered around. The evening air was warm on my skin. The sound of voices and feet cracking branches sent me scurrying back to Ryker.

He knelt at the entrance of the bush and helped me back into our hideout. We stared at each other. He pointed to the sides of the hideout and moved toward one.

I moved to the other side. Leaves rustled under my hands and feet as I crawled. I'm sure no one heard it, but to me, it sounded louder than a freight train. My heart pounded.

I curled up, facing Ryker. I assumed he wanted us tucked into the sides so if anyone came to the back of our clump of branches and noticed the opening, they wouldn't immediately see us. What happened if they had the same outdoorsy instinct Ryker had and poked their head in to looking for a place to sleep?

I opened my PCD and texted Ryker.

Are these people from Memphis?

He shook his head and texted back.

Too soon. Anyone fleeing from the city wouldn't be here for hours, if not days.

A shudder ran through me. So far, I was zero for three in meeting random people on the road. Ryker found me unconscious, so I didn't count that one.

Sure, these people could be scared, looking for help, or on a supply run. But there was also a decent chance they'd try to kill us.

Ryker swiped around on his PCD and turned it to face me. The cover of the Bible app appeared on his Holo-projection. I rolled my eyes so hard I swear he heard it.

Another text came through.

Psalm 23 and Psalm 138:7

I tapped an answer.

I don't believe what you do. You know that.

Now he rolled his eyes.

You don't have to believe something to read it. Read first. Call me crazy later.

I wanted to turn away from him, but since I still heard movement outside the brambles, I didn't dare. This was either an extremely large group of people or a smaller group who had decided here looked like a good place to camp.

FINE.

He smirked and lay back, still looking at his PCD.

I opened the Bible app and searched for the Psalm. What the heck was a Psalm, anyway? Whatever. As I read about how God overcomes fear, I couldn't help but wish I had some of Ryker's confidence.

I looked over at him. He lay on his side, curled along the inner wall of branches as I was. But he didn't flinch at every cracked stick. He didn't peer out between the branches with every footfall or rustle. His body seemed relaxed, not ready to spring up and fight at any given moment. He trusted something or someone would protect us.

Peace. The word came out of nowhere. Ryker had peace, and I wanted—no, needed some of it.

CHAPTER 59

RYKER

I FELT Z's eyes on me as I read the same things I hoped she was reading. I tried to ignore her, so she'd go back to the app, but she kept staring.

> What?
> How do you do it?
> Do what?
> Stay so calm. I'm ready to jump out of my skin, and you look like you're relaxing on the beach.

I had to stop myself from laughing out loud, but a snicker slipped through.

She shot me a glare and tried to peer through the dense branches. From the sound of things, people outside weren't going anywhere for a good while. Having this conversation over text would not be productive.

> We'll talk later when it's safe.

She sent me an image of a kid sticking their tongue out.

Aw, is that you?

She stuck her tongue out at me, closed her hand and then her eyes, ending our conversation.

Sleeping probably was a good idea. If the people outside our hideout set up camp, the best time for us to leave would be at night, and we'd need sleep to do that. I closed my eyes, not thinking I'd actually sleep, but still attempting to try.

I woke to Z shaking me. At least, I assumed it was Z. Darkness surrounded us, and I couldn't see anything. Forgetting I should whisper, I spoke in a normal tone. "What's up?"

She pressed her finger to my lips.

Oh, right. Quiet.

I mouthed sorry, even though I knew she couldn't see me.

She opened her hand to text me. Light spilled from her PCD display. I looked toward the last place I heard the people moving outside and quickly closed my hand over hers.

She trembled.

I tuned her out and forced myself to pay attention to the woods, like I did when I hunted. At the moment, these people were my deer. No sound. I took a deep breath, and the faint smell of smoke hit me. They'd built a fire but had put it out a while ago. Either the people moved on or slept.

I sat up. Using my body to block most of the light, I opened my hand.

Z grabbed my hand.

I kept my voice low this time. "It's okay."

She shook her head.

I sighed and closed my hand. "I think we're safe to move."

"I don't know where they are." I had to lean in to hear her. Our heads almost touched. My heart pounded. She smelled like the woods, the crisp scent of fallen leaves mixed with a little dirt. Being so close to her, in the dark, made me want to wrap my arms around her and never let go. I shook myself. Now wasn't the time.

"I'll check." I got to my knees and started to crawl out of the opening.

She grabbed the back of my shirt. I backed up and knelt in front of her.

"What if you get caught?"

Did she actually care, or did she just not want to be left alone? "I'll be fine." I couldn't help myself. I leaned in and gave her a quick kiss on the cheek.

I crawled out again and sneaked around the front of the branches, keeping close, trying to blend in. Not that anyone could really see me, anyway. No light came from a fire or flashlight. Even the moon didn't shine tonight.

Sticks I couldn't see cracked beneath my feet. I prayed the people either wouldn't hear me or assume I was an animal. I just hoped they wouldn't shoot me.

I took another step, and my back foot caught on a branch or a root. My arms flailed around. I desperately tried to hold on to my balance. I crashed to the ground.

Someone shouted and a light swept the ground in my direction.

Scrambling to my feet, I ran to the entrance of the bush, not caring how much noise I made. I ran into Z, who already stood outside. I fumbled for her hand as the light found our heads, which stuck up over the bushes.

Z crouched, but I grabbed her arm and pulled her to her feet. She gasped.

I realized I held her bad arm in my hand. I didn't let go

or stop pulling, though. Right now, her shoulder was less important than getting away from this Zealot, gang member, bounty hunter, or whatever.

We crashed through the woods, leaving a much more obvious trail than I'd have liked. I didn't know what direction we were going. We'd forgotten about the bike. Even if we could find our way back, I didn't think I wanted to risk it. We'd have to leave it behind when we hit the river, anyway.

We ran until Z tripped and went sprawling to the ground. Since I still gripped her arm, she almost pulled me down, too. I tried to help her up, but she moaned.

"I can't." Her breathing came in gasps.

I looked around and listened. No footsteps rushed after us, no light searched the woods. We were alone in the middle of the wilderness. Completely exposed.

And completely lost.

CHAPTER 60

JADZIA

I LAY on the ground at Ryker's feet. My ribs throbbed. I tried to control my breathing, so they didn't hurt as much, but it didn't work very well.

Ryker crouched next to me. "You okay?"

"Y—yeah."

He felt my back and drew in a sharp breath. "Z, do you have the bags?"

I rose to my knees. Bags. Backpacks. My gun. More than a few swear words found their way out of my mouth.

"I'll take that as a no."

I needed water. My mouth felt like a desert. No food. No water. The days of being out of supplies as I neared home after fleeing New York were forefront in my mind.

Ryker opened his PCD. His voice shook. "We have about two more hours until it gets light. We can't do anything until then."

"We have to go back."

He stayed quiet.

I pushed to my feet, ignoring the stabbing pain in my chest. "We have to go back."

In the dim glow of his PCD, his face looked ashen. "Even if we risk going back, our stuff won't be there."

I clenched my hands. "What do you mean, it won't be there?"

"Think about it. That person didn't chase us, which means they probably weren't after us in the first place. They were most likely on a supply run or something."

"So what? That means it's safe to go back."

He shook his head. "No, it means whoever was out there now has our stuff. They knew exactly where we were and once they poked around, it wouldn't be hard to find."

Now what? I'd counted on not having transportation, but not having supplies changed things. Not that we could even make it back to the hotel without at least having water. I turned in a circle. "Where are we?"

"Uh. Well." I whipped around to where Ryker's voice came from. I couldn't see his expression, but I imagined it wasn't a happy one.

"You have no idea, do you?" I pulled up my PCD. When I had figured out what direction I was going before, I always knew my starting point.

I screamed, letting out all my frustrations. Cassie. Ryker even being here. Losing our bike. Our supplies.

Ryker hung back until I finished. "Feel better?"

"No." I ran my fingers through my hair and barely resisted the urge to yank each strand from my head.

"I'll be able to get us in the right direction when the sun comes up. We'll run into a place to get supplies and transportation, eventually."

I almost screamed again, but I took a few deep breaths. "Yeah, and we might end up dead from dehydration before then." I shoved him. "This is all your fault. I'd have been fine on my own. Why did you have to follow me?" I turned away. I wanted to storm off, but where would I go?

His voice rose. "My fault? How is this my fault?"

"You made us hide in that stupid bush." Not a good reason, but at this point I didn't care. I just wanted to be mad at someone other than myself.

He scoffed. "You're the one who ran away with no plan, no transportation, and barely any supplies."

"I'm not having this conversation again." I stomped a few feet away from him and found a tree to lean against. Arms crossed. Teeth clenched.

I heard him muttering behind me and really wanted to yell at him again, but it didn't get us anywhere.

We stayed like that until light began touching the sky. My stomach grumbled, my head pounded, and my mouth was dry.

When the light got bright enough to see by, I faced him. "We have to find water." I picked a direction and started walking.

I glanced over my shoulder when I didn't hear him following me.

He turned in a circle, looking at who knew what. Then he stopped and pointed in the direction opposite from where I headed. "You're going the wrong way."

I turned. "How do you know?"

He pointed to the ground. "Game trail. Follow the animals and eventually we'll find water."

I warred with myself. On one hand, he was right. On the other hand, I really didn't want him to be, or at least I didn't want to give him the satisfaction of letting him be right again. But we did need water. "Fine." I walked to him and held my hand out in a go-ahead motion.

We'd walked for an hour when I heard water bubbling

over rocks. I pushed past him and hurried to the stream. I knelt on the edge, plunged my hands in, and brought them to my mouth again and again and again.

Ryker knelt next to me. "Slow down there. You don't want to make yourself sick."

Water dripping down my chin, I turned to him. "I'm sorry. You're only trying to help me. I'm just scared." Saying the words lifted a weight from my shoulders.

"I'm sorry for intruding. For forcing myself into this trip and your space when you wanted to be alone." He looked at the stream. "I just couldn't stand the thought of you out here by yourself. Last time, you—" His voice broke.

"I almost got killed."

His face took on a faraway look. "I keep picturing the way I found you. Bleeding. Unconscious. Barely alive. I don't know what I'd do if something happened to you." I leaned in to catch his last words.

"But I wasn't alone this time."

He shot me a confused look.

I don't know how I managed my next words with a straight face, but I did. "I had Cassie."

We both lost it, laughing until my ribs ached and he ran out of breath.

We stayed by the stream for a few hours, drinking and talking. My headache went away as I hydrated, and Ryker even found some berries growing nearby. They weren't nearly enough to fill me, but it was something.

When we were both ready to go, he stood and helped me to my feet. "This stream has to lead to the river. As long as we don't lose it underground before it gets there, we'll be good."

"Off we go, then."

CHAPTER 61
JADZIA

THE SUN GREW HIGHER, and the temperature soared.
Sweat poured down our faces. We stopped often to splash
in the stream and drink. Ryker took his shirt off, wet it, and
tied it around his head. I had to admit I liked the view.

The trees thinned and we stepped out of the woods to
face the Mississippi River.

I looked up and down the shoreline for anything we
might use to float across. Nothing.

Ryker skipped a rock across the water. "How's your
swimming?"

The river looked to be at least a mile across. "I'd drown
if I had to do two lengths of a normal sized pool."

"So not good, then?"

I stared at him, and he laughed. So I smacked him.
"This is serious."

"Okay, okay. Sorry." He pulled up a map on his PCD
but quickly shut his hand. With no reference point, maps
were useless. "We could look for a fallen log and hang on to
that while we cross."

I shifted from foot to foot.

Ryker frowned. "Or not."

"We need food and supplies, anyway. Why don't we look for an abandoned town? Maybe we'll find a bridge."

He shrugged. "I assuming we're still south of Memphis since we haven't run into it yet. We should head that direction."

We turned downriver.

We walked about an hour before we started seeing looted convenient stores, a few houses with busted out windows, and a sign for the Mississippi Limestone Company.

Ryker pulled up his PCD. "This place has got to be on the map."

Of course, he was right. He was always right. Ugh. At least we knew where we were now. But we still had to cross this stupid river.

Ryker pointed to the quarry yard. "We should check in here."

"What if there are people? It's a quarry. They're using it. I'm sure the war effort needs limestone for something."

"It's Sunday. I doubt anyone's there."

Huh. Sunday. I'd stopped caring what day it was a long time ago.

We poked around the empty quarry and work yard but didn't find anything to help cross the river. We managed to find a vending machine filled with snacks and water pods. Ryker grabbed a chair and approached the machine.

"What are you doing?"

He motioned to the vending machine. "I don't like it any more than you do. But without food, we'll never make it to Houston. They'll get over it."

"That's stealing, though."

He looked at me like I was crazy. "You haven't stolen anything the whole time you've been out here?"

I stared at my feet. "Okay fine." I mean, we were starving, and anyone who could still stock a vending machine had to be doing okay.

He smashed the glass, and we feasted on chips and jerky.

We checked out the employee locker room. Jackets, hats, work boots too big for either of us, and duffle bags. We grabbed four bags, and I shoved the rest of the contents from the vending machine into three of them. Not the most nutritious food, but it'd keep us alive. At least I hoped it would. While I did that, Ryker took the fourth bag and disappeared from the office.

When he came back, the bag looked full. "What do you have?"

"You'll see."

I squinted at him. "Whatever, weirdo."

We grabbed soap from the shower room and a first aid kit. We couldn't find any weapons, though. A gun would have been nice.

We followed the river until Ryker stopped and pointed toward the tree line. "Come on."

"Now what?"

A few feet into the trees, I saw he was headed for a wooden shack. Yay.

He walked around the back of the ramshackle structure instead of opening the door. Then he poked his head around the back wall, a huge smile on his face. "Check it out." He motioned me to him.

I walked around the building and found him pulling a rowboat from under an overhang. Maybe someone was looking out for us, after all.

We searched inside the shack and found fishing poles. Ryker insisted on digging up some worms and trying his luck before we crossed. I sat on a nearby rock and watched the outdoorsman catch us dinner. We built a fire and ate.

When we finished, Ryker kicked dirt on the remnants of our cooking fire. "We should either cross before dark or spend the night here and cross in the morning."

"Let's get this river behind us."

He helped me into the boat and pushed us into the water, then hopped aboard and settled into the middle seat while we drifted into the river.

I remembered how sore my arms were after crossing the rivers in Pittsburgh. "Want me to help row? It's a long way across."

He flexed. "I'll be fine."

I rolled my eyes.

Crossing the river took at least an hour. Ryker splashed into the water at the shoreline and pulled the boat onto the bank. He stretched his shoulders and moved them in circles. "See, told you I could do it."

He held out his hand and helped me out of the boat. I stared at the river and sank to my knees. I swiped my cheeks. My breath came in ragged gasps.

Ryker knelt next to me and rubbed my back. "You okay?"

I nodded. The biggest obstacle standing between my family and me now lay behind us. "I'm going through all of this to be with my family, and you left your dad behind you."

He picked a rock up and skipped it across the water. "My dad is safe. I couldn't live with myself if something happened and I wasn't there for you."

I hung my head. "Why? I've been such a jerk. I'd think you'd be happy to be rid of me."

He put his hand under my chin and gently lifted until I looked him in the eye. "You're upset. Maybe even scared. But I see the real you. The brave, loyal, individual who'd do anything for the people she loves."

My insides went gooey. He really cared for me. I wanted to lean in and kiss him, but Brent's face flashed in my mind. Would I always be like this? Never able to move on to another relationship because of what could have been with my dead best friend? I pulled away from Ryker and stood.

Hurt flashed in his eyes, but he quickly hid it behind a grin. He pulled the boat farther from the waterline so if the river rose, it wouldn't float away. "We should keep moving and find someplace to camp."

With the river behind us, we walked until we hit a back country road. Overgrown fields stretched as far as I could see in the waning light.

I motioned to the field on our left. "This spot is as good as any. I doubt we'll find a car around here."

We stepped into the field and walked ten feet or so through the weeds and cornstalks.

Ryker stopped and started walking in a circle, breaking stalks and flattening weeds.

"What are you doing?" I was tired of asking him that question.

He stopped and pointed to the open spot behind him. "Making us a place to sleep."

I walked with him and within minutes, we had created a nice little hollow to sleep in. The stalks were scratchy, but at least the ground was free of rocks, and we were hidden from view.

We watched the sky as the stars came out. Not long ago, we were in our meadow watching the eclipse. It seemed like a lifetime ago. "Can we talk about how you're always so calm now?"

Ryker rolled onto his side and faced me. "Sure, but what exactly do you mean?"

"You're never afraid. Is it the faith thing?"

"I've been scared plenty, and I mean plenty of times. When my mom died. When you almost got shot, and I pulled a trigger. And almost every moment since." He scooted close to me. "Just because I have faith doesn't mean I'm not scared."

"You're just always so confident. Like you know nothing bad is going to happen."

"I'm putting up a good front."

I mulled that over. "You don't have to do that for me."

The last of the light left and I couldn't see his face anymore. "Mom and I used to watch the stars together." His voice caught. He pointed out several constellations.

Not only could he hack, hunt, fish, and track, he knew the stars, too. Truly an amazing guy. Even if I could put Brent behind me, I wasn't sure if I deserved him. His gentle voice lulled me to sleep.

CHAPTER 62

JADZIA

THE NEXT MORNING, I woke to find my arms bleeding and a corn husk under my shirt. I picked an ear of corn from the stalk next to me and threw it at Ryker.

He sat up and whipped his head around. "What? Huh? What's going on?"

I cracked up. "That's the last time we sleep in a corn-field." I rubbed the scratches on my arm.

His body relaxed. "It was your idea."

I opened my mouth to protest but realized it had been my idea. I hated it when he was right, and he always seems to be right. Instead, I rummaged through our packs and pulled out some water pods, crackers and two candy bars. The breakfast of kings. "We're running low. Not to mention the nutritional value of this food is zilch."

"Since when do you care about eating healthy?"

"Since I have to walk ten thousand miles to see my family."

He rolled his eyes. "Five hundred. Tops."

I shrugged. "Same thing. Especially if we're walking."

He threw an ear of corn at me. I threw a cracker and

within minutes we were throwing everything we could reach at each other. "You're wasting our wonderfully nutritious food." He gasped.

That did it. I laughed until I had tears streaming down my face at the absurdity of it all. We were in the middle of nowhere, throwing corn and broken potato chips at each other.

Ryker put his arm around me. "Hey, hey. I'm sorry. You okay?"

Gasps forced their way out of me as I remembered the last time I laughed this hard—the sock war with my little brother. I nodded at Ryker but still couldn't stop the strange laugh-sob sounds that came out of my mouth.

Ryker pulled me to him, and I leaned into his chest. His lips moved in my hair. "Breathe with me." His chest expanded as he took a deep breath. "In," he held the breath, then released it, "and out."

I followed along as best I could until my breathing normalized. "Sorry."

He shook his head. "No problem. You want to talk about it?"

I told him all about Jonathan and the sock fight. He laughed. "I wish I had a sibling. Being an only child got lonely sometimes."

"Leaving your sibling behind to go fight a stupid war can be lonely, too."

He grew quiet, and we sat in silence for a few minutes.

He picked up a half-crushed cracker and handed it to me.

"Gee, thanks."

I took it and flicked it at him. "Let's get going. We have five hundred miles to go, tops." I stood and grabbed a bag.

He opened his map. "Looks like Mellwood is the next

town we can run into if we keep going southwest. It's not listed as a safe city, but I have no idea if it's still populated or not."

"We can try it. If it looks busy, we can skirt around." We'd probably be totally fine to hang out in a small town for a few days. It's not like anyone there knew I was a wanted criminal. But because I was wanted, I couldn't just use my bank account to pay for things like food and a place to stay. Ryker had been recorded as being in Tennessee and it'd look suspicious if his account was used in. . ."What state are we in?"

"We passed into Arkansas when we crossed the river."

"So you're good at geography too, huh?"

He smirked. "No. I can just read a map."

"Right."

We walked for hours. Sweat dripped off my face. "It's only June. Why is it so hot?"

"June is always hot this far south."

"We're lucky if we break seventy-five in the beginning of June where I'm from."

We talked about the seasons and snow and how different our lives had been before the war.

We found a stream and drank. Around three in the afternoon, a storm rolled through. The cool rain washed over me. I threw my arms out and spun around in circles.

"I wouldn't get too excited if I were you."

I stuck my tongue out at him and splashed in a puddle.

"I'm just saying."

Twenty minutes later, I understood. The humidity soared. The once cool rainwater turned hot, and my clothes stuck to me. My jeans chafed as I walked. I couldn't tell whether I was covered in sweat or if the rainwater still soaked me. Not only that, but Ryker had been right. Again.

We made it to Mellwood, a small, one streetlight town, by twilight. I couldn't tell if it was abandoned. The weight of my bag, or lack thereof, made any risk worth it. "I guess we should check the place out."

We walked down the sidewalk of what appeared to be Main Street. Stores still stood intact. No broken windows or busted doors to indicate the places had been looted. I peered through the window of store and saw items on the shelves. Not a ton of stuff, but more than in the looted places.

"I'm guessing there are still people here." I looked around more. "Somewhere."

Ryker pointed to a lone hover truck in a parking lot. "We need food and transportation."

"I thought you said a car wouldn't work. Too hard to maneuver through traffic jams."

"True. But it's the best we've got. For now."

The truck stood taller than me, even though it sat on the ground instead of hovering. Some red paint peeked out from under the mud-covered sides. I pointed at the top of the bed. "Why the heck does it have an exhaust pipe on it? They stopped using fuel for cars almost fifty years ago."

He shifted his weight, and his cheeks reddened. "It's decorative. Some guys like that kind of stuff."

My mouth formed an 'o'. "Tell me you didn't."

He looked at his feet. "I might have."

"Oh. My. Gosh. Ryker." I started to cross the street. "I'm walking over there from now on."

"Hey."

I stepped back to his side. "Just teasing you." I linked my arm through his. "So, about this thing." I pointed to the truck in front of us. "It's on the ground. There's no charge."

I glanced down the street. No streetlights, no lights in any of the buildings. "And no electricity either."

"I've got it covered." Ryker lifted the duffle bag he'd kept to himself. He pulled out a portable charger with cables.

"That's what you've been hiding? It should charge this truck in no time." I threw my arms around him. "You're awesome."

He wrapped me up in a hug. "If I'd have known I'd get this kind of reaction, I'd have told you a while ago."

I broke away from him. My face flushed hot. "Let's get this fired up."

A thick southern accent made me jump. "You ain't touchin' my truck."

I reached for my gun, only to remember I didn't have it. Ryker and I both turned to see the guy who spoke. A heavyset man, probably in his late twenties or early thirties, stood about two feet away. He held a laser pistol aimed at my chest. I swallowed hard and put my hands up.

Ryker's hands were at his shoulders, palms facing the guy. The charger wires dangled from his right hand. "I'm sorry. We didn't think anyone lived in this town anymore."

The guy didn't take his eyes off me. "I tell you what. You can have the truck if I get to spend the night with her."

My skin crawled at the thought.

Ryker stepped in front of me and swore. "Not on your life."

I moved next to Ryker and slid into a fighting stance. We'd practiced disarming in the military, and I had plenty of hand-to-hand combat training. Ryker didn't have any. Finally, something I was better at.

Before the guy, or Ryker, could react, I reached out and grabbed the guy's wrist. I twisted his arm, forcing him to drop the gun. He lunged at me, and I swept his legs out from under him with a kick.

The guy went face first onto the pavement. I scooped up his gun and pointed it at his head. It wasn't my rifle, but having a weapon again gave me confidence. I glanced at the cartridge on the gun. A stun cartridge. Good. At least if I had to shoot, I wouldn't kill him.

I stepped out of his reach and waited for his next move. My heart pounded in my chest.

He picked his head up, eyes wide. Blood streamed from his nose. He spouted words so bad I'd never heard anyone else say them before. Never taking his eyes off me, he felt around on the ground.

"Looking for this?" I waved the gun. Ryker stood next to me, his fists clenched for a fight.

The guy got to his knees and glared at me.

"I have a better idea. You let us take the truck, and I don't knock you out for the next four hours." Normally, I wouldn't have taken the guy's truck. Everyone was in a bad situation, and yes, I'd stolen things before, but never directly from someone. But this guy ticked me off.

He called me a few choice names, got to his feet, and stepped toward me.

Without hesitation, I pulled the trigger.

CHAPTER 63

RYKER

AN HOUR LATER, we were on the road. Z sat on the left side of the truck's bench seat. I sat where the drive would be, if the truck had needed one. Space big enough for a third person stretched between us. Adrenalin still flooded my system, and I had to work to keep my legs from shaking.

"You were awesome back there."

She rolled her eyes. "You've told me that five times already."

"I guess I have. It's still true." I couldn't get over what she'd done to that guy. The military might have been good for me after all. I mean, sure, I could fight—in a scrappy-kid-in-the-schoolyard kind of way. Nothing like what Z just did.

She looked at her lap. Come to think of it, she hadn't looked me in the eye since she shot that guy. "You good?"

She nodded. Now I knew something was up. "You can tell me."

"I shot another person."

I could barely hear her. "You just stunned him. He'll be okay."

She turned to me, threw her arms in the air, and let

them slap down on her legs. "I still shot him. What kind of normal person goes around shooting people and stealing their stuff?"

I took her hand. "The war has changed us all." My chest tightened as I remembered shooting the redheaded girl. I took some deep breaths. "We've all done what we've had to do—to stay alive."

She shook my hand off. "I betrayed my friends. I've killed like five people. I think. I don't even know anymore."

She started muttering names and ticking them off on her fingers. I closed my hand over hers. "It doesn't matter."

She flung my hand off. Her voice rose. "What do you mean, it doesn't matter? I'm a horrible person. How can you even be near me?" She hunched over with head in her hands, breathing coming hard and fast.

I wanted to pull her to me and take away all her pain, but I only knew one person who could do that, and I certainly wasn't Him. "I love you, Z."

Her head whipped up. Her entire face contorted. She cringed against the door as if I just burned her.

"Are you insane? I'm tainted. I'm vile. I'm no good." Her hands clenched on her chest like she was trying to rip her heart out.

I reached for her, but quickly pulled back. Bad idea. Very bad idea. I'm an idiot.

"You've killed someone too." She pointed at me. "How can you stand it? Why don't you hate yourself?"

She might as well have punched me. The air went out of my lungs. I had killed someone. But God. I sucked air in through my mouth. "I don't hate myself because I know I'm loved despite what I've done." I paused. "And so are you."

"No one should love me. Ever. Do you hear me?"

"Your mom loves you. Jonathan loves you. Your cousin. The rest of your family."

She cowered into the seat as if trying to disappear.

I steeled myself for her rejection this time. "I love you. And so does God."

She shook her head, tears flying from her cheeks. "I—I've been reading that book. I'm not worthy of anyone. Especially G—God."

I lowered my voice. "Then you haven't been reading it right. No one is worthy. But God loves us anyway."

I scooted toward her, taking up the middle of the bench seat. She shrank back even further, somehow. There had to be something I could do. Some way to help her. "Please, Z." I reached for her.

She nodded once. I touched her knee, which she drew up by her face. I begged God to give me the words to help her.

She didn't uncurl right away, but I felt her relax at my touch. I wiped a tear from her face and stroked her cheek. She leaned her head into my hand. What I wouldn't give to be able to read her mind. I brushed her hair behind her ear. "I'm here. I'll always be here."

She threw herself at me. I rocked backward but caught us and wrapped my arms around her. She muttered a string of words I couldn't understand between her sobs into my chest. I held her. Trying to whisper comforting words into her hair, to let her know she was worthy of love. I told her I loved her over and over.

It took a while, but she calmed eventually and pulled her tear-streaked face away from me. "I want what you have."

Thank you, Lord.

"But I don't deserve it."

I stroked her hair. "No one does." Please, God.

She shook her head. "I c—can't."

My heart ached. "It's okay." No matter how much I wanted her to open herself to the gift of unconditional love from God, I couldn't force anything on her.

We sat wrapped in each other's arms until the truck came to a stop behind another grouping of abandoned cars. "I'll clear a path this time. You hang here."

Even though she was in my arms, I strained to hear her. "Okay."

I jumped to the ground and ran my hand down my face. I paused for a minute and focused on my breathing. One of these days, she'd believe she was the strong, amazing person I knew her to be.

I shook my head and walked to the first of many vehicles I needed to move.

CHAPTER 64

JADZIA

RYKER MADE me eat dinner that night. Well, what passed for dinner, anyway. A protein bar and a bag of chips left from the vending machine. A stack of pancakes would be amazing right now.

The food settled my stomach and helped numb the pounding that had settled in my head.

The nice thing about Hover-cars and trucks, as opposed to Hover-bikes, was they kept driving when the passengers were eating, sleeping, or having mental breakdowns.

By the end of the day, we covered almost two hundred miles. We stopped several times to shove abandoned cars out of our way, take bathroom breaks, and stop in an abandoned town to look for food and water pods. The search was fruitless, literally and figuratively.

We stopped for the night. If we came across a cluster of vehicles, we didn't want to have to wake up and move them. We also needed to charge the battery.

I dreamed of Brent that night. But for the first time, he wasn't covered in blood. We were together. Talking, hanging out, just like we did before the world went to hell.

We laughed and teased each other. He grew serious, and he said two words I doubted would ever leave me. "Be happy."

I woke before dawn with those words ringing in my ears. Ryker snored like a bandsaw next to me. I wanted to grab a duffle bag and stuff it over his face so I could find my dream again, but I figured a quick, firm shake would work, too. He jerked, mumbled, and went back to snoring. Ugh. I gave him a sharp kick.

He bolted awake. "What's going on?"

I quickly closed my eyes to slits and tried to regulate my breathing. He turned his head from side to side, rubbed his eyes, and adjusted his position. He rested his head against his window and went back to sleep.

I snickered under my breath. I'd give him an earful in the morning.

The second time I woke, daylight reached through the grimy truck windows. My muscles ached and my left foot tingled. I stomped my foot, trying to get feeling back.

"Morning." Ryker opened his eyes and stretched.

I smirked. "Sleep well?"

He ran his hand through his hair, brushing a few stray locks from his forehead. "Mostly. I had a weird dream, though."

"About bears, or loud construction zones, maybe?"

"Huh?"

I waved him away. "Never mind." I leaned over and turned the truck on. Eighty-seven percent charged. "Think we're good, or should we fully charge the battery?"

"We can go longer if we let it charge all the way."

True. We both got out. I breathed in the already warming air and stretched. While having a truck beat walking, my body didn't seem too happy with sitting all day and sleeping in the cramped cab. "We should sleep in the truck's bed tonight. More room to stretch out."

"More of a chance of drones spotting us, too."

I groaned, not sure if I was ready for another full day of Ryker being right.

"Think I can find a stream to wash off in while we wait?"

He shrugged. "Maybe a runoff or something you can splash your face in." He went to the truck door, leaned in, then tossed the laser gun at me. "Take this with you."

I caught the gun. Good thing they couldn't fire unless they were being held. I turned to the woods and headed west, praying I'd find something. I stopped short. Huh. I prayed. A real prayer, not just a sarcastic thank God. A genuine prayer for help. A first. Wow. What had come over me?

I walked fifteen minutes before I found some water dripping over a rock. Not a stream and not much, but something. Making sure I was alone, I pulled off my shirt and let it soak up the water. When it was damp, I rubbed my face and arms with it and slipped it back on. Not the best shower in the world, but better than nothing and better than using our drinking water to cool off.

When I got back to the truck, I found Ryker packing up the charging pack. "Finished?"

He smacked the hood like a car salesman. "She's good to go."

THE NEXT THREE days were the same. Drive about two hundred miles. Sleep, charge the truck, push cars out of the way, and raid small, abandoned towns. We found food here and there—mostly junk food—but we were still constantly hungry.

My body cramped and ached from so much sitting. I tried to find different positions or stretch, and I always helped Ryker move cars when we came on an impassable part of the road, but I'd still kill for a soak in a tub.

When we crossed the border into Texas, I squealed. So, so close. "Can we drive through the night?" I folded my hands and gave Ryker the face I used to give my dad when I really wanted something. Big eyes. Exaggerated pout.

He shook his head. "We can't risk wasting the battery if we're asleep and we end up hovering by a roadblock."

"I'll stay awake all night. Please." I stuck my lower lip out further.

He sighed.

"I'll even move all the cars in our way myself." I flexed my arms, showing off my not-so-impressive muscles.

He rolled his eyes. I could almost feel his resolve weakening. "Fine. I'll help you move the cars."

I threw my arms around him. "You're the best."

He hugged me back.

I pulled away, ran my hands over my pants, and looked at the floor. "Thanks." Embarrassment didn't last long as my excitement surged. Every mile we drove was one fewer to separate me from my family. By evening, I practically bounced in my seat. Just an hour or so so now.

Sleep never even threatened to take me over as night fell. The truck stopped twice after Ryker fell asleep. True to his word, Ryker woke up each time and helped me move the vehicles. Why did he have to be such an amazing person? It'd be a lot easier to sort out my feelings for him if he were a jerk.

As we got closer and closer to Houston, I still didn't recognize anything. I'd been here so many times over the years, visiting Uncle Mark's family. I knew the place like I knew my own town.

The auto navigation showed we were close. Darkness didn't help matters, but there should be landmarks I could pick out, even in the dark. In the half moonlight, the only things I could make out were heaps of . . . something. Rubble, maybe?

Uncle Mark's family lived about twenty miles north of the city. Houston itself lay in ruins, but out here? It couldn't be. Why would they have bombed the suburbs?

"Pull over and stop." I instructed the truck.

The truck pulled off the road. I hopped out and walked to the biggest heap. The smell of old fire and concrete dust met my nose.

I turned on my PCD's flashlight. The beam of light swept across at least a half a mile of rubble in a straight line.

What on earth had been here? A government complex? A medical building? I walked closer to the debris field. My foot crunched on something. I shined my light on a large red sign with white lettering that lay under my boot. T A R G then a jagged edge.

I kept walking. Another sign caught my light, Ulta.

T A R G—Target. Ulta. I stopped moving. This was a strip mall. My breathing came in gasps. No. Surely this mall had no strategic value. Just a lot of people going about their lives and someone decided they had to die. Because the owner of the place believed in a higher power.

I crouched into a fighting stance when a hand landed on my shoulder.

"It's me." Ryker stood behind me, hands in the air. "Sorry. Didn't mean to scare you."

My hand went to my chest. "Geeze. You're lucky I didn't punch you."

"Again."

I smirked.

"You—"

Our PCDs emitted the same ear-piercing alarm I'd heard the day my entire world changed. I really didn't want to open my hand. Ryker opened. In the glow of his display, I saw all the color drain from his face. He stood, not moving, opened-mouthed, reading whatever notice scrolled across his display.

Another attack? They hadn't alerted us like this when Memphis got blown up. Something worse? My mind raced with possibilities.

Ryker bent over, hands on his thighs.

Shudders ran through my body and my legs gave out. My knees stung when they hit the pavement. "What?" I whispered. I still didn't want to see for myself.

He choked out. "Dad."

Huh? That didn't make any sense. I swallowed hard and opened my PCD, preparing for the worst.

The words "New Law in Effect Immediately" scrolled across my display followed by a link. Okay. What could possibly be so bad? Ryker sank to his knees and sat on his heels. Head in his hands he muttered to himself.

I took a deep breath and opened the link.

To end the war, any and all forms of religion, religious gatherings, beliefs, texts, and anything having to do with a belief system were now illegal. The Bible that I carried on my PCD would land me in jail. Which meant almost everyone living at the hotel was now an outlaw. My stomach clenched. Poor Ryker.

I crouched next to him and put my arm around his shoulders. His whole body shook. I still wasn't sure where I stood on the issue of faith, but now I didn't even have the option, unless I wanted to become even more of a criminal. And as for Ryker. He had spent his entire life believing in God and being a member of a community of believers. Now he had to deny everything he believed in, just to meet some stupid law. Would he be able to do it?

I pulled him close and held him.

We stayed like that until the hum of a drone caught my attention. I sighed and tugged him to his feet. "Come on. We need to move."

CHAPTER 66

JADZIA

WE GOT BACK in the truck and crouched down in the footwells, waiting for the drone to pass. When the danger cleared, I double-checked that I'd entered the correct address in the auto navigation, and we kept going.

My breath hitched at the thought of going to Aunt Dawn's house, knowing Uncle Nick wouldn't be there. But Mom and Jonathan would.

When the truck exited the highway, I still didn't recognize anything. Piles of rubble stood in place of the stores and a movie theater. Who blew up a movie theater? What was the point? People seemed to get crazier the longer this war went on.

The truck left the business district and moved into neighborhoods. I was relieved to see most of the houses were intact.

Fifteen minutes after we left the highway, I recognized the gated community my aunt lived in. Ryker sat silently beside me, looking out the window. He didn't even acknowledge me when I rubbed his back. His breath hitched and come in silent bursts. I wished I could read his mind.

The truck pulled up to the familiar two-story red brick house. "We're here." My hands trembled. No light shone from the house. Of course, no light shone from any of the houses at one in the morning. Even people in demolished cities needed sleep. I hated to wake anyone by pounding on the door, but I couldn't wait.

Ryker still kept his back to me. He sniffled.

I fidgeted. I didn't want to leave him, but Mom was right there, no more than thirty feet away. "You can stay here. I'll get you in a little while."

He nodded and sniffled again. I gave his shoulder another squeeze. I stepped out of the truck and slammed the door behind me. Oops.

I ran to my aunt's house and pounded on the door. A few seconds later, I pounded again. "Mom, it's me." I probably should have been a little more courteous toward the neighbors, if there were any, but I hadn't seen my mom or brother in three months. The neighbors would just have to deal with the noise.

I stopped short. Three months. Is that all it had been? Felt like forever. I hoped they still recognized me. I'd changed so much, I barely recognized myself.

I glanced around. A river rock hastily painted blue on the porch caught my attention. Just like the smaller one Mom gave me when I left. I smiled and crouched down to get a closer look. A swing set had been drawn on it. The paint looked fresh. Not chipped or worn. Strange. Why would this be here? A decoration? A reminder?

A message?

I picked up the rock, slipped it into my pocket and brought my hand up to knock again. I heard movement inside. The door opened.

I stared down the barrel of a laser rifle.

My heart tried to beat its way out of my chest. I threw my hands into the air. "It's me." My voice cracked.

A figure stepped out of the dark doorway. A figure in a very familiar uniform, holding a very familiar gun. I stepped back and almost tripped off the single step up to Aunt Dawn's porch.

The figure, a guy with dark hair, stepped out of the house. "Jadzia Mills, you're under arrest for desertion and for crimes of terrorism against the United States Military."

Terrorism?

More uniforms converged on me from the sides of the house. Someone even popped out from behind my aunt's palm tree near the door. They'd been waiting. How long had Mom been gone? Where was my family? Were they cuffed inside?

The military must really want me if they pulled all these people from the front lines to wait at my aunt's house. How did they even know I'd show up here? Unless—I looked at the truck. Crap. The auto navigation. When I entered Aunt Dawn's address, it must have triggered some kind of alert. How could I be so stupid?

"Please don't shoot me." I stepped backward off the porch, only to have another gun barrel poke me in the back. Sweat ran down my temple.

A weird noise came from behind me. I turned. A woman lay at my feet. All the rifles that were aimed at me swiveled to the surrounding area. Another guard went down.

Ryker. He held the gun I had taken from the owner of the truck. But there were at least five more guards pointing rifles at us. From my training, I knew there were more inside, and the only weapon I possessed was rock. Great.

I spun and kicked the man closest to me. Bones

crunched. He screamed and went down, knee probably broken. More soldiers came out of the house, for a total of fifteen. My mind raced. That should be all of them.

I plunged my hand into my pocket and pulled out the rock. Maybe I could bash someone in the head with it. I punched and kicked and dodged gun barrels as some of the guards tried to shoot me and others defended against Ryker, who moved in to fight hand-to-hand.

"Z. Run," Ryker yelled as he punched a guard who'd raised her gun to shoot me. "Run." He screamed again.

I couldn't leave him. I grabbed the nearest guard's gun, pulled him off-balance, and sent him sprawling to the ground.

Five soldiers surrounded Ryker.

"Go. Please." He kicked out at anything that moved.

I fought to get to him, keeping my back toward the house, to prevent enemies from ambushing me. I grabbed the planter on the front window and smashed it over a guy's head. It shattered. He wouldn't be getting up anytime soon.

"Z. Go." A quick glance at Ryker showed me he was now on the ground, his arms being zip-tied behind his back.

I lunged for him, but someone grabbed me from behind and slammed me to the ground. The rock slipped from my grasp.

A female voice growled in my ear. "Traitor."

I reared my head back and smashed it into her face. Her nose crunched. Pain burst through my head, but I didn't have time to deal with it. She crumpled to my side, unconscious. I jumped to my feet, grabbed her fallen rifle, and ran.

CHAPTER 67

RYKER

THE GUY who had pinned me down hauled me off the ground by the zip-tie. My wrists burned as the plastic cut into them. I could feel blood oozing from where they dug in. At least Z got away. They sent six soldiers after her, but she was fast and knew how to hide. I prayed she'd be okay.

Someone checked my ear implant with a scanner. I couldn't believe I'd never thought to hack into the implant and change my identity.

"Ryker Jenkins. Nineteen." Yep, there it was.

The guy spit at my feet. "I hate draft dodgers."

I wished my arms were free. This guy wouldn't have any teeth left. "I didn't dodge the draft. I was exempt because of religious beliefs."

The guy smirked. "Didn't you hear, Draft Dodger? Religious beliefs are illegal." He punched me in the stomach.

I doubled over and acid rose in my throat. It would serve him right if I threw up on his boots, but I swallowed hard.

His colleagues snickered.

I kicked out at him, but he backed up and laughed louder.

They threw me in a Hover-jeep and zip-tied my feet together. I squirmed, trying to get loose. "Sit still." The guy who hit me slid in next to me and poked my side with a handgun.

An older woman hopped into the front seat and tapped her ear. "Mark, you have her yet?"

I held my breath and waited for the answer.

She swore.

I cheered inwardly. Z had eluded them.

She tapped her ear again. Her voice grew official as she reported in to her commander. She explained the situation, then fell silent for a moment. "Yes, Sir." She tapped her ear again and ended the conversation.

I sat on the edge of my seat.

She turned to me. "Looks like you're going to boot camp." She rolled her eyes. "Welcome to the Army."

The guy next to me laughed. "Guess you're not dodging the draft anymore." He smacked me in the back of the head.

Moron.

A big soldier leaned against the doorjamb of the Hover-jeep. "We still have to find the girl."

She pointed to him. "Sarge said he'd send another twenty guys and thermal drones. You and Mark set up a perimeter and run standard search patterns until they get here. She couldn't have gotten far."

The fight left me. If I hadn't been sitting down, I'd have fallen. Thermal drones. No one could hide from those.

A guy in the front seat hopped out. He saluted the woman and left to join the search for Z.

I closed my eyes and prayed some more.

The jeep started, and we left the neighborhood.

I'm not sure how long we drove. The guy next to me muttered complaints about having to take me all the way to the nearest training camp. I tuned him out and kept praying for Z. And for myself. How could I do this? The war was against everything I believed in.

I shuddered at the thought of being forced to kill someone. Not in the heat of the moment like I had to do to protect Z, but knowingly and willingly mowing down groups of people. Believers didn't deserve to be wiped out. But Zealots didn't deserve to be attacked either. I wouldn't kill them.

As light streaked the sky, we pulled up to a complex with a barbed wire topped fence surrounding it. Guards at the gate checked the woman's ID and let us through. She pulled into a common area and stopped.

The guy next to me grabbed my arm and jerked me out of the vehicle. Since my feet were tied together, I couldn't find my balance and fell to the pavement. He gave me a small kick, knelt, and cut the plastic on my ankles. "If you end up in my unit, Draft Dodger, you'd better watch your back."

For the hundredth time, I wished my hands were free.

He yanked me to my feet, and I purposely stumbled into him to knock him off-balance.

He punched me in the face. Blood dripped from my nose. I had no way to wipe it.

A man with gray hair and a gruff voice walked toward us. "What's going on here?"

"Delivering your newest recruit, Sir." The woman saluted, then motioned to me.

The man returned her salute, then glared at the idiot standing next to me. "What'd you do to him?"

"He put up a fight, Sir."

The older man sized me up like I was a horse he wanted to buy. "Is that so? I like a fighter. Leave him."

Both of my escorts saluted again, got back in the Hover-jeep, and left.

The man pulled out a laser knife and cut the zip-ties from my wrists. "I'm Staff Sergeant Turner."

I massaged my wrists, trying to get blood flow to my hands.

Turner looked at my hands. "Let's get you to medical to take a look at that."

"Okay."

"The correct answer is 'Yes, Sir.'"

My voice shook. "Yes, Sir."

He led me to a white pod building. A woman who introduced herself as Doctor Madison put some salve on my wrists. "This will keep infection away. You'll be good as new tomorrow morning."

Turner stayed with me the entire time. When the doctor finished, Turner motioned to the door. "Let's get you to your dorm so you can get a few hours of sleep. I expect you to be at lunch and afternoon training."

I couldn't figure out if I liked this guy or not. But I knew he wouldn't like me. I pulled myself up to my full height and looked him in the eye. "I refuse to serve."

He sneered. "Yeah, they told me about you. Religious objections and all that." He took a deep breath. "In that case, we'll see how you feel after a few days in P block."

"P block?"

I winced when he squeezed my shoulder a little too tight. "Prison."

CHAPTER 68

JADZIA

I RAN until my lungs were ready to burst, crossing random streets, scrambling over fences, and checking behind me for soldiers.

How was this my life? Running from the people I used to serve with. Running from the people my dad used to lead. He would be so disappointed with who I'd become. Traitor. The word rang in my ear with each beat of my heart.

Traitor to my unit, to my commander, to my friends. Traitor to Dad. To Brent. To Ryker. I spun to go back for him. But should I? He sacrificed himself so I could get away. It seemed a slap in his face if I got arrested now.

Then there was the rock on the porch. The more I thought about it, the more I knew it wasn't sitting on that porch by accident or even random chance. Mom put it there for me, as a message no one else would understand. But why a swing set? I wiped the sweat from my forehead. Think.

Sure, I loved swinging when I was little. I'd always begged Mom to take me to the local park. I stopped moving. My chest heaved and I bent to put my hands on my knees.

The park. Had she somehow avoided capture and was hiding in a park? No. When would she have had time to paint a rock? I gripped the sides of my head and tugged on my hair. None of this made any sense.

But why else would the rock be there? With nothing else to go on, I pulled open my PCD and found my aunt's house. I moved the display around until I found the community playground, six streets from Aunt Dawn's place in the direction I'd come from. Of course.

I walked back toward Aunt Dawn's but stayed a few streets away from her house to avoid the military search parties, I knew were still looking for me. I skirted through backyards and hid behind cars, pools, bushes, and doghouses.

When I made it to the park, I ducked behind a bush and peered through the branches. I couldn't tell if anyone was around. I certainly wasn't about to call out. Not in a wide-open space with only a few play structures. Surely Mom wouldn't be at the playground for the entire day.

Finding her tonight wasn't going to happen. This morning. Whenever it was.

I kicked in the door of a house I hoped was abandoned. Using the flashlight on my PCD, I cleared the place, then lay down on the couch and set my alarm. Three hours until the sun came up. I would give myself three hours, and then I'd find Mom and Jonathan.

When my alarm finally woke me, I shut it off and realized it had been blaring at me for an hour. I swore and jumped off the couch. My stomach rumbled. I didn't have a pack or any provisions. I doubted there would be any in this ransacked house. I went to the kitchen just to be sure. Nothing. I put my forehead on the counter. I couldn't remember the last time I'd eaten.

Standing here wouldn't get me food, though. I turned on the faucet. At least there was still water. I drank as much as I could hold and went to the window facing the park. I'd wait here and hope Mom showed herself.

The hours ticked by. I scanned the park from my perch at the window. At one point, a guy, who was definitely not my mother, shuffled through and headed south. Ugh. Come on, Mom. I couldn't sit here all day, but I didn't want to leave in case I had missed something.

How long had she been waiting for me? It had been at least a week since I called her. Did they leave then? No. She wouldn't have left knowing I was on my way. Were Jonathan, Aunt Dawn, and Carina with her? Maybe the military arrested them. Maybe the stupid rock had been on Aunt Dawn's porch for years and I'd never noticed it.

I squirmed and crossed my legs. I shouldn't have guzzled all that water. I gave in and went to the bathroom as fast as I could. When I got back, everything looked the same. I wanted to bang my head against the wall, but I'd only give myself a headache.

A blue lawn flag caught my eye. It fluttered on a short, ornamental flag post, by the street, three houses to my right. I looked closer and saw a yellow watering-can on the bright blue background. The flag was in good condition, like it hadn't been out in the elements for the past three months.

Of course, she wasn't in the park. I smacked my forehead. I'd already determined that was a terrible place to stay. I walked to the back of the house. Somehow, it felt safer than leaving by the front door.

Everything was quiet. Still, I stood by the door for fifteen minutes, scoping out the backyards. I couldn't see much. The house had a ten-foot privacy fence around the backyard. Nothing moved, so I figured it was safe to step outside at least.

I walked through the yard and peered through cracks between the slats into the next yard. I could see at least six houses down. Most of the houses had trees, flowers, and plenty of bushes to hide behind. I climbed the fence and landed in a roll, like we'd learned in basic training. I made my way to the third house from the one I'd slept in. What if it was a trap? I wiped my sweaty palms on my pants, squared my shoulders, and tried the back door. Locked.

I kicked the door in. The bang echoed through the house.

I wanted to call out, but I might have a better chance of escaping if I didn't give my position away every few steps. I crept through the kitchen. Dining room. Living room. Down the hall. Bathroom. No one was here. I checked the first bedroom. Bedroom number two.

A rifle clicked. A voice I knew well said, "Put your hands in the air."

CHAPTER 69

JADZIA

"MOM." I whirled around and threw myself at her.

She dropped the gun and pulled me into a hug. "Jadzia."

My breath came in gasps. "Y—you're here."

"You found the rock." She laughed through her tears. "And the flag. I knew you'd figure it out."

I couldn't speak. I just squeezed her tighter and took in her scent and the familiar feel of her arms around me to reassure myself she was real.

We held each other for the longest time. My body relaxed. All the tension I carried the past few months drained out of me. Everything was perfect . . . except.

I pulled away and stepped back. "Where's Jonathan?" I blew my nose on the bottom of my shirt and wiped my cheeks.

Mom's face fell.

My voice rose, near hysterical. "Where is he?"

She held up her hand in front of her. "He's safe."

Air rushed from my lungs, and I slumped against the wall.

"He's with your Aunt Dawn and Carina. When the military came to the house, they gave us some crap about you being a traitor and they thought you were on your way to the house. They insisted on taking us to Dallas." She paced and swore. "While your aunt packed some clothes, I painted the rock. Then I slipped away at a rest stop. I knew you'd be coming, and I had to warn you or meet you if I could."

I gasped and stared at her. First, Mom never swore. Second, she'd escaped from a military escort. Who was this woman? I guess the war really did change us all. "Are they safe?"

She nodded. "Last I talked to your aunt, yes. They weren't happy I went missing, but they won't hurt civilians. Especially civilians who are related to your father."

Dad's reputation might have protected my family, but it sure didn't extend to me. My stomach growled.

"Hungry?"

"I haven't eaten in at least a day. My pack is back at Aunt Dawn's. At least it was. We could try to get it."

Mom gave me her best mom stare.

Man, I'd missed her.

"No way you're going back there." She flashed me a smile. "Besides, we don't need to." She tugged on my arm and led me to the kitchen. She opened a cabinet full of food packs and water pods.

My mouth dropped open. "How?"

She laughed. "Thank your father. He was such a prepper, and he passed it on to your aunt and uncle. They have a storage unit full of supplies under a fake name." While she talked, she pulled two MREs off the shelf and prepared them using the heating kit the MRE came with. "As long as

I'm not seen, I can get food whenever we need it." She slid the hot meals toward me.

"Aren't you eating?"

She shook her head. "I ate a little while ago."

I dug into the ravioli meal first. With my mouth half full, I said, "We can't stay here, you know."

"I don't intend to. We have to contact your aunt somehow."

"And we have to get Ryker."

Mom's hand went to the base of her throat. "I forgot about him. I'm so sorry." She looked out the window like she expected him to pop out from behind a bush. "Where is he?"

My voice cracked. "He let himself get captured so I could get away."

She wrapped me in a hug. "Oh, honey. He must really care about you."

I nodded. And I cared about him.

"Finish eating. We'll figure something out."

My stomach tightened. I put the plastic fork down. I'd been expecting Mom to be angry. To lecture me about deserting my unit instead she was willing to plan a rescue mission. She hadn't even asked me what the military meant when they told her I was a traitor. She only believed the best about me. But she was wrong. "I have to tell you something." I kept my eyes on my food. My arms crossed over my chest.

She rubbed my back. "You didn't get captured by Zealots."

My vision blurred. "How did you know?"

Her voice was caring. "I'm your mother. I can tell when you're hiding something. After what the soldiers said at your aunt's, I figured it out."

I buried my head in my hands. "I'm sorry. I t-tried. But Brent. I just—"

"Ssssh, honey. It's okay."

I looked for any sign she was just telling me wanted I wanted to hear, but her face showed sincerity. I wiped my nose with my hand. "It is?"

"I love you. Nothing you do could change that. I'm just happy you're alive."

Unconditional love. Just like Ryker talked about. I threw my arms around her waist. She stroked my hair.

When I finished crying, a weight had lifted. I no longer had to worry about what mom thought of me or whether she would cast me aside.

Mom held me at arm's length and gave me a sly look. "Now. Let's talk about how we're going to get your man."

Heat rushed to my cheeks. "He's not my man. He's just a friend." Heat rushed to my cheeks. "I think."

ACKNOWLEDGMENTS

There are so many people who have helped bring this book to life and I cherish each and every one of them. A huge thank you goes too:

My family: My wonderful husband and three daughters. Thank you for putting up with countless hours of me typing away on my computer, going to conferences, and attending meetings and classes. Without your constant love and support, none of this would be possible.

My parents: Mom. Dad. Thank you for encouraging me and supporting me on my writing journey. Thank you for always being there when we need you.

My mentor: DiAnn Mills, almost fourteen years ago you took a raw, untrained writer and saw potential in her. Thank you for always believing in me, especially when I didn't believe in myself. Thank you for all of the brainstorming, the critiques, the pushes to keep going, and the unwavering support you have given me.

My sisters: Suzanne Ruggieri and Chrissy Whiting. Thank you for listening to me whine and complain when I had a bad day, for your constant love and support, and for always knowing the right thing to say to make me laugh.

My friends: There are so many names that belong here, and I am grateful for all of you. But for this project particularly, I would be remiss if I didn't thank Molly Jo Realy, Shannon Thomas, and Vincent Brent Davis II. MJ, thank you for always checking up on me, for being there when I needed to vent or cry, and for praying for me. Shannon, thank you for supporting me and for being there for me. Vincent, thank you for sharing your marketing expertise and for always lending a listening ear.

My writing coach: Larry J. Leech II, thank you for your constant support, belief in me, and encouragement. You have helped bring this project to life. Thank you for being there every step of the way and for not letting me give up.

540 Writing Community: I thoroughly credit finding the time to finish his novel to the 540 Club. Without their write-ins, this novel would still be a work in progress. https://beckyantkowiak.com/join-the-540-writers-community/

My Beta Readers: Suzanne Ruggieri, Chrissy Whiting, Hannah Bruschi, and Emily Bova. Thank you for being the first to read Jadzia's story and for all of your feedback.

ABOUT THE AUTHOR

Heather Kreke is passionate about showing teens and young adults that they can find hope in God's plan for their lives—even through the darkest times. She is the Blog Manager for Blue Ridge Mountains Christian Writers Conference, and a Coordinator for the Blue Ridge Readers Connection. In her spare time, she teaches writing classes, shoots archery, and camps with her family. Married since 2004, Heather has three daughters. She loves connecting with readers on her website heatherkreke.com, Instagram, Twitter, and Facebook.

Made in United States
Orlando, FL
26 October 2022